**"Is this all about acting for you?"
Raymond asked as he began
smoothing lotion on Imani's leg.**

"Maybe. But you're here just for the money, so why don't we make it work for both of us?"

Her skin was smoother than his favorite John Coltrane jam and softer than Egyptian cotton. He couldn't focus on what she was saying because he was transfixed by those lips. All he wanted to do was kiss her.

"So?" Imani questioned. "What do you think?"

"About?"

"You and me teaming up? You get the money you want and I get the screen time I need. We already have a story line. Were you listening to anything I said?" she asked as she sat up straight and placed her hands on her hips. "I can't—"

He cut her off quickly as he captured her lips with his, swallowing whatever words she had been about to say. Her lips were sweeter than anything he'd ever tasted, and talk about soft. Her lips were like rose petals. . . .

Also by Cheris Hodges

Just Can't Get Enough
Let's Get It On
More than He Can Handle
Betting on Love
No Other Lover Will Do
His Sexy Bad Habit

Published by Dafina Books

Too
HOT
For TV

CHERIS HODGES

Kensington Publishing Corp.
http://www.kensingtonbooks.com

DAFINA BOOKS are published by

Kensington Publishing Corp.
119 West 40th Street
New York, NY 10018

All Kensington Titles, Imprints, and Distributed Lines are available at special quantity discounts for bulk purchases for sales promotions, premiums, fund-raising, and educational or institutional use. Special book excerpts or customized printings can also be created to fit specific needs. For details, write or phone the office of the Kensington special sales manager: Kensington Publishing Corp., 119 West 40th Street, New York, NY 10018, attn: Special Sales Department, Phone: 1-800-221-2647.

Dafina and the Dafina logo Reg. U.S. Pat. & TM Off.

ISBN-13: 978-0-7582-6571-5
ISBN-10: 0-7582-6571-9

First Dafina mass market printing: September 2011

10 9 8 7 6 5 4 3 2 1

Printed in the United States of America

To D. C., thank you for all of the inspiration.

*To my parents, Doris and Freddie Hodges,
thank you for always supporting me.*

*To my sister, Adrienne Hodges Dease,
thanks for listening.*

Acknowledgments

I'd like to thank all of the readers who have supported my work over the years, especially *His Sexy Bad Habit*. Your e-mails and Facebook posts were very much appreciated.

I'd like to thank my editor, Selena James, for her patience and support with this project. A big thank-you to my agent, Sha-Shana Crichton, for always being there and giving that critical eye.

To the various book clubs who have picked my work as their book of the month, including the SBS Book Club, the PWOC Book Club of Jacksonville, Lavender Lilies of Jacksonville, Sistahs Unlimited Book Club in Columbia, S.C., those pink sisters of the SistahFriends Book Club, and the Round Table Readers Literary Group in Danville, V.A.

I'd like to thank the best friends a tattooed girl could have, Mr. and Mrs. Hart. You guys make love look so easy.

Chapter 1

If looks could kill, Edward Funderburke would
have been dead under Imani Gilliam's icy stare. Her
agent must have been losing his mind along with
his silver hair for suggesting such a thing. A reality
TV show?

Imani was a serious actress, not someone seeking
fifteen minutes of fame, like those people who signed
up for those shows. Obviously, Edward must have
forgotten that. Imani was Broadway, feature films—
not reality TV. Instead of getting her a part in a cheap
reality show, he should have worked harder to get
her the role in the reprisal of the hit play *Kiss of the
Spider Woman*. According to Edward, the producers
were looking for someone with more of a recogniz-
able name, even though she had wowed them at
her audition. But how did anyone think Imani would
become a bankable name if she couldn't get a big
role that would make her a star?

What Imani lacked in name recognition, she made
up for in talent. She was the classic triple threat—she
could sing, dance, and act. That should have been

enough, or at least that's what Imani thought. But in this industry, sometimes it didn't matter how talented you were, which was why so many rappers and singers had lead roles in so many movies, yet only a few of them were actually good enough to pull it off.

She'd do a film with Common, but he was the only rapper who she felt deserved the screen time he received. The rest of them needed to stick to their day jobs and studios needed to put their faith in actresses and actors—people who trained to do the job.

Imani wasn't naive enough to think that the studios weren't in it for the money. That's why 50 Cent and T.I. starred alongside Denzel and Samuel L. Jackson. And if it wasn't the rappers, it was the stars who stayed in the tabloids who got all of the plum roles. Imani would've loved the chance to play the lead in *Salt*. Of course, she didn't have the name recognition of Angelina Jolie or the headlines.

Folding her arms, she glared at Edward, letting him know that she wasn't warming to the idea of doing a reality show.

"It's a really good concept, and think of the national exposure," Edward added, hoping to open Imani's mind to the notion.

"Eddie, I know you don't really expect me to say yes. I'm a real actress," Imani said indignantly, flipping her curly locks behind her ear. "These shows are for has-beens or wannabes. Maybe if you would get out of the office more often, you'd find a script for me that would give me the name recognition that I so badly need."

"All right, Imani," he said, leaning across his desk

and looking her directly in the eye. "Let's be real here. You haven't worked in months, no one has sent you a script since you did *Fearless Diva* and, need I remind you, that wasn't the best vehicle that you could have taken. *Monster's Ball* could have been your breakthrough role. Halle won the Oscar for that role. You would've been great in that role and I tried to tell you that. You just think that you can do anything you want to do and you can't. It's about building a career, a portfolio that people identify you with. Those regional plays you've done, most of them have been for free and no one, not a soul, is trying to put them on Broadway. You have to do something to shake the stagnant off your career."

Imani rolled her eyes. "I didn't want to do a drama. I had just come off a dramatic role on Broadway and I needed a break," she said. "And if you gave me better advice, then maybe I would listen. You weren't too happy about the *Monster's Ball* role either; now all of a sudden it was the best thing that I ever passed up?" She folded her arms underneath her breasts and pouted.

Unfazed by her temper tantrum, Edward leaned back and propped his feet up on the desk. "You gambled and we lost. Now, Imani, I like you and I believe in your talent, but you're not one of my most profitable clients. If either of us has a plan to make any money, we have to get you out there and make your name stand out in a crowd. This is a start. I don't want to have to drop you, but you've got to do something. This show can build your image. Look at how famous lots of people who have no acting ability have gotten—all from the exposure of reality

TV. We can turn that fame into big movie roles and those Broadway shows that you want."

Imani chewed on the end of her sculptured nail, pondering what he'd said to her. It had been hard for her to get signed by a reputable agent. Before meeting Edward, she'd been scammed by so-called talent agents who wanted to put her in B-list movies and soft-core pornography films.

At least Edward had done his best to get her roles in blockbuster movies and hit stage productions, even if she didn't agree with him at the moment. He'd steered her away from the typical chitlin' circuit plays that young actresses found themselves acting in and from becoming typecast as a neck-rolling, finger-wagging stereotype.

But now, he and Imani were desperate.

"Eddie, I'm trying, but these reality shows are just so beneath me, and the images that they portray are not the best. Sometimes the women on these shows are just dumb looking, slutty, or bitchy. I'm none of the above."

"It pays fifteen thousand dollars up front. It's only ten weeks and you might even get voted off before the show is over. The concept is simple. You get teamed up with a bachelor, do some physical challenges, and America votes to see if you and your partner should get married. Just make a splash and watch the scripts and offers come rolling in."

"No," she said, and then stood up. "I'd rather starve." Imani turned to her left, ready to walk out the door.

"Aren't you doing that already?" Edward called out.

Imani slammed the office door behind her. *The gall*, she thought as she headed for the subway terminal. She wanted to take a cab, but with only three dollars in her pocket and a box of raisins for dinner in her apartment, a taxi trip was a luxury that she couldn't afford. Besides, a taxi trip from Manhattan to Brooklyn would wipe out her savings in the bank—if you could call it a savings account. She barely had a hundred dollars in her checking and savings accounts combined. Calling her parents for a loan was out because the first thing her mother, Dorothy, would say is that she needed a real job and acting was a dream she needed to give up. Her father, Horace, would tell her that it was time for her to join the family business of home restorations.

She could be in charge of the interior design aspect of it, even live in a historic home in beautiful Savannah, Georgia. Imani wanted no part of it. Her dream was to act, sing, or dance. Her career of choice was considered an insignificant pipe dream by her family. She'd graduated with a degree from the Juilliard School and hadn't asked her parents for a penny, despite the fact that she went into major debt paying for the expensive performing arts college.

Frowning as she headed to the subway entrance, Imani tried to figure out how she was going to take a free trip on the subway because she wasn't sure if she had the money to make it home. When she saw three New York City Transit officers arresting a group of teenagers who were also trying to get a free ride home, she knew she'd have to walk. She was only about two miles from her place in Fulton Ferry and she could use the exercise. Besides, the walk would give her a chance to think about the reality show.

"I'm not doing it," she mumbled to herself. By the time she had walked five blocks, her feet were throbbing like a heartbeat. "Maybe I should do it. *The Apprentice* made Omarosa a star and she's not even an actress. But then she did that stupid dating show on TV One," Imani said to no one in particular as she unsnapped her Steve Madden sandals, took them off, and flung them over her shoulder. "But," she continued musing to herself, "I trained at Juilliard. I shouldn't be subjected to this."

Imani was half a block away from her home when she decided that she wasn't going to go on the reality show. She held her head high and walked up to the door of her building, ready to prop her feet up and relax with her *Variety* magazine. Before she could put the key in the lock, reality sucker-punched her in the stomach. A pink note with big red letters was tacked to her door. "Eviction," it read. Imani snatched the note off the door. She pulled her cell phone out of her tote bag, pressed speed dial number three, and waited for Edward to answer.

"Funderburke and Associates, Edward speaking," he said.

"It's Imani. I've done some thinking," she said as she read the eviction notice for a second time. "I'll do the stupid show."

"Well, don't sound so excited about it," he replied. "What made you change your mind?"

Imani made a mental note of the thirty-day deadline she'd been given to come up with the back rent. Then she balled up the notice. "Let's just say I know this is what I need to do right now."

Storming into her place, Imani decided to watch a little television to take her mind off her current situation. But that was the wrong thing to do. As she flipped through the channels, lamenting her career, she stopped on a sitcom that she'd auditioned for.

"LisaRaye is not a better actress than I am," she exclaimed as she came across a rerun of *All of Us,* and then flipped the channel.

Next she landed on a Lifetime movie about an abused wife who'd killed her husband. As she watched the unknown actress overdramatize her lines, Imani knew that she would have done so much better in the role, had it been offered to her. She remembered that she'd once told Edward that the last thing she wanted to do was a Lifetime movie. Now, she wished that she'd never made such a crazy statement.

Then she came across her movie on the FX channel. *Fearless Diva* was a bomb, but it wasn't J. Lo in *Gigli* or Halle's *Catwoman.* If she was honest, she'd admit that it was worse. But she wasn't practicing honesty right now.

That role should have led to something, she thought as she watched herself prance across the screen in a skintight leather catsuit. *At least my clothes were fierce.* Twirling a lock of hair around her finger, Imani critiqued her performance. She was pretty awful in the movie, but it wasn't her fault. The script was horrible and the cameraman, who also called himself the director, didn't know how to operate the camera because every scene looked as if the wind had gotten hold of the equipment.

Maybe Imani did deserve those Razzie award nominations she'd gotten. But someone had to see her potential, didn't they? As tears welled up in her eyes, Imani wondered if her family had been right about her career. Were they right to have no faith in her? Was she chasing a pipe dream that had no chance of coming true?

The phone wouldn't stop ringing at the Palmer Free Clinic in Harlem. And that was the least of their worries. The receptionist had left for lunch three hours ago and never returned. That left Dr. Raymond Thomas juggling answering calls with seeing patients, writing down appointments, and taking messages. What he didn't have time for was a game-playing prankster. "Look," Raymond said, a frown darkening his handsome face, "this is a place of business. No one here has time to play with a lowlife small-timer like you."

"Sir, this isn't a joke. I'm Elize Harrington, a producer with the WAPC Network. You're a candidate for our new reality show, *Let's Get Married*. Your name was submitted to us and we reviewed your qualifications and we want you on the show," she said, her voice in a near plea.

"Ms. Harrington, who put you up to this joke?" Raymond dropped his pen on the desk and held his finger up to the patient in front of him waiting for her prescription.

The woman sighed. "Again, sir, this isn't a joke.

Our show is going to air later this year, but the ten weeks of filming starts in a few weeks. We just need you to come in and take a screen test and sign a waiver."

A rush of people were vying for Raymond's attention. All at once, he had a patient trying to make a follow-up appointment, a nurse questioning him about his orders for a different patient, and the same woman who'd been waiting for ten minutes still wanting her prescription. As Raymond's head began throbbing, he silently wished he could write himself a doctor's note and go home.

He mumbled yes to the producer, told her to call his cell phone, leave the details about the show on his voice mail, and he would call her back. Raymond hung up the phone and, putting his composed doctor face back on, turned to his patient. When things calmed down, Raymond was going to get to the bottom of this reality TV show mess. It was already pushed to the back burner.

"Mrs. Wentworth," he said, taking the elderly woman's hand, "can you come back in two weeks?"

The caramel-colored woman smiled at him. "I can do that and my grandbaby, Emma, can bring me. She's real pretty and she can cook, too. Our family is originally from the south and southern women know how to do one thing better than anyone else does, and that's cook. Dr. Thomas, you don't get many home-cooked meals, do you? You're not married, are you?"

"No, ma'am," he replied with a smile, even though he wanted to push her out the door. If Raymond had a penny for every elderly woman who wanted to fix him up with her granddaughter, niece, or daughter, he would be rich enough to fund the clinic himself.

Mrs. Wentworth shook her head. "That's a shame. You need a good woman to take care of you. You're way too skinny. I like a man with a little more meat on his bones, but my grandbaby would love you."

Nurse Karen DeSalis dropped a chart in front of Raymond. "Mrs. Wentworth, I've been telling him that for years, but he doesn't listen."

Raymond rolled his eyes. Who had time for love or romance? He and his fraternity brother, Keith Jacobs, had opened the Marion Palmer Free Clinic, named for their favorite first-grade teacher, three years ago in Harlem. They'd gone to Morehouse School of Medicine in Atlanta, Georgia, together and did their residency at Grady Memorial Hospital. When their residency was over, the native New Yorkers returned to Harlem ready to make a difference. Luckily for them, they had help. Keith and Raymond received a three-million-dollar grant from the Harlem Revitalization Group to buy equipment. The city donated the building and donations from businesses helped the men with the first year's operating costs. Then September 11 happened and everything changed. As donations began to dry up, Keith and Raymond poured their savings into the clinic. They could barely pay the staff, which was why they were on their fourth receptionist in a month.

"Karen, have you seen Keith?" Raymond asked as Mrs. Wentworth walked out the door.

"He's eating lunch in the doctor's lounge," she

replied. "But what about these orders?" She placed her hand on his sculpted arm, preventing him from leaving the front desk.

Raymond picked up the chart. "Discharge Loretta, give her meds for the pain, and have her come back in a month. What's the question?"

"Sorry, doc, I'm not fluent in chicken scratch."

Raymond playfully sneered at her and then broke out laughing. "Watch the door and phones for me. Five minutes, okay?" She nodded, and then Raymond took off for the doctor's lounge, which was more like a storage closet with a dingy window.

Keith was sitting at the small table, more akin to a TV tray, eating a salad and a roast chicken sandwich. "What's up, Ray?" Keith asked, catching his partner's stare.

"You tell me, brother."

Keith stood up, stuffing the last of his sandwich in his mouth. "The only time you call me 'brother' is when you're pissed off. What did I do now?"

Raymond raised his eyebrow. "You're going to stand here and pretend that you don't know what you did? I got a call that I'm sure you know all about. Some TV producer called me about the show *Let's Get Married.*"

"Finally! I'm glad they got to my letter," Keith said excitedly. "I thought all of my writing had been in vain."

Raymond was tempted to grab his best friend by the throat and choke him like a chicken ready to be plucked and fried.

"Keith, have you lost your mind? First of all, I

don't want to get married, and second of all, I'm not reality TV material."

"Think about it Ray. This show guarantees people will hear of the Marion G. Palmer Free Clinic over and over again. And I'm sure the ladies will swoon over tall, muscular Dr. Ray-Ray, just like they did in college. We can't pay for this kind of publicity. It's not as if we can afford it anyway. Bro, we're in trouble. At this point, we need to do anything to keep these doors open."

Raymond shook his head. "Why don't you go on the show?" he snapped.

"Number one, Celeste would kill me; she's been trying to get me to marry her for three years. Number two, I know the limitations of my charm. I'd be voted off the first show. And number three, I don't want my momma to see me on TV like that."

"I don't want to do it," Raymond said, "and I'm not going to do it. Besides, do you actually think you can run this place without me? Do you know how busy we've been today? There's no way we can afford to have either one of us out of pocket for any amount of time."

"It's fifteen thousand just to do it. That doesn't even include the prize money, should you win," Keith said. "This is a great way for us to get some free publicity. I know one thing for sure. If we don't start getting some income coming in, the doors aren't going to be open much longer."

Raymond rubbed his chin, thinking about the clinic's finances. The books were in the red. Medicare was slow to pay for the services the clinic provided, but that didn't stop Keith and Raymond from providing quality health care to the people in the community who wouldn't otherwise be able to get the help that they needed. The clinic had never been about the two of them getting rich. They wanted to help the people who reminded them of the women who'd help raise them. Keith's grandmother could've been Mrs. Wentworth, a hardworking woman who as she aged needed help managing her health but couldn't afford health insurance.

"That's a lot of money for a one-time gig. Maybe I can make myself get voted off after two episodes," Raymond said as he fingered his goatee.

Keith nodded. "See, that's the spirit. But don't be evil or anything like that. Just make yourself seem pitiful. You have to win them over if we plan to milk donations from people who watch the show."

Raymond looked at himself in the reflective material on the side of the file cabinet. He was hardly a vain man, but he knew there was no way he could make himself seem as if he were some pitiful soul who couldn't find a date. Raymond was the kind of man who made a woman's breath catch in her chest after she got a look at his creamy caramel skin, dark wavy hair, and shimmering green eyes— which had been known to put a woman in a trance if he looked at her just the right way. People often snagged him for charity fashion shows and bachelor auctions, and asked him to pose for bachelor calendars. Raymond always brought in top dollar when he was auctioned off.

"I'm going to do it, but I tell you what—you're going to pay for this," Raymond said, pointing his index finger at his friend.

Keith patted his partner on the shoulder. "All right. I knew you would see it my way. Now stop yakking and let's get to work."

Raymond took off his white lab coat. "You work, I'm going to lunch. First thing you need to do is relieve Karen at the front desk." Then he dashed out the back door.

Many people who saw Raymond walking down the street would peg him as another New York pretty boy player. Though he enjoyed having fun with the ladies, he was also hoping to experience the love that his parents had shared during their fifty-year marriage. Lorne and Helen Thomas never had much; however, what they lacked in material possessions, they made up for in the love they'd shared. He had memories of seeing his parents hugging and kissing every time either of them entered the room. Lorne had always showed his wife the utmost respect and affection, and if they'd ever argued, Raymond wasn't around. Until the end, they worked as a team, and that was the kind of life he wanted with the right woman.

Raymond was beginning to believe his woman wasn't in New York. He didn't think he was going to find her on a TV show, either. Marriage wasn't something to be entered into for the hope of a big payoff. Doing this show was not a good idea, because it made a mockery of marriage—in his opinion. If his parents were alive they wouldn't approve of him making a joke of marriage on national TV. *What am I getting myself into?* he asked himself.

Chapter 2

Imani sat across from Elize Harrington, producer of *Let's Get Married*. She fingered her chemically straightened hair as Elize read over her bio.

"So, you're a real actress?" she said.

Imani nodded and smiled, hoping that her acting experience would work against her. Despite the fact that she needed the money that she'd make from the show, she was still ambivalent about the gig.

"And I understand if you don't want me on the show, being that this is reality TV and all," Imani said, trying to keep the sarcasm out of her voice as she crossed her legs. She knew that there was nothing real about reality TV—except the fact that "reality" was in the title.

"No, no," Elize said, standing up. "This is New York City, where every waitress is an actress. Just when, I mean if, you are cast on the show, keep the acting to a minimum. This isn't a role on a sitcom."

Imani was hoping that she had blown the interview and would be sent packing, but the sparkle in

Elize's eyes told her that she was going to make the cut.

"Let me ask you something," Imani began. "Are you producers and writers just running out of creativity? Don't you have a show that needs someone like me for at least a guest starring role?"

Elize shook her head. "Imani, it's hard to pitch new shows. But America eats up reality TV like McDonald's French fries. Big bucks for both the network and the show's participants. No one is forcing you to do this show and if your career was all of that, you wouldn't be sitting here, now would you? So don't get all indignant with me. You got spunk, though. I'll give you that."

Imani stood up and looked at Elize. "So I guess this means that you aren't going to have me on your show, huh?"

"Are you kidding? You're in, Imani. I don't know how long you'll last. You might be the new woman America loves to hate. Welcome aboard." Elize extended her hand to Imani. She shook Elize's hand, all the while thinking how she should have taken her mother's advice, majored in criminal justice and become a lawyer or something else.

As Imani left, Elize punched the intercom button on her phone. "Who's next?" she asked her secretary.

Imani wasn't paying attention as she headed back into the waiting area where she had left her jacket. As she reached down to pick it up, she collided with a tall, hard body.

"Jerk," she mumbled.

"Excuse me?" a bass voice snapped. "I believe you bumped into me."

Imani locked eyes with the jewel-eyed man. "If you were a real gentleman, you could have seen you were standing in my way."

"And who do you think you are, the Queen of Sheba? If you get your head out of your behind you could see that you're in the way. The world does not revolve around you," he replied. "Excuse me." He pushed past her and headed for the producer's office.

"He thinks he's got so much to offer," she said as she grabbed her jacket from the chair. "I bet he's getting an audition for a real show. It's so much easier for men in this industry."

Elize smiled when Raymond walked into her office. "Dr. Thomas, it is truly a pleasure to meet you. I had no idea you were so, uh, tall," she said as she shook his hand, holding on a little longer than she should have.

"Thank you," he replied as he pried his hand out of her grip.

"Your story is so compelling I felt we had to have you on the show." She never took her eyes off Raymond. He was beginning to feel as if he was a male dancer being stripped. "I'm sure you're going to be a crowd favorite."

Raymond nodded. "If you say so," he said.

Elize handed him the show's waiver forms. "Look over this and sign at the bottom."

Raymond read the form. It was a standard contract; he couldn't talk about the show until he was either voted off or coupled off. "So, when do we receive payment?" Raymond asked after signing the agreement.

Elize laughed. "You don't waste any time, do you?"

Raymond smiled. "The money isn't for me; it's for the clinic I run in Harlem."

"Wow," she said. "That's wonderful . . . a doctor with a big heart. I hope you do well on the show. If you win, it would mean a lot to your clinic, wouldn't it?"

Raymond stood up. "It would. And seeing that this show is going to be filmed in Hawaii, I'm kind of looking forward to this." *As long as Miss Attitude from the lobby isn't there,* he added silently.

Raymond headed for the door feeling a lot less apprehensive about doing the show. Maybe he would even try to win the million-dollar prize. Nowhere in the contract did it say he had to stay with the woman. And if the other contestants were like the woman in the lobby, they wouldn't last two seconds off camera.

Raymond had run into women like her before. He couldn't deny she was beautiful. Her skin was creamy like milk chocolate. She had long black hair that reminded him of midnight, moon, and stars. Her eyes were striking, like a tiger's. But she had an attitude that proved she knew she was beautiful.

Raymond deplored that kind of woman. He had run into his fair share of Manhattanites whose lives were all about Prada, Cavalli, and Dolce & Gabbana. When a woman like that found out he was a doctor at a free clinic, her interest dried up like a desert in July. He couldn't stand shallow women, and any woman who was on a reality show to marry a man for money was beyond shallow. At least he was doing it for all the right reasons.

Raymond walked outside and was surprised to see Miss Attitude standing on the curb. He took a leisurely glance at her long, lean legs. They seemed to stretch from the sidewalk to the sky. She reminded him of a bronzed statue of ultimate womanhood. Her head was cocked to the side as she talked on a small cell phone. Her behind was round like a Vidalia onion.

Imani turned around and looked at Raymond. She snapped her phone shut and stared at him. "What is it now? You're stalking me?"

"You think highly of yourself, don't you?" Raymond retorted. "It's a public sidewalk. Or am I walking on your imaginary red carpet?"

Imani smiled, blinding him with her perfect white teeth. "Okay, maybe I was a little out of line in there, but I have a lot on my mind."

"Is that what passes as an apology these days?" he scoffed.

Imani flung her hair back. "Why would I apologize to you? Maybe I'm not the only one ego-tripping out here," she said, then turned to walk down the street.

As much as he didn't want to, Raymond watched until Imani's shapely figure disappeared from view. "Damn," he mumbled. "Why do the beautiful ones have to have such attitude?"

* * *

Imani's breathing finally became normal as she got away from Mr. Green Eyes. That man was so fine it was mythical. But he had some nerve! Why would she apologize to him when he ran into her? Imani figured he was an actor or a model. She silently hoped that she wouldn't see him again until she was a bona fide superstar. Then she would show him a real diva. But on second thought, having a man like that on her arm right about now walking down the red carpet would mean a boatload of publicity for her and would launch her career into the stratosphere. Imani dismissed the thought as she headed for the subway entrance, intending to go see Edward and find out when the show would pay her. She needed the money so that she could save her home. Before she had headed to the network's office, she received a disconnect notice from Con Edison.

To make matters worse, when she asked her landlord for an extension, he'd flat-out refused to give her more than thirty days to pay her back rent; instead he had proposed the unthinkable.

"I'm sure we could work something else out," he'd said lewdly, pressing Imani against the wall.

Grasping the doorknob, she shook her head vigorously. "Mr. Harper, I can have the money in about forty-five days."

"You can pay all debts just by, well, you know," he suggested as he ran his thick and dirty index finger down her bare arm.

"Oh, hell no." She pushed him into an end table, causing a reproduction Ming vase to fall to the floor and shatter.

"Thirty days and no excuses, unless you want to take me up on my offer," he'd replied with a wink.

The thought of using her body to pay her rent or even to get a plum role on Broadway was off-putting, and if she didn't find something quickly, she'd have to get what people called a real job. And she had to do it pretty damned quickly, unless she wanted to play the real life role of a homeless woman, like a member of the chorus in *Rent*.

Looking across the street, Imani saw that the soul food restaurant on the corner had a WAITRESS WANTED sign in the window. She sighed, feeling defeated. The last thing she wanted was to wait tables again, but if that was going to pay the bills . . . Just as she was about to force herself to cross the street to apply for the job, a yellow cab zoomed out of nowhere moving at break-neck speed and aimed right at Imani. Frozen in place, all she could think about was the many mistakes she'd made, the roles she'd been offered and passed on.

Closing her eyes, she braced herself for the impact of the car against her. . . .

Then out of nowhere, a body pushed her to the ground, causing the strap on her sundress to break. Imani grabbed the man and hugged him tightly, not caring that her black lace bra was showing. She felt his strong, warm embrace in return.

"You saved my life," she exclaimed, terrified. As she focused her eyes and discovered her savior's identity, she felt nauseous. It was Mr. Green Eyes. "It's you," she said caustically.

"Would you have liked it better if I let the cab hit you?" he asked.

Imani shook her head as she shivered and clung to him. If her near-death experience showed her anything, it was that she had a lot of life left to live. And she so wanted to live it.

He picked her up and, with an arm around her, pushed through the crowd that had gathered to gawk.

"We need room," he said. He walked Imani into a corner café and sat her down at an empty table. Imani tried to fix her dress while Raymond looked at her scraped knee.

"Do you have any pain in your leg?" he asked, noting her grimace when he touched her knee. He probed her wound with the skill of someone who knew what he was doing.

Physically, she was fine, but Raymond's touch sent an electrical charge through her nervous system. "Are you a paramedic or something?" she asked as he began checking the bruise on her forearm.

"No, a doctor," he said. "Maybe I should take you to the clinic and clean you up."

Imani shook her head frantically because she couldn't spend another moment around this man without sampling his lips. Gingerly, she rose to her feet. "I'll be fine," she said.

Imani shook her head again, her gaze once more focused on his lips. They looked soft, inviting and ready for her to kiss over and over again. "I'll be fine," she repeated. "I don't think my dress will be, though."

Raymond stood up and looked at her. "You can get another dress," he said. "Can I drop you off any-where? We can share a cab."

"Saving my life was enough. And I'm sorry about before," she said. "Maybe I don't pay enough attention." Imani fought the urge to run out of the café. She was overwhelmed by Raymond's masculinity. And he was a doctor?

He has to be married, she told herself. *There is no way a man that fine can be single, unless he's gay. That's probably it. And that would be just my luck. Who am I kidding? I don't need or want to get involved with anyone until I can at least pay my own way.* Imani shook the thoughts out of her head and walked out the door, making sure there were no wayward cabs shooting across the street. Applying for the waitress job at the restaurant was forgotten, and she headed home.

Raymond tried to get the woman from the street out of his mind as he rode back to Harlem. She was probably married or had a rich Manhattan boyfriend keeping her in the lap of luxury. She wasn't his kind of woman, if that was the case. *A woman like that is nothing but high maintenance,* he told himself as the taxi slowed to a crawl in the wall-to-wall traffic. That woman was probably like the last few women he'd been in serious relationships with, women who said he'd worked too much and had precious little to show for it. They'd been expecting a doctor who had money in his pockets, not a doctor who placed most of his profits back into his clinic. *I don't need the headache of a woman, no matter how sexy she is,* he thought.

When he got to the clinic, Keith was sitting in the

lobby with a barrage of questions for Raymond and he barely allowed his friend to get his foot in the door before he started. "So, are you going to do it? Did the producers like you?"

Raymond put his hand on his hip and looked at Keith. "You know they did," he said. "When I told the producers that I was raising money for the clinic, they ate that up. But, man, on the way over here, I saw this woman—ah, never mind."

"Wait, wait," Keith said, waving his hands as if he were an air traffic controller landing a 747. "A woman got to *you* and not the other way around? It must be a cold day in hell."

Raymond laughed. "She nearly got hit by a car; I took her to a café to look at her. She had skin like silk and a body that would make Jessica Rabbit jealous. But she probably has a man or something. A woman like that needs a man to shower her with gifts."

Keith drummed his fingers across his knee. "Oh, so she's one of those women? Pay to play type chicks, huh?"

Raymond shrugged his shoulders. "I have no idea. I'm just judging a book by its beautiful and sexy cover," he said. "All right, enough of that. Let me get back to work."

"We don't have any patients waiting. Tell me more about this woman. Did you at least get her number?"

Raymond shook his head. Keith slapped him on the shoulder. "Are you slipping or what? If this woman is all that you said she is, you should have at least gotten her number."

He shook his head. "It's all right. The moment has passed and if it is meant for me to see her again, then I will."

Keith raised his eyebrow. "There are millions of people in this city, and there is no way you're just going to run into her again. I can't believe you let one get away. Satan is zipping up his parka right now."

Raymond shrugged his shoulders. "I have charts to review." He headed down the hall, trying not to think about the mystery woman with the scraped knee, but he couldn't help himself. *Damn, I don't even know her name,* he thought.

Chapter 3

Imani rubbed her knee as she sat across from Edward's desk. She closed her eyes and imagined the handsome doctor stroking her knee.

"Imani? Are you all right?" Edward asked.

She nodded like a bobble-head doll. "Why do you ask?"

"Because you seem distracted," he replied. "So, how did the meeting go at the network? I really believe this show can lead to bigger and better opportunities for you. All we need is a foothold and reality TV seems to be the way to go these days. And before you protest, I know that you're a real actress, but unfortunately without a sex tape and some controversy, talent doesn't seem to be enough anymore. I'm still trying to figure out why the Kardashian family is famous. But I digress. Imani, we have to make this work. This reality show will lead you to the stardom that you want. Just don't pull the diva card out."

She sighed heavily and rolled her eyes. "This show is going be stupid. Couch potatoes call in and vote on who should get engaged. Really? That's what passes for entertainment these days? Then the couples go through these trials, testing their teamwork. And how long does America think the winners of this show are going to stay together?" Imani pulled her hair back and twisted it into a loose bun. "If I didn't need the money so badly, I would've told that producer a thing or two. She had the nerve to say, 'No one is forcing you to do the show.' I think Con Edison's disconnect notice is forcing me to do this nonsense. I'm not doing it on my own free will, believe me."

Edward looked at her and smiled. "That's a good look for you. I know how you wanted to keep your hair in its natural state, but this will make you a little more marketable. Now, here's the plan. You're going to be hot on this show and we're going to have to strike fast. Dana is in her studio and she's ready to take new head shots of you. While you're in Hawaii, hopefully showing off what you can do on this show, I'm going to sell you to some of Hollywood's best and brightest directors. And if you make a big enough splash on TV, I might even be able to get some Broadway shows lined up. But one thing is certain, Imani, if you're having the financial problems that you've been talking about, we're going to have to go commercial. That's why I love the straight hair.

"I have a source at the network that I'm going to lean on to get you a check cut early. Hopefully, I'll have some news for you by tomorrow and you can get some much needed money in your pocket. Despite what you think about this show, it's getting some buzz and people are going to be watching. I'm not just talking about the folks you call couch potatoes, either," he said. "You can't back out of this. I've dropped a few whispers in the ears of some industry insiders about you being on the show."

Imani groaned and shook her head. "Your industry friends who won't send a script my way? The same industry friends who have said that my career is dead because of one craptabulous movie?"

"But they're talking about you again and that's what's important. Stop being so negative and think about how this will change things for you."

Imani narrowed her eyes, wanting to ask Edward if he was sure that she'd have a check coming in soon. The sooner she paid off her back rent, the more secure she'd feel and she wouldn't have to deal with her landlord's creepy come-ons. "Do you really think you're going to be able to swing an advance for me? I really need that money," she said.

"Imani, I'm not going to let you down," he said. "You're going to have a check by the end of the week, all right?"

She wanted to shout hallelujah and dance a jig, but she played it cool. "So, do I need to call Dana and let her know that I'm coming?" Imani asked.

"She's expecting you," he said.

Imani stood up once she heard his answer. She was excited to see Dana, knowing this would be a chance to clear her mind. Dana was not only her photographer, but one of her best friends. As a matter of fact, Dana was the only friend she had whom she could be totally honest with—about everything—and not worry about that information being used against her. She didn't have to pretend around her. Dana knew the struggles Imani was going through. Dana and Imani had attended college together and for a while, they were both struggling. Dana considered joining the paparazzi and their endless quest for the candid celebrity shot, but her break finally came when a talent scout saw her portfolio. The man, who just happened to be Edward Funderburke, asked her to take some pictures of his clients. From those head shots, Dana became one of the most sought after photographers in the city. Imani was glad to see her friend's star rise, but she was also ready for her own time to shine.

Imani walked into Dana's studio space. "What's up, girl?" she said, catching the lanky photographer's attention. Dana turned around, swinging her ink black dreadlocks.

"What's going on, superstar? I see Edward talked you into that relaxer," she noted as she looked at her friend. Imani flung her hair back as if she were in a shampoo commercial. "I'm surprised that it looks so good on you. But at least you can go back to the curls whenever you want to."

"This is what Hollywood is going for," she said. "Besides, it will grow out and I can't wait. I'd rather have my straight hair than a lace-front wig or a bunch of tracks sewn into my scalp."

Dana shook her head. "I know acting is your dream, but how much of yourself are you willing to give up for this?"

Imani rolled her eyes. "Relaxing my hair does not equate to me giving up anything about myself. I just want to be marketable, a bankable star." She waved her hands in the air. "Just take my pictures." Imani hobbled over to the camera.

"What happened to you? Trip up the ladder to stardom?" Dana asked when she noticed Imani's gait.

"I almost bought it on Fifty-ninth Street. But luckily, there was this fine doctor there to save me from becoming the finest chalk outline in the city," she said.

Dana opened a box of batteries for her camera. "A doctor, huh? And he was fine? So, when are you guys going out?"

Imani reached into her purse, pulled out a brush and began brushing her hair. "We're not. I don't even know his name. Besides, the way he looked, he has to be married, gay, or otherwise involved. But he had the biggest hands and emerald eyes that sparkled in the sun. He was such a man, though. Arrogant, cocky, overconfident . . ."

"Just your type," Dana interrupted.

Imani put her hand on her slender hip and scowled. "What is that supposed to mean?"

Dana walked over to her friend and pushed her hair behind her ear. "Let's take some test shots, and then you can go change and put on some makeup."

Imani grabbed her hand. "Dana, what do you mean by that little statement?"

"You need makeup for your picture," she replied. "You want to put your best face forward, don't you?"

Imani sucked her teeth and folded her arms across her chest. "You know what I'm talking about," she retorted. "I don't have a type. I just have bad luck when it comes to men."

Dana rolled her eyes and clicked her tongue against her teeth. "Bad luck? That's what we're calling poor choices these days?" She laughed, then fired off two shots of a frowning Imani. "You know the kind of men you have dated. This man sounds like a chip off the old dating block."

Imani walked over to the vanity set up behind the camera. She opened the drawer and pulled out the stash of foundations and blushes that Dana kept on hand. Imani pulled her hair back in a ponytail and began applying the makeup. "You know what? I don't want a relationship right now. I'm just going to focus on my career and that's it. I'm never going to see this guy again, so I don't know if my bad luck will continue."

Dana raised her eyebrow. "So, why are you going on a show to get married?"

Imani shrugged her shoulders and continued to put her makeup on. "It is a means to an end. Who says that I'm going to last long enough to get paired up with some desperate man looking for a wife on TV?"

Dana laughed. "I hope you find the fame that you're looking for," she said. "Because I couldn't go through with it. What has happened to marriage in this country? There was a time when it meant something. My parents have been married for thirty years."

"Dana, marriage is up to the individual. No one cares about lasting marriages these days. You have people like Britney making headlines for quickie marriages in Vegas. Hell, if getting married on a reality show will get me a movie role, then fine," she said. "No one said I had to stay married."

"Whatever, Imani," she said. "Now, let's get started."

Keith and Raymond closed up the clinic Friday around seven and decided to hit the town for a guy's night out. They headed to BlackFinn for some women watching and to take their minds off their troubles and the clinic's financial issues. The place was the ultimate happy hour destination and both of them decided they needed some happy in the long hours they'd worked this week. More bills had been rolling in and the MRI machine, which had been threatening to break down for months, finally bit the bullet. They'd been trying to work out something with Harlem Hospital Center to get their most important cases looked at with some priority. But of course, the hospital wanted to be paid and that's where the problems came in.

Tonight, Keith and Raymond said they weren't going to talk about work or anything health related. They planned to eat food they'd told their patients to avoid and drink until they needed a cab. Raymond had gone for a casual look, dressing in a pair of ivory linen pants and a tan tank top that showed off his luscious body—sculptured arms and flat stomach. Raymond's black and red phoenix tattoo peeked out from underneath his shirt on his right shoulder. While Keith was no slouch in the fashion department, his blue jeans and vintage Jimi Hendrix

T-shirt could have been a set of rags, because all eyes were on Raymond.

"All right, this might be the last chance you have to come out as a single man," Keith ribbed as they walked into the bar. "What if you win this thing?"

"It won't matter, because I'm not making a mockery of marriage. Marriage is a serious thing. I want a marriage that will last until my wife and I die. I want to love my woman so much that my day is incomplete without her."

Keith began playing an imaginary violin. "Brother, please," he said. "In this instant world, if a marriage lasts two years, you're doing well. Women are just as commitment shy as men these days. They aren't looking for Mr. Right, just Mr. Right Now."

"Even Celeste?"

Keith shook his head. "No, but I'm not sure that I'm ready to settle down. I love her, but I'm not in a stable position right now. Look at how we're struggling to pay our bills. Sometimes, I'm not sure if Celeste understands that when I'm working all of these long hours and don't have a pocket full of cash to show for it that this is what my being a doctor means. And, honestly, I need to be sure that I'm ready to settle down before I say, 'baby, let's get married.' It's the only way to be fair to Celeste. Why should we get married if one of us plans on cheating on the other one or if we're not sure about spending forever together?"

Raymond shrugged his shoulders and waved for the bartender to come over. The woman, who kept her brown eyes focused on Raymond, smiled as she sauntered to the end of the bar where he and Keith sat. "What can I get for you gentleman?" she asked in a husky voice that was sexy and seductive.

Keith eyed the woman and smiled. "Can you pour yourself in a glass?"

The bartender rolled her eyes at Keith and turned her attention back to Raymond. "What are you drinking?" she asked, gently touching his hand.

"I'll have Royal Grape," he said. "And get my boy a Cîroc and orange juice."

She smiled and fixed the drinks. She placed Raymond's glass in front of him and winked as she placed a stirrer in his glass, then she turned to Keith and slid his drink to him without much of a second look. "Are you having a good time tonight?" she asked Raymond, ignoring Keith's request for a stirrer of his own.

"Yes, so far, so good," he replied. "Does this taste as good as you look?"

She placed her hand on top of Raymond's and stroked it. "Maybe. But if you want something tasty, you should stick around for a few hours until my shift is over."

Raymond winked at her and said, "I just might take you up on that."

"Don't tease me with a good time," she said with a wink, and then sauntered over to a new group of customers at the bar.

"You know I hate you, right?" Keith quipped.

"What? A little harmless flirtation with the bartender means we're going to drink all night without waiting."

Keith shook his head. "I'm willing to bet that you will be invited to go home with her tonight as soon as she's off the clock. No wonder you're in no hurry to settle down."

Raymond shook his head and took a sip of his drink. "I'm in no hurry to settle down because when I get married, I plan to do it once."

"You know what they say about the best laid plans," Keith said, then drained his drink. "That was pretty good. Call your girl over so I can get another one. Being that I don't rate on her radar."

Raymond caught the bartender's eye and waved her over. "Yes, sir," she breathed.

"He needs a refill and I need to know your name," Raymond said. He could tell by the wide grin on her face that he would get that invitation Keith had alluded to.

"Namina," she replied as she picked up a cocktail napkin and scribbled her number on it. "I'm off in three hours." Before he could reply, another customer called her away.

Keith punched Raymond on the arm. "And you claim you're looking for the one," he said.

Raymond turned around and grinned at his friend. "I didn't say I was looking for her right this minute."

Before Keith could reply, his cell phone vibrated in his pants pocket. When he pulled the phone out and saw it was Celeste, he excused himself from the bar.

Namina walked over to Raymond with a smile on her plump lips. "So, you know my name. What's yours?" she asked.

"Raymond."

"Are you going to use that number tonight?"

"We'll see," he replied, returning her smile. "But it's looking that way."

She leaned in closer to him and stared into his emerald eyes. "You have beautiful eyes, but I'm sure you've heard that before."

"Yes, but it sounds great coming from a beautiful woman like you."

"What is it that you do?"

"I'm a doctor at a free clinic," he said.

Namina cocked her head to the side. "That doesn't sound really profitable."

Great, he thought, *she's another one of those.* His attraction to the bartender was waning. While he thought about telling her that he made more than a bartender, he just took another sip of his drink. He wouldn't be using that number after all. Glancing over his shoulder, he saw Keith making his way through the crowd.

"You know what," he said to her. "I'm going to have to take off. My friend has to get home to his wife."

"Umm," she said, obviously showing that she'd lost interest in him because his job didn't reach her expectations. Raymond rose from the bar stool and met Keith.

"What's up, man?" Keith asked. "I figured you and the bartender would be sucking face by now."

"Funny. Is everything all right with Celeste?"

"Yes. She was just wondering what time I'm coming home tonight, so I'm going to make it an early evening. She's been watching the Food Network again and wants to feed me," Keith said, then glanced over at the bar. "What's up with you and Hot Lips, the bartender?"

"She's not interested in a doctor who works at a free clinic. As if we were building a relationship tonight," Raymond said as he shook his head.

"Maybe you'll meet your wife on the show and she'll bake cookies and bring them by the clinic," he replied with a chuckle.

"Yeah right. I know Celeste has you watching those reality shows. It's probably going to be another crop of women like Namina. Looking for the big bucks instead of a quality relationship. Let's break," he said.

"At least you're heading to paradise tomorrow and we can keep the clinic open for another month when you get your check from the studio. You still have nothing to complain about. I have to go home and pretend dinner's good."

Raymond laughed and nodded. "You're right. I'm going to go home and eat something I know will be good—a slice from John's."

"You really make me sick right now," Keith said as he and Raymond headed for the subway.

Imani tugged at her hair, deciding that she hated her relaxer. She was going out of her mind sitting in her house doing nothing. *Hard to go out when you're broke,* she thought as she pulled her hair down again. Since her cable had been disconnected, she was stuck with three channels and she'd grown tired of the reality shows that every network seemed to be showing. There was a cooking reality show, a reality show where people ate rats, and then there were all of the relationship shows. Reaching for her phone, Imani decided to call Dana and see if her friend wanted to do anything that would get her body out of her house and her mind off her upcoming trip to Hawaii. Of course that trip would've been amazing if she was going to film a real movie or a real series. But no, she was going to be on a reality show.

"Yes, Imani?" Dana said when she answered the phone.

"What are you doing? Don't you want to get out of the house this evening?"

"Who's the director that we're chasing tonight?" Dana asked with a laugh.

"No one," Imani said. "But I want to go to Broadway."

"Not another Imani pity fest," she groaned. "That, I'm not interested in."

"Come on. I'm going to be away from my city for at least ten weeks. I need to soak up some Manhattan, eat some street meat or maybe a slice from somewhere. You know the kind that is just oozing with cheese."

"And how are you paying for this?"

"Another reason why I called you," Imani said with a laugh. "As long as I owe you, you will never go broke."

"All right, Imani, I'll meet you at the station," Dana said. "But the moment you start lamenting about why your name isn't in the lights on Broadway, I'm gone."

"Oh, you're such a good friend," Imani quipped.

"Wear sensible shoes," Dana said, then hung up.

Imani glanced at the four-inch-heeled Steve Madden booties she'd pulled out of her closet. They were sensible enough, she thought as she slipped the shoes on. After all, she'd been sitting down all day. And Imani always had a dream of being discovered on the streets of New York. That's why she never walked outside without looking camera-ready. She knew Dana was going to laugh at her when she saw her slinky Napa leather dress and booties, but she'd also have to admit that Imani looked damned good.

Grabbing her purse, which only held three dollars and her identification, but matched her outfit perfectly, Imani dashed out the door. As she walked to the subway station, she ignored the catcalls from the brothers hanging out on the stoops she passed. But she did put an extra twist in her hips as she strolled to show those men what they would never have a chance at enjoying, touching, or seeing live and in living color—unless they bought a ticket to her Broadway show.

When Imani arrived at the station, Dana shook her head and laughed when she looked at Imani's outfit and shoes. "Always camera-ready. Hollywood is going to love you when you make it," she said "The paps, not so much, because it's going to be hard to get a bad picture of you."

Imani twirled around. "I know. I'm guessing leather isn't going to go over well in Hawaii, so I had to wear this dress tonight."

"Tell me something," Dana asked as the train approached. "What's sensible about those shoes?"

"They make my legs look good."

"All of this to eat a hot dog? You're a trip."

Imani shrugged her shoulders and smiled as they stepped on the train to Manhattan. A group of men sitting next to the doors stood up and gladly gave Imani and Dana their seats. She smiled sweetly at them and turned to Dana. "Gentlemen still exist," she said, then crossed her legs at the ankle. One of the men tapped the other one on the side.

"We don't even get a damned peek," he said in a loud whisper.

"Real princes," Dana replied.

Imani shook her head and told Dana that they should get off at the next stop. "We can get a hot dog from anywhere," Imani said as she tugged at the tail of her dress, which did little to cover her thighs.

"What about the Broadway stroll?"

"We can skip it. Hopefully when I get back from Hawaii, I will be on my way to being a star."

"From your mouth to God's ear," Dana said as the women rose from their seats and waited for the train to come to a complete stop.

Chapter 4

Raymond polished off his last slice of cheese pizza and leaned back in the chair, still wondering if going on this show was a serious mistake. Sure, the money would help save the clinic, but was it smart to put his face on national TV pretending that he wanted a wife?

On the other hand, he surmised, it was a free trip to Hawaii. And that was a far cry from New York. Yes, he loved his city, but he needed a break from all of the noise, the relentless pace. Too bad he had to pretend he wanted to get married to do it.

"Sir," the waitress asked when she walked over to Raymond, "can I get you another slice?"

Looking at the crusts of the three slices he'd already eaten, he decided that he'd had enough. "I'm ready for the check," he said. "It was great."

She winked at him. "Well, if I can get you anything off the menu, let me know."

Raymond nodded, but wasn't interested. Though the waitress was just as attractive as the bartender who'd shot him down earlier, a one-night stand was not the send-off he wanted before going to Hawaii. As he waited for the check, Raymond wondered what happened to the days when men actually had to work for a woman and not have sex offered to the highest bidder.

Everybody's a call girl these days, he thought as the waitress handed him his check and a napkin with her phone number written on it. Raymond thought about wrapping his tip in the napkin, but deciding that he liked the pizza here too much to piss off the staff, he left the money for the bill and the tip on the table and stuffed the napkin in his pocket. He could toss it out later, he decided, as he waved at the waitress and headed for the door.

When he made it out into the street, he ran into a woman he'd never wanted to see again—his ex, Mena Harrison. He wasn't surprised to see that she was draped in diamonds and had her arms wrapped around a well-dressed man who looked as if he had enough money to keep her happy—for a while at least.

"Raymond," she said, squeezing her mate's bicep tighter. "*Quelle* surprise. I learned that when Harrod and I went to Paris last year. How've you been? Still trying to save the sick?"

"Yeah," he said flatly. "Some of us do care about other people."

Harrod cleared his throat as if he was waiting for an introduction. Mena flung her expensive extensions back and said, "Raymond, this is Harrod Wagner, Wall Street broker with the firm Smith

Barney, and my fiancé." She elbowed him in his side, prompting Harrod to extend his hand to Raymond.

As the men shook hands, Raymond said, "I hope you know what you're getting into and that you're recession proof."

"What's that supposed to mean?" Harrod asked, his eyebrows furrowed in confusion.

"Thought you should know, she's a gold digger. You guys have a good night," he said, walking away from the couple. They stood motionless on the sidewalk with their mouths wide open.

As he headed to the subway, Raymond thought about his relationship with Mena, how they'd met at a bachelor auction and how impressed he'd been with the caramel-skinned beauty with auburn hair and a slight English accent. She'd been impressed— at first, anyway—because Raymond had MD behind his name. Their first date, some four years ago, had been dinner at Maroons, because she'd seen it pro- filed on G. Garvin's cooking show. He should've known after that first encounter that she wasn't the one for him. All Mena talked about was the people she knew, the Broadway shows she'd attended, and how she was hoping to make a lot of money through her marketing company. Had she not been dressed in a tight low-cut dress that showed off her fantastic cleavage and toned thighs, he would've left her sitting at the table alone. But as she smiled at him and placed her hand on top of his, all he'd been able to think was how he could talk her out of that tiny dress.

The night had ended just as he'd hoped, in her bed in the Village. She had been a minx in bed and that's why they'd wasted two years together. No matter how he'd tried to explain why he wanted to run a free clinic and not get into a private practice, she didn't get it.

She didn't understand his dedication to helping people with his medical knowledge rather than making money. That rift in their relationship never healed and they drifted apart. When they broke up, he didn't even care that the relationship was over. Raymond wanted a relationship, but it wasn't his main focus. He needed a woman in his life who could understand his commitment to his community. But it seemed that the women he met in New York were only about the almighty dollar. He didn't want to paint all women with the same broad brush. He was sure there had to be women out there who wanted something more than money.

Raymond didn't mind that he was going home alone tonight. But he hoped with all his heart that his cynical side could be proven wrong.

Imani took a big bite of her hot dog as she and Dana headed down Broadway. "I can't believe Papaya still has fifty-cent hot dogs."

"You're lucky that they do," Dana replied as she wiped relish from her hand with a napkin. "Who would've thought that this is how we'd spend a Friday night in New York."

Imani swallowed her food and raised her eyebrow at her friend. "It's hard to have fun when you're broke."

"That's not what I'm talking about. I love you,

Mani, but I'm tired of spending my weekends with you. I need to do something different, experience the New York that I dreamed about when I was in Savannah."

Imani tilted her head to the side and smiled. "Bright lights, big city."

"Excitement and romance."

"I never came to New York for romance," Imani said, then took another bite of her hot dog.

"Yes, fame is your lover," Dana said. "But with all the men in this city, why are we still single?"

"I don't know about you, but I'm single because once a man figures out that I'm not going to hop into his bed, he loses interest. And you won't believe how many men tell me that I'm wasting my time with acting and if I had a real job, I could find a man. What happened to men who supported your dreams and encouraged you?" Imani asked as she kicked off her left shoe.

Dana rolled her eyes and tossed her half-eaten hot dog in the trash. "They died, got married, or never existed anyway."

"That's horrible," Imani said as she picked up her shoe and slipped it back on her foot. "I really thought by now I'd be wearing Jimmy Choos."

Dana shook her head. "Well, if you win the million dollars on the show, you will not only have the money to buy Jimmy Choos, but you'll have that supportive husband that America wants you to have."

"Please," Imani said with a finger snap. "I am not trying to win on this show. But I will show off my phenomenal acting skills. If the man they team me up with falls in love, I feel sorry for him."

"That's the Imani I know and love—career first and everything else be damned," Dana said as she looked down at her watch. "We'd better get moving."

"Thanks for coming out with me tonight. Who knows what Hawaii is going to be like, or these other contestants?" Imani said as she pulled the bread from around her hot dog and dropped it in the trash can. "Hopefully, I'll be able to work out and drop those ten pounds the camera adds. Then, I will be able to get another superhero role."

"And that's why I'm behind the camera. Imani, your figure is fine, and if you lose any more weight, you're going to be unrecognizable. Kind of like Lindsay Lohan when she went blond and lost all the curves that made her a star."

"Please don't compare my career to hers. She's a train wreck, in and out of rehab. Didn't *Law and Order* do a ripped-from-the-headlines story based on her life? Ugh, I was so hoping that I'd get a cameo on that show and then NBC ups and moves it to Los Angeles."

"Why haven't you moved to LA?" Dana asked as she and her friend started walking toward the station.

"Please, I can't afford New York. Imagine me in LA without you? Who would buy me hot dogs there?"

"I'm keeping a running tab of what you owe me," Dana joked. "You're either going to pay me back when you get your first big paying gig or thank me when you win your first Oscar."

"You got it. And I promise you—you're going to shoot my first magazine layout. Eat your heart out, Annie Leibovitz," Imani shouted as the train pulled into the station and the two hopped on.

"How are you getting to the airport in the morning?" Dana asked as they took a seat on the nearly empty train.

"I would say I'm taking a cab, but—"

"What time does your flight leave?"

"Seven."

"And we stayed out this late because?"

Imani shrugged. "Because we live in the city that never sleeps!"

"If this acting thing doesn't work out for you, you should really look into working for the tourism board," Dana joked.

"Ha, ha. Hell, if this show doesn't do everything that Edward says it's going to do for my career, I might have to see if they are hiring," Imani said as she chewed on her bottom lip. "I don't want to give up my dream."

"Don't. But be realistic. If you have to get a real job, don't let pride stop you."

"I'm hoping that doesn't happen," Imani said. "That's why I'm going to make this reality show one long audition tape."

"Only you would say that," Dana said with a laugh. "I like that, though. When you become the next Meryl Streep, I'm putting that in the biography that I write about you."

"As long as you include pictures that capture my best side," she said. Imani crossed her legs and leaned back on the seat. She wanted to close her eyes and imagine Dana snapping photos of her for a spread in *Elle* magazine after she won the best actress award for a movie that starred Denzel Washington and Idris Elba. Double fine and her ultimate dream. But the way the man seated a few feet over on the bench had been inching closer and closer to her, closing her eyes and dreaming about her future was not a good idea.

"Your eyes are glossing over," Dana said as she glanced at her friend. "Denzel or Idris?"

Imani turned to her friend, gave her a camera-ready smile, then said, "Both."

"You're crazy and I hope if that movie ever happens, you get cast in it."

"Yes, because I was ready to get some kind of role in *American Gangster.* Unfortunately, when most casting directors look at me, they see *Fearless Diva* and "Flop" with a capital F written all over my face."

"I thought I knew you," the old man said, hopping into Imani and Dana's conversation. "That movie sucked."

"Excuse me," Imani snapped. "I guess you feel the same way about soap and water."

The man folded his arms across his chest. "Your movie stunk worse than my ass ever will." He rose from his seat and headed to the other end of the train.

Imani closed her eyes and shook her head while Dana fought with her laughter and lost.

"That movie wasn't that bad," Imani said weakly. "But who is he to say—"

"Give it up, Imani. That movie was the biggest mistake of your career."

"Do you think this is another one?"

Dana shrugged. "Have you seen how reality shows are making nobodies stars these days? Imani, you're talented, there is no doubt about that. But people have to get past that movie. This show could be a step in that direction."

Imani nodded. "One more question," she asked.

"Umm. What?"

"Do you really think I have what it takes to be a star or should I listen to my parents and give it up and get a real job?"

"Absolutely not. Imani, you're good at what you do, your material for your movie wasn't great, but you can't allow other people to tell you what to dream and how big to dream," she said. "If it wasn't for you, I wouldn't be doing my thing now. So, I'm going to support you, until you are on Broadway or on the big screen in a movie that doesn't suck."

"See, Dana, that's why I love you," Imani said.

"Umm, I think you love me because I have a car and unlimited patience with you," Dana replied as the train reached their stop.

"You'd better be nice to me or I won't bring you a lei," Imani said.

"How about you better be nice to me or you won't make it to the airport?"

"Good point," she said as she and Dana broke into a fit of laughter.

As they walked to Dana's car, Imani took a deep breath of the New York air. Tomorrow, she'd embark on that journey to fame and fortune.

When the women arrived at Imani's, they were both tired, but as Imani walked inside, retrieved a blanket, sheet, and pillow for Dana, she didn't dare think about going to sleep. Her excitement about heading to Hawaii was overwhelming her need for rest. Of course, she wasn't fully packed.

"Only you would decide to go out the night before your trip and not be packed," Dana said as she made up the sofa and watched her friend flitter around packing her suitcase.

"I thought that I had everything, but as we were coming back, I decided on the character that I want to portray," Imani said. "It's easy to be the vixen, but I want to be the sexy, yet smart contestant. That way, when and if some movie producer sees me, I can be considered the lead for a romantic comedy or something like that."

Dana laughed and rolled her eyes. "And how do you dress smart and sexy?"

"That's what I'm looking for. Cute dresses are key, number one."

"I'm going to bed. What time is your flight again?"

"Seven," Imani said. "I have one more thing to pack and I will be off to bed."

"I hope so," Dana said. "Because the way security is at JFK, I'm going to have to drop you off by five."

Imani looked up at the clock on the wall; it was five minutes to one. "Then I guess I'd better set the alarm and the coffee pot."

Imani dashed into the kitchen and realized that she didn't have coffee or filters to set up her needed dose of morning caffeine. "This being broke crap sucks," she muttered as she decided it was time to go to bed.

Later, Imani didn't have trouble getting up for

her trip. Her night had been filled with dreams of Edward calling her and saying that she needed to come back to New York because a Broadway producer wanted her for a new show and she was playing the lead. She'd almost thought the dream was real and checked her cell phone when she woke up at four-thirty to see if the call had actually happened. But she soon realized that she was still in Brooklyn and her phone hadn't rung at all. *It's going to be a reality soon,* she thought as she hopped in the shower. After her shower, Imani dressed in a pair of leggings and a tank top so that she wouldn't set off too many bells and whistles going through security. Then she grabbed her bags and headed into the living room, happy to see that Dana was walking in the door with two cups of coffee from the bodega around the corner.

"You really are my BFF," Imani said as she set her luggage next to the door.

"Whatever. I know how you are without coffee and I didn't want to deal with that," Dana replied as she handed Imani a cup. "Only two bags?"

"Yep. Smart and sexy romantic comedy stars don't overpack. Besides, I got enough bathing suits in here to last me just in case I make it to the finale."

"And why do you think you won't make it?" Dana asked, then took a sip of her coffee.

"I had a dream," Imani said. "It was all about Broadway and I can't help but believe it's going to come true."

Dana nodded. "But if we don't get going, you're

not going to make your flight to paradise and I'm not going to get home to get some real sleep."

Carefully guarding her coffee, Imani grabbed her keys and luggage, then she and Dana headed for the airport.

Raymond wanted to ignore the blaring alarm clock. But he couldn't ignore his ringing cell phone.

"Yeah?" he said when he answered his annoying BlackBerry.

"Man, you need to pull yourself out of bed and get to the airport," Keith said, sounding wide awake at four-thirty. "Or did you get some good-bye nookie that wore you out?"

"One day, I swear you're going to stop living your bachelor fantasies through me," Raymond said as he swung his legs over the side of the bed. "I swear, if we didn't have so much debt and if that clinic didn't have Mrs. Palmer's name on it, I'd skip this flight." He shook his head and groaned. Early mornings to head into the clinic, Raymond didn't mind. Heading to an emergency room because one of his patients didn't want to see another doctor, that was fine as well. But this, heading for a reality show, was giving him pause.

"Are you sure this is the only way we can keep the clinic open?" Raymond asked as he glanced at his luggage in the corner.

"Yes, otherwise, we'd be in the black right now," Keith replied. "Do I need to go over there and drive you to the airport to make sure you get on the plane?"

"Nah, man. I made a commitment and I'm going. A car will be here in an hour."

"Then don't you think you should get out of bed?" Keith asked. "No one wants to sit on a plane with a smelly doctor. What if you run into one of the other contestants and you smell like the inside of a filthy cab?"

"First of all, speak for yourself. Second of all, you're keeping me from my shower," Raymond said, happy that his friend called him. "Hey, where is Celeste?"

"Sleeping. Like I'm going to be when I'm sure you're going."

"I said I was, didn't I? And if your woman is lying in bed, why are you up?"

"Her dinner did a number on me. I've had heartburn all night. I should've gotten pizza with you and I might've gotten about two hours of sleep tonight."

"Are you sure that's all it is?" Raymond asked out of genuine concern.

"Yeah. You know I have acid reflux. She used extra sauce on that pasta and I forgot to take my purple pill."

"Have you gone to the doctor to make sure you don't have GERD?"

"I think I would know that."

"Doctors always make the worse patients. When I get back, we got a meeting in exam room three," Raymond ordered.

"Whatever. You need to worry about charming those babes on the show and stop worrying about me. I'm going to be fine."

"Keith, you need to start taking better care of yourself."

"So do you. Had your prostate exam yet?"

"Touché," Raymond replied. "We'll take care of all that when I get back, and if I'm lucky, I won't be in Hawaii that long."

"You'd better try and win this thing," Keith said, then laughed. "And I'd better go; Celeste is looking at me wondering who I'm talking to."

"All right, I'll call you when I land." Raymond hung up the phone, glanced at his watch, and hopped out of bed. After a quick shower, a bagel, and a cup of coffee, he heard his car honking outside to take him to the airport. As he loaded his luggage in the car, Raymond prayed he wasn't about to make a fool of himself.

Chapter 5

Imani sat on the plane, heading for the show's location, Maui, Hawaii, trying not to be excited about the reality show. But as the hours ticked away, her excitement grew. Okay, she wasn't going to film a big budget movie and Terrence Howard wasn't going to be shirtless on the beach waiting to shoot a love scene. But damn it, she was going to Hawaii. *Fearless Diva* had been filmed in Southern California, but all Imani had seen of the West Coast had been soundstages and back alleys in East Los Angeles.

This trip would be different because even if she was going to do something that she felt was beneath an actress of her skills, the location was a slice of paradise. Imani's plan was simple: the longer she stayed on the show the more money she would make. So, she needed to find a guy who was docile enough to let them fly under the radar and make America at least like them well enough not to vote them off until she caught the attention of someone who could further her career.

She had to make herself stand out; however, she

didn't want to be a stereotype. It would be a tough road to walk, but Imani was confident that she could do it. As a matter of fact, this would be the ultimate screen test. She pulled her oversized sunglasses over her eyes and leaned her seat back. Sleep took over as the plane reached its cruising altitude. Imani dreamed of receiving an Oscar for best actress, beating Halle Berry, Gwyneth Paltrow, and Sissy Spacek. Denzel was her date and he kissed her deeply when she stood up to get her award. Cameras flashed as she walked up the steps to accept the award from Julia Roberts, who had won last year for some movie where she showed her breasts, something Imani refused to do just to get an Oscar nomination. Her coral and blue Roberto Cavalli dress swayed as she walked. Just as Imani was about to give her acceptance speech, a jolt of turbulence awakened her.

The captain began telling everyone to put their seats in the upright position and lock the serving trays. Imani did as she was commanded and prayed silently that this wasn't the end. She hadn't made it yet. Imani promised herself that when she reached superstar status, there would be no more flying, just like Aretha Franklin. If someone wanted her to audition for a movie role, they would have to drive her out or pay for the train ticket.

The turbulence soon subsided. Imani looked at her watch. Only six more hours. *What am I going to do with myself for six hours?* she thought as she pulled out her month-old *Variety* magazine and read the articles again. That took about twenty minutes. Imani looked out the window, hoping to see some breathtaking view, but all she saw was clouds and blue sky. She tried to go to sleep again, but she knew as soon as she got comfortable there would be more turbulence. A flight attendant walked by with the food and drink cart. "Would you like something to drink, ma'am?" the petite blond girl asked.

"Just water," Imani replied. The flight attendant eyed her as if she knew her.

"Were you on TV or in a movie or something?" she asked. "Oh my God. You were in *Fearless Diva.* I love that movie." Her voice went up an octave. "'You don't scare me, I'm fearless!'" she quoted from the movie. "That is my favorite line. I used it on my boyfriend once and he just stood there and looked at me. Needless to say, we did everything I wanted to do that night."

Imani smiled, glad to see that she had one fan. "Well, I'm glad."

"I need your autograph. He's not going to believe this," she replied excitedly, and handed Imani a paper napkin and pen. The flight attendant waited with bated breath as Imani signed the paper for her.

"You're the first actress I've met on a flight who isn't a bitch," the woman said as Imani handed her the napkin. "Here," she said as she handed Imani a can of soda. "Just keep it for later. This is going to be a long flight."

"Thanks," Imani said with a smile. Little did her fan know, but Imani was just happy to be recognized by someone who didn't think *Fearless Diva* sucked. Imani smiled and relaxed in her seat. She glanced at her watch—only four more hours to go.

* * *

Raymond didn't enjoy flying, but loud people on a plane could double the discomfort level. The flight attendant kept talking about some actress who'd saved her relationship and signed a cocktail napkin for her. Wonderful, but could she hold this conversation somewhere else? All he wanted to do was sleep.

"She was so down to earth and just as pretty as she was in the movie," the flight attendant gushed to another attendant, who was clearly uninterested.

"She should be nice because that movie was horrible," the other woman said.

"It was not horrible," she replied.

Raymond cleared his throat and then said, "Excuse me."

Both flight attendants turned to him and smiled. "Yes?" one of the women asked.

"Can I get another blanket and a pillow so that I can finish my nap?" he asked, when what he really wanted to say was, can you two take this inane conversation elsewhere?

"Oh, yes, sir," the flight attendant said as if she'd read Raymond's hint loud and clear. "Can I get you some Earl Grey tea as well?"

"I'm fine, but I appreciate the offer," he said. The women smiled at him and as they walked away, Raymond heard one of them say, "Oh, I'd like to offer him something, all right."

Looking down at his watch, Raymond smiled. Only two more hours until the plane landed and he could put his feet on solid ground. The flight attendant returned with a blanket and an extra pillow. "So, are you meeting someone special in Hawaii?" she asked as she spread the blanket across his lap.

"That's the plan."

"Well," she said, then licked her lips seductively, "if things don't work out"—she handed him a business card—"call me."

"All right"—he looked down at the card—"Kara."

She winked at him and sauntered down the aisle. Shaking his head, Raymond wondered if it was worth it to join the mile high club with Kara and her shapely hips.

Nope, he decided. *The last thing I need is a fling this high up in the air. But if I'm lucky, she'll be on my return flight.* Leaning back in his seat, Raymond snuggled against his pillow and drifted off to sleep. And just as his nap was getting good, he felt a tug on his shoulder.

Opening his eyes, he saw Kara standing over him. "We're preparing to land," she said. "You need to put your seat in the upright position. Pity, I thought you'd wake up sooner and join me in the bathroom."

"Maybe next time," he said as he adjusted his seat and turned toward the window to watch the landscape of the island grow closer and closer.

"I'm going to hold you to that," she replied as she watched Raymond's eyes sparkle at the sight of the Hawaiian island, for many people an exciting sight to see.

Raymond released a sigh of relief as the plane bounced on the runway. He couldn't wait to kiss the ground.

"*E komo mai*. Aloha and welcome to Hawaii," the captain said over the speaker. "Thank you for flying with Delta Air Lines. It's a sunny day here in Maui, eighty-five degrees this morning at Kahului Airport. Enjoy your stay in paradise and we hope to see you soon."

"Paradise lost," Raymond muttered. "Too bad I'm not going to be on the beach with Kara on vacation." He got out of his seat and grabbed his pack from the overhead compartment as people rushed off the plane, just as happy to be on the ground as he was. He waited as everyone got to the exit door before he moved. The last thing he wanted was to be crushed by the wave of humanity dashing for the exit. When he finally left the plane, he and Kara locked eyes and she mouthed, "Call me."

Raymond winked at her, but was really thinking that women should allow a man to be the hunter at least some of the time. Still, he wouldn't complain about getting caught by Kara for a couple of hours. After heading to the baggage claim and retrieving his bags, Raymond followed the signs the hula dancers were holding for the reality show contestants. Outside, a Hawaiian band played, hula dancers and fire stick tossers put on a show as two limousines, a black one and a pink one, pulled up. Raymond reached into his carry-on bag and put on a pair of aviator sunglasses. He scanned the other contestants, paying close attention to the women heading for the pink limo. He had to hand it to the show's producers, the female contestants were very sexy. He'd only counted eleven women, though.

There had to be one more since he was standing in a group of twelve men.

"Man," one of the men said out loud, "I hope there are no drama queens over there."

"Here, here," a man standing close to Raymond chimed it. "As long as there are no chicks from Boston over there, we're good."

Raymond laughed. "Or New York."

"Oh yeah," the man from Boston said. "New York women, high maintenance. What's up, man? I'm Harvey."

"Raymond."

"And you're from New York?"

"Best city in the world," Raymond said.

"Unless you're talking about baseball."

"That would matter to me if I weren't a Mets fan," Raymond replied.

Harvey laughed and nodded. "You're a cool guy, then," he said. "Damn, look at her."

Raymond followed Harvey's gaze and saw a shapely sister dressed in a white halter dress with a pair of oversized sunglasses on. She walked liked a gazelle, graceful and with a purpose, and she seemed so familiar to him.

"I'm going to need America to put me with that sexiness in that white dress," Harvey said. "Excuse me."

As he walked over to her, Raymond tried to think where he'd seen her and chalked it up to his most erotic dream.

* * *

"Hey," a man called out. Imani turned toward the voice, wondering who this idiot was hollering as if they were at some kind of sporting event. Lifting her sunglasses, she saw someone else, a familiar man, standing near the black limo.

"Yo," the screaming man called out again. Now, everyone was looking at him. But Imani knew he was bellowing for her. "In the white dress."

She found herself regretting going into the restroom and changing her clothes when she'd gotten off the plane. Her new friend Kara, the flight attendant who'd loved *Fearless Diva,* had walked her off the plane and shown her where to freshen up.

"Yes?" Imani replied.

"What do I have to do to get to know you better? You know you're fine, right?"

Imani raised her right eyebrow as she surveyed him. This man wasn't going to make any friends or fans and there wasn't enough acting in the world that she would do to pretend she liked this loud-mouthed, annoying man.

"There's nothing you can do," Imani replied.

"Ouch. Damn, baby, that's harsh." His eyes roamed her body like a hungry man at a buffet. When his stare landed on her breasts, Imani folded her arms across her chest.

"Your breath is harsh. What I said was the truth."

Snorting, he turned his head to the side. "You must be from New York. Stuck up b—"

"And you must be mentally challenged," she said, then stepped away from him. As she continued to look at the men lined up by the black limo, she saw the man who'd caught her eye standing there. He looked as if the last place he needed to be to find love was on a reality show. There was something vaguely familiar about the tall man in the aviator sunglasses. *Please don't let him be an actor. This is my chance to shine, not compete with others in the business. I don't need the odds stacked against me like that,* she thought as she watched him lift his suitcase with one hand as if it weighed less than a pound.

His hands . . . She wondered if they were soft and tender. She forced herself to look away because if she didn't, she'd get caught up in the fantasy of those muscular arms being wrapped around her and those lips pressed against hers. Imani liked kissing. She wanted to kiss him. She wondered what was behind those sunglasses. An admiring gaze? Or lovely green eyes like the doctor who'd cleaned her knee on the street in Manhattan?

No, she wasn't going to think about the one who got away. She was looking for a partner who would allow her to show off her acting chops, nothing else. Still, she stole one more glance at Mr. Aviator Sunglasses as he climbed into the limo. What a fine ass that man had.

"All right, ladies," one of the producers called out. "It's time to go!"

Imani headed for the pink limo that was taking the contestants to the resort. Just as she suspected, when she got into the limo, it was full of Barbie dolls—busty, blond, tanned, and half dressed. She made a mental note to tell Edward that she didn't appreciate being the token black woman on the show.

"Hi," a Latina said, when she climbed in and sat beside Imani.

"Hello," Imani replied. No one else in the car had spoken to her, not that it mattered. She was there for one reason and making friends wasn't it.

"I'm Lucy Chavez," she said. "Isn't this exciting?"

"Thrilling," Imani replied sarcastically.

"I hope I meet someone really nice," she said. Her eyes sparkled with hope.

"You're serious?" Imani asked incredulously.

Lucy nodded enthusiastically. "I've been trying to meet someone at home in San Diego, but I haven't had any luck. I was so happy the show called me."

Imani held back a sarcastic comment. Another contestant, who introduced herself as Marilyn Tanner, smiled at Lucy. "Dating is so hard. That's why I jumped at the chance to meet someone who actually wants to get married. And from what I saw out there, those guys are gorgeous. I just hope America gets it right and pairs me with someone tall and sexy. I did see a few toads out there, but that's life."

The two women turned to Imani. Their eyes seemed to urge her to tell a sappy story about wanting to get married. But Imani only offered them a silent smile, because inside she was simply laughing at the fact that they thought true love was a made for TV competition.

Lucy finally asked the question. "So, Imani, why are you here?"

"For the fame and the money," she said bluntly. "Do any of you actually think a relationship formed on TV in front of a live audience is going to last?"

The collective gasp in the car was more than

enough to make Imani wish she had kept her mouth closed. She had given those eleven women ammunition to use against her. Now, she was going to have to watch herself even more if she didn't want to get booted from the show before securing a chunk of prize money or a great movie script. After her outburst, everyone was silent the rest of the way to the Blue Diamond Resort. Imani avoided eye contact with the others, but she could feel their daggerlike stares stabbing her. *Great job, Imani,* she thought woefully. *You should have just painted a bull's-eye on your back.*

The pink limo pulled up to the breathtaking resort, and moments later the black limo followed. The doors on both cars opened. Imani wondered if Mr. Aviator Sunglasses had taken his shades off yet, but she forced that thought out of her mind as Lucy and the other women hopped out of the car as fast as greased lightning. Each one of them made a fuss over their hair and pulled at their clothing for maximum cleavage exposure.

Imani decided to play it cool as she scoped out the crop of desperados. The dark tint on the limo's windows made it practically impossible to get a good look at the men. Reluctantly, she got out of the car. After all, she did need to make it look good.

"All right, who came to win? I need to avoid you if you're looking for a wife," she mumbled as she gave the male contestants a closer inspection than she had at the airport. She'd almost forgotten about Mr. Aviator Sunglasses until she saw him without the mirrored shades covering his eyes. Her heart fluttered when she recognized his bewitching green eyes. It was him—the doctor from New York. Their eyes met and for a moment, Imani forgot about the other women jostling for position and partners. She'd nearly forgotten that she was in Hawaii to film this ridiculous show, and felt like she was there only to meet him.

"Wow, look at green eyes over there," Lucy said to Imani, loud enough for everyone around to hear her. "If America loves Jesus, they will pair us up."

Not if I can help it, Imani thought as she and the doctor locked eyes. Either he was remembering her or Lucy's extreme cleavage drew him in their direction. Imani prayed that he wasn't coming to fawn over those mounds of silicone that Lucy claimed were breasts.

When he stood in front of Imani, all she could think about was his hot hands touching her when she'd fallen. Had he introduced himself that day? She couldn't remember his name, if he had introduced himself—but those eyes were unforgettable.

"Hello," he said, looking directly at Imani, and she could barely keep the coolness in her voice when she replied.

Lucy quickly hopped into the conversation, nearly pushing Imani to the ground with her hips. "I'm Lucy," she said with her hand extended. He took her hand and shook it, but his eyes never left Imani's face.

"Nice to meet you," he said to Lucy, then he smiled at Imani. "Nice to see you again. How's the knee?"

"Great," she said. "I have to say, I'm surprised to see you here."

He shrugged, dropping Lucy's hand. "Thought I'd give it a try so that I could raise money for the clinic," he replied. Obviously, Lucy felt ignored and stormed off. "What's your name?"

"Imani. And you are?"

"Raymond."

"Nice to officially meet you," she said.

"Now, what is a beautiful woman like you doing here looking for a husband? I'm sure you have no problem finding a man." He folded his arms and Imani's mouth watered as she watched his muscles flex. She wanted those arms around her, wanted to feel his warmth and have those lips pressed against hers. They would make a perfect picture on the cover of *Us Weekly* or *Essence* magazine.

"Are you all right?" he asked.

"Yes," she replied with a smile. "I was just thinking about how we had to come all the way to Hawaii to get a proper introduction."

"Funny how life works out sometimes," he said with a laugh. Then he did it, he reached out and took her hand in his.

Her skin was soft, Raymond thought as he stroked the back of her hand with his thumb. Their eyes locked and he was transfixed by her quiet beauty, her smooth caramel brown skin and elegant brown eyes. Her hair, pushed behind her ears, looked real. But being that she was from New York, it could be a weave. Either way, he wanted those silky strands against his cheek after he tasted her lips, wrapped her legs around his waist and dove into her wetness and made her scream his name.

"I wonder if they're filming us now," Raymond whispered.

"Oh, God," Imani exclaimed, "I hope not." She fussed over her hair and ran her tongue across her lips. "I'm so not camera-ready right now."

Raymond shrugged as he watched her smooth her dress. "You look good to me," he said with a smile. "So, what do you do?"

"I'm an actress," she replied proudly. "I'm hoping this show will give me some great exposure."

"Broadway?" Raymond's mind immediately flashed to Imani in a sequin leotard and a pair of sky-high heels showing off those long, curvy legs. He loved her legs.

"I've done a few commercial spots and a movie. Have you ever seen *Fearless Diva*?"

He narrowed his eyes at her as he recalled that horrible movie with the sexy star. "Wow, that was you in that movie?"

"You saw it?" she asked with a smile.

"Yeah, and if you weren't so cute, I'd ask you for my ten-fifty back. That movie was horrible."

"Excuse me?" she said, narrowing her eyes into little slits.

"You can't be proud of that movie," he said with a laugh. "What were you thinking when you read that script? Cult following? I laughed a lot, but I don't think some of the things I laughed at were supposed to be funny."

The evil look Imani gave him made Raymond shiver in the tropical heat. "You're going to stand there and insult my craft? I worked hard on that movie and it's not my fault that you can't appreciate a movie that thought outside the box."

"The box of good taste."

"And what have you done?"

"Saved a couple lives, opened a clinic, and wasted my money on a damned sorry movie."

"I would say that it was nice to meet you, but that would be a lie," Imani said, then stormed off. Though she was angry, the sway of her hips, with a little extra ummph, still had Raymond mesmerized.

Chapter 6

Producer Tres Ellis watched Imani and Raymond interact on closed circuit TV. She took a pull of her clove cigarette. "I see stars being born," she whispered as she exhaled a puff of smoke. Tres could see the attraction that both parties were trying to deny. Raymond looked as if he wanted to kiss Imani, then tell her off. And Imani looked at Raymond with a gleam in her eyes that screamed "make love to me." Tres had seen this on other shows and she was happy to have it on hers.

"Elliot," she shouted. "See these two? I want a camera on them at all times. No matter what America says, they are going to be a couple on this show. I knew we had a strong cast on this show, but who knew the actress and the doctor would look so good together on camera? First thing in the morning have them in the interview room."

"Yes, ma'am," he replied as he turned to the monitor. "What's so special about them, though?"

Tres smiled and blew out another puff of smoke. "They sizzle like bacon."

* * *

For the next two hours, the contestants explored the resort, finding its treasures—such as the hot tub, a grotto with a pool built for four, and an indoor waterfall—and their rooms.

Imani prayed to everything holy that she would avoid Raymond. But every time she turned a corner, there he was. His eyes seemed to peer through her soul and she wanted to open it up to him—but he had insulted her craft and that was an unforgivable sin. Yes, her movie sucked and she'd heard people say worse things than he had about *Fearless Diva,* but she took it personally when Raymond said it. When Imani found the door to the room she claimed as her own, it seemed that fate was playing with her again, because Raymond was letting himself into the room across the hall from hers. He didn't seem to notice her. She looked over her shoulder and drank in his delectable frame. She wondered how he would look in a tight pair of boxer briefs and no shirt. His skin damp from a shower. With arms like that, he could wrap them around her and pull her against his hard body and . . .

"Is there a problem?" Raymond asked, causing Imani to break her stare.

"What?"

"You're staring at me."

"I was not. You're so conceited."

Raymond smiled and walked into his room. Before he closed the door, he turned to Imani. "I'm locking my door, in case you have ideas about coming over here and kicking my ass because I didn't like your movie."

She sucked her teeth, then slammed her door behind her. Imani was embarrassed that he caught her staring, but she couldn't help but smile. He wanted her and she wanted him. *What am I going to do?* she thought.

Raymond sat in his room, staring out the window. He watched the waves crash against the shore. Why was Imani this close to him? He closed his eyes and imagined being on the beach with her. Their bodies would be intertwined. Her hair wet and plastered to her face. Raymond could almost taste her tongue. Was her kiss as sweet as she was vicious? Raymond felt a fullness in his pants as he thought about lifting her bikini top. Her breasts would spill out like a Hawaiian waterfall. The ocean spray would give her nipples a salty taste as he took them into his mouth. Raymond shook his head. *She's not why you're here. Ignore her and keep your eye on making money for the clinic,* he thought.

Raymond knew that was going to be easier said than done. Knowing that Imani was across the hall was going to wear on him, drive him crazy and haunt his dreams. But, this was a TV show, Imani was an actress, he reminded himself. He couldn't be sure that she wasn't just here for the camera time and thought of everyone as a prop. Still, she was sexy as hell and there was no way he could deny that. Raymond told himself not to lose focus. He was on this show to raise money for his clinic.

Falling for a moody actress was not a part of the plan. *Why is she here anyway? Why isn't she doing another movie?*

Raymond had to admit, Imani was the only bright spot he recalled in that dismal comedy/drama that was *Fearless Diva*. He couldn't even remember the plot. But he remembered Imani getting out of a hot tub in a pair of panties and no bra. She had the most perfect breasts he had ever seen. He wondered how much of that was studio magic and how much was actually her. Raymond wanted to walk across the hall and talk to her. But what would he say? He was the one who said he was locking his door to keep her away. "Open mouth, insert foot," he mumbled as he walked over to the window and pulled the curtain back.

A knock on the door interrupted his thoughts. Raymond smiled, thinking that it was Imani. He bounded to the door, but paused for a few seconds before opening it. He didn't want to look too excited to see the sexy siren.

However, when he opened the door, any excitement about seeing Imani faded when he found Lucy standing there with a smile on her face and a bottle of wine in her hand.

"Hi," she said. "Earlier, we didn't get a chance to talk or get introduced properly. Want to have a glass of wine and get to know each other?"

Raymond looked at the barely there pink bathing suit she wore and the sheer sarong wrapped around her shapely hips. Lucy had a nice body, but she was no Imani. Her curly black hair looked damp, as if she had just gotten out of the pool. Beads of water glistened on her brown shoulders. Sure, she only wanted to talk. He knew those signals and they had nothing to do with talking.

Forcing a smile, he replied, "Why not? I have a wonderful view from my balcony. Come on in."

"A bunch of us are swimming and hanging out. I was looking for you," she said, not hiding her attraction as she followed him inside the room. "I'm glad you're not in here with our resident actress."

"You know, I'm a little tired. It was a long flight from New York, but thanks for thinking of me," he said.

"You do have a great view," she said as she joined him on the balcony. "The ocean is beautiful." Lucy set the wine on the table and pulled her chair beside Raymond's. He reached for the bottle and looked out at the ocean. He wondered if Imani enjoyed the water or if she was too vain to get her hair wet. Glancing over at Lucy, he decided that there was nothing wrong with spending time with a less dramatic woman. She was cute . . . but wait, what if she was actually seeking a man who wanted to marry someone he met on TV? He opened the bottle with the corkscrew Lucy handed him and sighed.

"What's wrong?" she asked.

"Nothing. Just thinking about how far people will go for love."

She folded her arms and cocked her head to the side. "What do you mean?"

"Just thinking out loud."

"So, you don't think the one for you is here?" Lucy asked. "I believe in love at first sight."

Raymond gave her a sidelong glance and exhaled slowly. "Love at first sight is a myth," he said. "Lust at first sight is more like it." Imani immediately popped into his mind as he poured himself a glass of wine.

Lucy took the bottle from his hands and set it on the table. "So, what did you think when you saw me standing at your door? Love or lust?"

Neither, he thought as he stared at her. "Let me get back to you on that."

Lucy wasn't taking no for an answer as she rose to her feet and crossed over to him. Before Raymond could say a word, she'd perched herself on his lap, her arms wrapped around his neck and legs around his waist. Her grip was as tight as a vise. Raymond shifted, but Lucy wouldn't let him go. "I think I feel lust," she moaned.

"Lucy, come on," he said as he finally pried her off him. "I'm not trying to be that guy."

"What guy is that?" she asked as she tried to press her lips against his.

"The reality show boy toy," he replied, pushing her away. "Besides, if you're looking for love, you're going about it the wrong way."

"Really? I don't think you're going to fall in love with me right away, but once we win the show, then we can go from there. I just want to give you a taste of what I have to offer."

"I'll pass," he said as he turned toward the door. "I'm going to take a nap. Maybe we'll see each other later."

"Oh, we will see each other later," Lucy said. "Are you sure I can't join you for a nap?"

"I just want to sleep," he said as he led her into the room and toward the door.

"All right, Dr. Raymond," Lucy said, walking into the hallway. "Make sure you dream about me."

Before he could respond, he saw Imani's door open. She stepped out dressed in a white, red, and orange bikini with a sheer sarong wrapped around her waist and no shoes. Raymond looked down at her feet and realized that calling them perfect would be the understatement of the decade. Imani looked at Raymond and raised her eyebrow. Their eyes locked and he wanted to say something to her. But she turned away from him quickly.

Lucy seemed to notice their spark. "She's just here for the money and fame," she whispered to Raymond. "She told us that in the car."

"I don't doubt it," he said, not taking his eyes off Imani as she sauntered down the hall without even looking back at Raymond. Her hips had a beat of their own. Why couldn't she have been the one trying to kiss him? Turning to Lucy, he offered her a weak smile. "Thanks for the wine," he said.

"Sure I can't interest you in anything else?"

Raymond shook his head and reached for the doorknob. "Maybe we'll see each other later," he said. Lucy walked down the hall, putting an extra twist in her hips as she went. Raymond wasn't watching, though. He shut the door behind him and strode across the room. His attention had turned to the island beauty he saw from his window. Imani. She was lounging on the beach, head back and eyes covered by a pair of diva sunglasses. Did she know that she was right underneath his window and giving him a show that he wouldn't mind spending way more than ten dollars to see?

He figured she wasn't going to the pool with everyone else because that's where the majority of the cameras would be. Raymond couldn't say that he was disappointed to find Imani alone on the beach. He smiled as he thought about the fantasy he'd had about her on that same stretch of sand that she was lying on right now. He quickly put on a pair of Speedos and dashed down the stairs. Raymond tried to make sense of what he was doing. He'd just said he didn't want to be the reality show guy who had sex with a contestant, but Imani was too damned irresistible to leave alone. At least with Imani, he knew that she wasn't on this show to find a husband and she probably didn't believe in love at first sight like Lucy. He just wanted to talk to her, alone and away from the cameras. Yeah, right. He didn't want to simply talk to her. He wanted to feel the crush of her breasts against his bare chest as he kissed her and explored her mouth. That's what he wanted to do. Talking could come later.

When he reached the shore, Raymond was rendered speechless as he drank in her image in the waning sunlight. She looked like a mythical goddess who'd washed up on the seashore to find a man to put under her spell. Well, it was working because she had him mesmerized. Raymond cleared his throat to announce his presence. Imani pulled her sunglasses off her face and frowned at him. "You're blocking my sun," she said.

"Why aren't you at the pool with everyone else?" he asked.

"Why are you concerned about what I'm doing? Where's your friend?" Imani asked as she placed her glasses on her face and propped up on her elbows. Her body was elongated and he wanted to ski on those curves.

"My friend is right here. If she can forgive me for insulting her movie."

Imani ran her hand down her throat. "I'm not your friend. I'm talking about the girl who was leaving your room looking all wet. Does she know you kicked her out of bed so you could come down here and block my sun?"

"See what happens when you assume things? I didn't kick anyone out of bed," he said.

Imani rolled her eyes, then looked at Raymond as if to say "are you kidding me?" "Either way," she said, "you're still blocking the sun."

Raymond leaned down beside her and looked into her enchanting brown eyes. God, she was beautiful—but like a jagged coral reef. Raymond knew he was going to get hurt if he got too close.

"Are you getting into character?" he teased as he took up residence on her blanket. She formed her mouth into an O as if she was about to say something snappy; instead, she handed him her sunscreen bottle. "If you're going to be out here, you really should make yourself useful."

"You still didn't answer my question," he replied as he squirted a glob of cream into his palm. "Is this all about acting for you?"

She flung her leg onto his lap. "Maybe. But you're here just for the money, so why don't we make it work for both of us?"

Raymond began smoothing the lotion on her leg. Damn, her skin was smoother than his favorite John Coltrane jam and softer than Egyptian cotton. He couldn't focus on what she was saying because he was transfixed by those lips. Luscious was the only way to describe them and as he finished smoothing the lotion on her legs, all he wanted to do was kiss her.

"So?" Imani questioned. "What do you think?"

"About?"

"You and me teaming up? You get the money you want and I get the screen time I need. We already have a story line. Were you listening to anything I said?" she asked as she sat up straight and placed her hands on her hips. "I can't—"

He cut her off quickly as he captured her lips with his, swallowing whatever words she had been about to say. Her lips were sweeter than anything he'd ever tasted, and talk about soft. Her lips were like rose petals.

She's going to slap me at any moment, he thought before slipping his tongue between her parted lips. And when Imani wrapped her arms around Raymond's back, he moaned, easing closer to her. In his arms, she felt like heaven. Felt like the ripest mango ready to be peeled and devoured. Raymond kissed her deeply, sucking on her bottom lip, enjoying the feel of the curve of her breasts pressed into his chest. A wave crashed against the shore, covering them in a salty mist. She pulled back from him and their eyes locked.

"I have to go," she said as she quickly rose to her feet and dashed back into the hotel. Raymond watched her run away and realized that she'd left her blanket, sarong, and beach bag. He could've caught up with her and returned her things, but he had to wait until his heart rate returned to normal and his erection faded. A single kiss had never caused him to be so aroused. Damn.

When he could breathe normally again, he gathered her things and walked slowly into the resort.

"Did you see that smolder? Oh, this is going to be a huge fire," Tres said as she ripped the cap off a bottle of water and took a big swig. "Makes sure Lamont gets a bonus for following my directions to a tee."

"Yes, ma'am," Elliot said. "They do make a hot couple. But in fairness to the other contestants, how are we going to fix these two up without—"

Tres held up her hand, cutting him off. "If we don't get good ratings on this show, you and I are going to be out of a job. Do you want to be on the unemployment line or do you want a successful show?" She pointed to the screen. "Those two are the key to success."

"How are we going to make sure the people watching the show won't think it's fake? This is reality TV, Tres."

She smacked her lips and shook her head. "Fiction without having to deal with writers—it's the best television money can buy. Just remember that Imani and Raymond are our stars." Tres rose from her chair. "But we can't have stars without some villains.

Play back some of the other footage and let's see who we're going to pit against the golden couple."

"I know the woman we can put up against them. Look at this. Lucy has an eye for Raymond." Elliot showed Tres footage from earlier when Lucy had arrived at Raymond's room with the wine.

"I love it!" Tres exclaimed. "This is going to be ratings gold!"

Chapter 7

The moment Imani barreled into her room, she stripped off her clothes and headed for the shower. She had to cool the heated lust that Raymond had stirred up in her on the sand. She'd never been so thoroughly kissed, touched so intimately and so passionately. She hadn't been ready for her body's response to Raymond. The liquid lust that pooled between her thighs had shocked her and excited her at the same time. It was a new feeling for her. Never had she been that turned on from a kiss. The last guy she'd dated, Carlton something or other, had called her a frigid tease because she hadn't even kissed him with tongue. Yet this stranger was able to make her body respond in ways that she'd only read about or heard her friends talk about.

Imani stepped underneath the cold shower spray, trying to clear her mind of the feel of Raymond's lips and hands on her body. But as the water beat down on her, she couldn't think of anything else but his hands roaming her body and she got all hot and bothered again. Was there a setting on the shower for ice?

Imani turned the water off, wrapped up in a towel, and sat on the edge of her bed, her wet hair hanging on her shoulders like seaweed. She exhaled loudly. *This must be what sexual frustration feels like,* she thought as she twisted her wet tresses into a sloppy braid and leaned back on the bed.

"Why did I kiss him? I should have slapped him," she mumbled. Imani stood up and walked over to the door and placed the palm of her hand on the door as if she was stroking Raymond's smooth, sculptured torso. His kiss was like a gourmet candy that she had never tasted.

Imani had protected her virginity. In her business, sleazy producers always tried to bed actresses. She never gave anyone a chance to force her on the casting couch. She didn't mind playing a sexpot on screen, but she couldn't do it in real life, wouldn't do it in real life. But, if that was the case, why had it been so easy for Raymond to turn her on like a light switch?

Imani went back to the bed, lay down and gazed at the ceiling. *I am not going to lose my virginity on national TV,* Imani thought as she pounded the pillow beside her.

Imani knew that avoiding him was going to be impossible, but she wasn't going to tell him that she wanted him. Did he already know that?

So much had changed in a day. It wasn't about the money anymore. It was about a desire to be with Raymond. "What have I gotten myself into?" she bemoaned.

* * *

Tres was beyond excited as she watched footage of Raymond and Imani on the beach again. There wasn't even going to be a need for a lot of editing on this scene.

She hadn't thought the couple would've connected this quickly, but she wasn't upset about it. This show was make or break for her career after the last two scripted shows she'd produced were canceled after two episodes.

"I've got a feeling this show is going to be great," Tres said more to herself than her staff. She began running promos in her head. She had to make sure the votes put Imani and Raymond together.

"Darcy," Tres barked into her walkie-talkie cell phone, "bring me the bios on Imani and Raymond."

"Yes, ma'am," Darcy replied.

Within minutes, Tres had the information she had requested. She looked over the biographies. Both of them were from New York. And she wanted to play up the fact that Imani was an actress. The public needed to *think* this show was keeping it real. Tres laughed. If people only knew the truth about reality TV, how much was staged to get the most ratings. But Imani and Raymond had one thing that didn't need to be staged, Tres knew, and that was real chemistry.

"I want interviews with Lucy, Raymond, and Imani, first thing in the morning. People, looks like we may have a hit," she barked to her staff.

* * *

Raymond wanted to knock on her door. As he stood there with her bag and towel in his hand, he knew he looked ridiculous. Raising his fist, he thought about that kiss again. Was it play acting? Lucy said Imani was here for the fame and money and he knew she was an actress. She'd even tried to pull him in with the offer of an alliance. But, that kiss was real, wasn't it?

Hanging her belongings on the door, he turned away because knocking on that door and entering her room would be walking into temptation and he wasn't sure if he could resist it.

She could have been acting on the beach, he thought as he walked over to his room. He turned and looked back at the door. What if she wasn't acting? Suppose that fire he felt had burned Imani too? Should he expect a knock on his door and a lustful thank-you kiss for returning her items? He wanted that, yearned for another chance to feel her lips on his and her body pressed against his. He didn't believe in love at first sight, but he was definitely struck by lust at first taste. And Imani tasted so damned good. He wanted to lick her all over, slowly, methodically, until she screamed his name. Lost in the fantasy of feasting on Imani, he was shocked when he heard a woman call his name. Turning around, he'd hoped to see Imani, but it was Lucy.

She eyed him, in his near naked and aroused state, as if he were the main course for dinner.

"Were you heading to the pool?" she asked with a lick of her glossy lips.

Raymond shook his head. "I went down on the beach. Pools are nice, but it seems a little sinful not to dip in the ocean when it's this close."

Lucy smiled. "I never thought about it like that. What are you doing for dinner?"

"I think I'm going to order room service," he said, though if he could have the perfect meal, it would involve his mouth between Imani's thighs. "I may have overdone it on the beach."

"You don't want to eat alone," Lucy said as she cozied up to him and ran her index finger down the center of his chest.

He took her hand in his and before he could say a word, Imani's room door opened. Lucy smiled when she saw the scowl on Imani's face as she stared at her and Raymond.

"I'm going to eat alone," Raymond said, quickly dropping Lucy's hand. He tried to catch Imani's glance, but she slammed into her room and that pretty much killed his fantasy of having her for dinner.

He unlocked his room door, hoping that Lucy would leave, but she stood there as if she was waiting for an invitation to come in. Sighing, because he couldn't have what he really wanted, he wished Lucy could take a hint. "Well. I'll see you later," he said.

Lucy was visibly disappointed as she said goodbye to him. "Hey," she said, "if you want to have breakfast together, you know how to reach me."

Raymond closed the door and lay on the bed. He

looked out the window and watched the waves crash against the shore. He closed his eyes and remembered his interlude with Imani on the beach. The memory of her kiss made his body tingle, his body harden. And it frustrated him. No other woman had ever made his body so alive with desire. *Get a grip,* he thought. *You have to focus on what you're here for and it isn't to get that woman into your bed. Besides, you've probably blown any chance you had with her because she saw Lucy with you.*

Raymond wondered what would happen once the cameras started to roll. Did Imani still want to team up with him or was she going to saddle up to someone else because she saw him with Lucy? *Maybe she's in her room working on her character right now,* he thought. Raymond pondered if he should go across the hall and . . . do what? She wasn't his woman and he didn't have to explain anything to her. Rising from the bed, he headed for the balcony and watched the setting sun. The sky was painted with hues of orange, lavender, and deep blue. He noticed a set of clouds in the distance that looked like two lovers intertwined in a deep kiss. As if he needed another reminder of her. He thought about walking across the hall and clearing everything up with Imani or better yet, just kissing her again.

A knock at the door interrupted his thoughts. Thinking it was Lucy, Raymond almost didn't answer. But he did and to his surprise, it was Imani. "Hi," he said.

"I hope I'm not interrupting anything, but I thought it would be rude if I didn't thank you for returning my bag," she said with her arms folded across her chest.

Raymond's gaze slowly meandered across her body. She'd changed into a bandeau dress that hugged her delectable curves as he wished he could. Her feet were bare, toes polished a cherry red color that made his mouth water.

"Well," he said once he found his voice, "I didn't want to leave your things on the beach and I wasn't sure if you—"

"Just tell the truth, you were distracted by silicone and sex," she said in a tone that sounded as if she was jealous.

No way, he thought. "I wasn't distracted," he replied with a smirk. "Had you given it about three more seconds, you would've gotten an invitation to dinner."

She rolled her eyes. "I'm nobody's second choice. Did she turn down your offer?"

"You got it backward. I turned her down. And you're right—you're not second choice. We're partners, remember?"

Her lips curved into a bright smile that sent a shiver from the base of his neck to the tips of his toes. "That's good to know," she said. "So, I guess when filming starts, we should really work on how we're going to play off each other. There should be some conflict, some tension, and some . . ."

"Kissing," he said as he pulled her against his chest. Imani tilted her head upward and stared into his eyes. Her lips quivered, telling Raymond that she wanted to kiss him as much as he yearned to kiss her. So when she gave him a stiff arm that would put

Jets' running back LaDainian Tomlinson to shame, he was taken aback.

"Why don't we wait until someone's watching?" she said, then wiggled out of his embrace. "So, you want to talk strategy over dinner?" Imani backed against the door and Raymond took a deep breath, deciding that he would stop torturing himself.

"Why not," he said. "I'm here for the money and you're here for the fame," he lied, because now that he had a taste of Imani, he wanted so much more than money. "But I will kiss you again. Not right now, because you want the camera to capture it."

Imani turned her head away from Raymond because she wanted to kiss him, wanted his lips on hers so badly that her body ached and her mouth watered. And now, she was supposed to sit there and have dinner with him while keeping her hands, lips, and tongue to herself.

Where are these thoughts coming from? Imani wondered as she watched Raymond reach for a room service menu. Those arms. When he wrapped them around her, she felt heat. She felt both protected and horny. At least that's what she thought she was feeling. She had all the symptoms she'd heard other women talk about: wet panties, shortness of breath, and a craving for skin to skin contact.

She expelled a sigh and headed out to Raymond's balcony, glancing over her shoulder at him as he ordered dinner. "I didn't even tell him what I wanted," she muttered. "And he doesn't know me well enough to . . . Who am I kidding? If I go in that room, it's not going to be pretty."

She turned around and watched the waves of

the ocean beat the shoreline as the full moon shone down on the beach. Imani was beginning to become a fan of the beach. She closed her eyes imagining being down there underneath the stars and wrapped in Raymond's arms as he kissed her and, parting her thighs, tenderly entered her valley. With slow and gentle strokes, he'd introduce her body to the art of lovemaking. Asking her if she felt all right as he touched those secret places that made her weak. Places no one had ever come close to touching in her past. Lost in the fantasy of Raymond thrusting in and out of her awaiting body, she moaned and whispered his name.

"Yes?" Raymond asked, his warm breath tickling her earlobe and causing a tingling in her spine. Imani's knees buckled and she nearly fell backward. He wrapped his arms around her, bracing her fall. "Are you all right?" he asked.

"What are you doing sneaking up on me?" Imani demanded, masking her desire with anger.

Raymond loosened his grip on Imani and nearly allowed her to tumble to the balcony's floor. "Would you have preferred that I just let you fall? Besides, I heard you call my name."

"I didn't call your name," she said, though she knew it was a lie. "Are you delusional?"

He winked at her as he lifted her in his arms and placed her in a chair. "Seems as if you have the market covered on that. I was going to order dinner, then I realized I had no idea what an actress eats."

What Raymond didn't tell her was that he'd been standing in the doorway of the balcony, watching her hips sway to and fro, wondering if the moon was not only controlling the ocean's waves but Imani's hips as well. Then he heard her moan, as if she was in the midst of a passionate encounter, and when he slowly advanced toward her, ready to wrap his arms around Imani's waist, he heard her moan his name. So, he couldn't help but answer her call. She was a vision in the moonlight and his ultimate wish had been to rip her clothes off and make love to her against the railing. But when she saw that he was standing there behind her, he noticed something in her eyes—an innocence that didn't match the sexpot image that she was portraying. "Well," he said, finally able to speak again, "what do actresses eat?"

"Food. Please stop acting like I'm some sort of mythical beast. I'm a woman and I'm hungry," she said.

"For?"

Imani shrugged. She really was hungry, hungry for his kiss, his touch, and so much more. "Any kind of seafood would be nice," she replied after catching her breath.

"All right. I'm going to place the order and you can keep not calling my name."

She glared at him but didn't say anything. However, she did turn away from the ocean and sat down on one of the chairs near the table in the center of the balcony. Imani noticed a bottle of wine and two cups surrounding it. *I guess he's been entertaining. Wait, why do I care what Dr. Raymond does? This is an audition. I want a lead role in a romantic comedy and I just need him to be kind of mindless, pretend he's into me and stop looking at me as if he wants to rip my clothes off,* she thought as she glanced over her shoulder and locked eyes with Raymond as he talked on the phone. *He's going to be really disappointed when he finds out that I'm not giving him a chance to do what any woman would love to do at the drop of a hat. I wonder if Lucy has already given him a sample. Slut.*

"Imani?" Raymond said, breaking into her thoughts. She hadn't even realized that she'd picked up the half-empty wine bottle until she nearly dropped it and spilled some of it on her lap.

"Hmm, what?" she asked as she tried to blot the wet spot from her dress. Raymond walked over to her and smiled. He pulled a handkerchief from his pocket and handed it to Imani. "Are you all right?" he asked. "Missed your mouth with the wine?"

She rolled her eyes. "Like I would drink from the bottle. Who knows where it's been or where it came from."

"You have a smart mouth, but I'm sure you've heard that before," he said.

"What are we eating?" she asked, ignoring his comment.

"I ordered coconut shrimp and pasta salads. A chardonnay will go nicely with that," he said. "Not this." He held up the bottle of old wine. "Room service is bringing us something fresh."

Imani stood up and gathered the cups. "Then I'd better freshen up the table. Do you mind if I grab a towel and clean up my mess?"

"Have at it," he said with a smile. As Imani walked into the room, he watched her hips sway and forced himself not to get aroused. It was an epic failure.

When she returned with the towel, he took if from her hands. "I'll clean this up. I wouldn't want you to get that beautiful dress wetter."

He would talk about wetness, she thought as his fingers grazed hers when he took the towel. "Okay, and I'll go inside and wait for the food." Imani just needed to get away from him, needed a moment to collect her thoughts and get back into the scene she'd been writing in her mind. No, not that scene, because it ended with her in the middle of his king-sized bed. She glanced over her shoulder, looking at the made bed, and was glad there was a knock on the door before her wanton thoughts could develop.

"Yes?" she said as she looked out of the peephole.

"Room service," a muffled voice replied. Imani opened the door and smiled at the man as he wheeled the cart holding dinner into the room.

"Do you need me to open the wine?" he asked, smiling brightly at Imani.

"I can handle that," Raymond said as he walked inside from the balcony. "As a matter of fact, I'll take it from here." He crossed over to the attendant, handed him a five-dollar bill, and promptly ushered him out of the room.

"Wow," Imani said. "That was kind of rude. The man was just doing his job."

Yeah, while staring at your breasts and probably thinking exactly what I'm thinking right now, he thought as he looked at her. "Want to head outside?" he asked as he stood behind the cart, hiding his erection from her as they headed back to the balcony.

The ocean breeze had cooled the evening and as it blew across the balcony, the wind briefly lifted her dress, showing off a pair of panties that were all lace. She tugged at the tail of her dress and tried to cover up what Raymond had already seen.

"Cute," he said.

"What?"

"The lace."

"Perv. A gentleman would've turned his head the other way," she said, then laughed.

"Imani, you seem like a nice girl. How is it that we've never met in New York before?"

She shrugged and plucked a juicy shrimp from the dishes Raymond uncovered. "Probably because you hang out in doctor spots and seek out women with letters behind their names."

"That's not true. I like all kinds of women and I appreciate the letters behind their names and not in front of them," he said. "What about you? Are you one of those high-maintenance women who assume that all doctors are rolling in big dough? Let me guess, you live somewhere in Manhattan?"

Imani rolled her eyes again as she polished off her piece of shrimp. "First of all," she said after chewing, "I live in Brooklyn. Thank you very much. Second of all, I don't look at a man and see a bank account, because when things start going my way and I'm a star, I won't need anyone else's money."

Raymond sat down, opened the chardonnay, and set it in the middle of the table to allow it to breathe. "That's refreshing," he said.

Imani cocked up her right eyebrow. "What's that?"

"A woman wanting her own and no one else's. I see why we've never met in New York. You're too good to be true."

She smiled as she reached for her pasta salad. "I'm not too good to be true, but I didn't go to Juilliard to wait tables and not put my skills to use. And I am not anybody's trophy wife."

"And doing this show was the only way to translate your talent into something big?" he asked. "I mean, Juilliard is nothing to sneeze at."

"I wish you were a movie producer or the head of a studio," she said after swallowing her bite of food. "These days, talent doesn't seem to mean much. That's why you have rappers starring in movies—movies that I might add are worse than *Fearless Diva*. And I know Halle Berry is an established actress, but she still got work after *Catwoman* without having to appear on a reality show." Imani took a big swig of wine.

Raymond raised his eyebrow at her as he took a bite of his shrimp. "So, it's all about the business, huh?"

Imani nodded. "I've had so many people tell me that acting is a waste of time and that what I'm doing is just a pipe dream. I want to make them eat those words when I get an Academy Award. But everyone is judging me on one bad movie. Even you did it." She pointed a half-eaten shrimp on a fork at him. "That's why this god-awful show is so important."

"What would happen if you made a connection with someone on the show?" he asked, then took a slow sip of wine.

Imani watched his lips on the rim of the glass and sighed. "Really, Raymond? Can I call you Ray? Raymond just sounds so formal."

"Depends on how you answer my question," he replied.

"I'm really not here to make a connection with anyone," she said. "This is my audition tape, you know?"

Raymond didn't respond. On the one hand, he could respect and appreciate her honesty. But damn, what was he supposed to do with the desire building in him toward her? "So, how do I help you live your dream?"

Imani smiled. "Can I call you Ray?" she asked again.

"Sure."

"All right, Ray, you help me by being the cute Bradley Cooper type."

"What? The dude from *The Hangover*? I know I'm not an actor, but I need better inspiration than that," he replied with a laugh.

"Well, you can't be Denzel from *Mo' Better Blues*, though I'm sure Lucy might enjoy that. But I need all of the camera time I can get and she needs to stay away from you."

If Raymond hadn't listened to Imani say that she wasn't trying to make a romantic connection with him or anyone else on the show, he would've sworn that she was jealous of the interest Lucy had shown in him. Especially as he watched her drop her head after telling him that Lucy needed to stay away from him.

"More wine?" he asked rather than getting into what she really meant by Lucy staying away. *Leave it alone. Imani has made her intentions clear. Besides, you didn't come here to fall in love with any of these women.*

Still, if I'm going to help Imani blaze her path to stardom, I should get something out of it.

"I think I've had enough wine," she said, then turned toward the ocean. "Want to take a walk?"

"Sure," he said. "What is it with you and the ocean? I've noticed that you've been looking at it all night. For a Brooklynite, I find that odd."

"What's that supposed to mean? Because I'm from Brooklyn, I can't enjoy nature?"

Raymond liked the way Imani's nose crinkled when she was on the verge of getting angry. Maybe she had an expressive face because she was an actress. Or maybe she just happened to be the most beautiful woman he'd ever seen and she could cross her eyes and stick her tongue out and he'd still be impressed.

"I'm not saying that at all," he said as he stroked her smooth cheek. "You know something? You're a beautiful woman and even though we just met, I believe you are going to get that Oscar, those prime movie roles, and anything else you want. Because I see Miss Imani doesn't believe in accepting no for an answer."

She smiled and his heart skipped four beats. "Thank you," she said, then slipped out of her shoes. "And when I get my Oscar, you're going to be one of the first people I thank."

As they headed for the door, there was another knock. "What now?" Raymond muttered. He looked out of the peephole and saw a man standing there with a pair of black-rimmed glasses on and a headset around his neck. "Yes?"

"I'm Elliot Reynolds, a producer from the show. I need to talk to you."

Raymond opened the door and the man smiled when he saw Imani leaning on the dresser. "Great, this saves me a trip. Like I told Raymond, I'm a producer with the show and we're doing cast confessionals with a few contestants in the morning. You two are at the top of the list."

"Why?" Imani asked.

"I'm just following orders from the EP—executive producer," Elliot said. "Imani, you're scheduled for eight, Raymond, you're scheduled for ten. We've set wake-up calls for your rooms. Or should we set them for just one room?"

Imani smacked her lips. "What kind of woman do you think I am? Of course you need to set them for each room. I'm a lady, thank you very much."

Elliot nodded. "Right. See you two in the morning. Lady, Doctor," he said, then left the room.

Raymond turned to Imani, who was laughing hard now. "Let me guess, that was acting?"

She nodded. "Kind of. I mean, I am a lady, but I didn't have to get so indignant with him. I just wanted to try a new emotion. Ready for that walk?"

Raymond offered her a blank stare. He wondered how often she brought acting into her real life. Did she act in bed too? "Yeah, let's go," he said.

Moments later, they were walking along the beach, underneath a sky filled with sparkling stars that looked like diamonds against black velvet. Imani looked up at the sky and smiled. "It is so beautiful out here. I've never been to Hawaii before and

I see why all of my friends who've been here gushed about it for years and years."

Raymond took her hand in his after they took a few more steps and she squeezed her fingers around his. Was this real, he wondered, as she continued looking at the sky and talking about its beauty? Or, was she trying a new emotion?

"Am I talking too much?" Imani asked when she noticed his silence.

"No, not at all. I'm just admiring the beauty along with you," he replied, looking directly at her. What he didn't say was she was the most beautiful thing he saw on the beach. He didn't care about the stars, the sky, or the ocean. "It's too bad we didn't bring a blanket. We could've laid it out and gotten a really great view of the stars." *And your breasts, your lips, and those lovely legs,* he added silently.

"Umm, I don't believe that. You wanted a blanket out here in the dark so you could look at the stars with me?"

"Maybe not. Maybe I just want to kiss you underneath the stars."

She turned her head upward and looked him square in the eye. "So, what's stopping you?"

"You do realize there are no cameras out here," he said. "This isn't a made for television kiss."

She stood on her tiptoes and brushed her lips against his. "If I wanted a made for TV kiss, I would've looked for the cameras first," she said, then grabbed the back of his neck. He brought his lips down on top of hers and kissed her slowly and gently. That just wasn't good enough for Imani as she slipped her tongue between his parted lips.

Raymond responded to her hot tongue by sucking on it until she gasped. He slipped his hand underneath her dress and stroked her smooth thighs.

A soft moan escaped Imani's throat as Raymond ran his finger down the valley of her breasts. She placed her hand on his chest and pushed him back.

"What's wrong?" Raymond asked, taken aback by her quick change in attitude. She was the one who'd deepened their kiss. Did she expect that he wasn't going to respond to the signals she was sending out?

"I don't think this is the right time for this. We're just moving too fast and I don't know what I was thinking when I kissed you," she whispered. Imani drew in a deep breath, trying to collect her thoughts and return her breathing to normal.

"The right time for what?" Raymond asked. "This walk was your idea and you kissed me. I don't want you to do anything you don't want to do."

"I didn't say you did," she replied. "We should head back, we have an early morning."

Raymond nodded. "All right," he said. "But can I tell you something?"

"What?"

"I like kissing you and unless you tell me to, I'm not going to stop," he said.

"Raymond—I, um, really don't want you to stop, but that's not part of the plan."

"I keep forgetting, this is just a game for you," he said. "One long audition."

"That's right. And even though I like kissing you too, I can't get confused as to why I'm here." Imani tore away from him and ran back to the hotel.

So, she liked kissing him? Then what was she fighting? Why couldn't they connect on camera and in the bed? She wanted him and he definitely wanted her. Wanting didn't even begin to describe the animalistic need that he felt for Imani. But he wasn't going to chase her. She was right, they needed this show as a means to an end and nothing could stand in the way of that. Especially his libido. Closing his eyes and groaning, Raymond headed back to the hotel. He was surprised to see Imani sitting at the bar. Just as he started in her direction, he felt a tap on his shoulder.

"My man Mets," Harvey said. "Man, there are some fine women on this cast. But I still want that one."

Raymond followed his lecherous gaze to Imani's frame. "I don't know why she's playing hard to get. Been hiding out all day. She knows she wants me."

"Why don't you leave her alone? She's not interested."

"How in the hell do you know?" he demanded hotly. "She's just playing hard to get. I know just what she needs."

"Leave Imani alone," Raymond said harshly as he grabbed Harvey by the neck.

Harvey pushed Raymond's hand away, then stroked his neck. "What the hell is wrong with you? Trying to write your name on that? Afraid of a little competition?"

Raymond smirked at Harvey. "You're hardly competition. But the lady doesn't want you."

"I'm going to let her decide that," he said as he stomped off toward Imani.

Raymond started to follow him, but stopped when he saw Imani toss her drink in Harvey's face. He chuckled, thinking that she was one feisty woman who knew how to take care of herself. He liked that. But what he didn't like was the scowl on Harvey's face as he reached for Imani's arm. Raymond dashed over and grabbed Harvey's hand.

"I think she's made it clear that she doesn't want to be bothered with you. There are eleven other women you can harass."

"What are you, Captain Save a . . ."

"Your mother isn't here for him to save," Imani snapped, then looked up at Raymond.

"Let's get out of here," Raymond said as he extended his hand to Imani. "I'll see you to your room."

She took his hand and shot a contemptuous look at Harvey, who was glaring at the couple as they walked away. "That guy is nuts. I thought they did better screening for these shows," Imani said.

"He's not going to be a problem for you," Raymond said, suddenly feeling very protective of Imani. "I'm not going to let him bother you again."

She sucked in her bottom lip as they stepped onto the elevator. This man was too good to be true. Why did they have to meet here? she wondered as she slipped her arm around his waist.

Chapter 8

When the elevator opened on their floor, Raymond wanted to take Imani into his room and just watch her sleep. He wasn't worried about Harvey, but he didn't want Imani out of his sight. Not when she was such a vision and they needed to clear up something.

"Imani," he said, "can we talk for a minute?"

She nodded. "Why don't we go inside my room?"

Raymond looked down the hall and saw Lucy coming their way. "Sounds good to me," he said as he followed her inside.

The scent of her perfume greeted him at the door and slammed his heart against his rib cage. This woman was damned intoxicating in every way and he had to keep his hands to himself. Somehow.

"So," she said when she turned around, "I guess this is about what I said on the beach."

"Pretty and smart. I like that in a woman," Raymond quipped. "What I don't understand is if we're both attracted to each other, why do you want to pull back?" He inched closer to her, wondering for a moment if he could get another kiss from that beautiful mouth.

"This isn't the best time to start anything. We're being filmed and I don't want my sex life all over national TV. I had no idea that I'd meet someone like you and want to be wrapped in his arms and . . ."

"Kissed by him all the time?" he asked, staring into her eyes. "Imani, why do you want to fight the feeling?" Raymond wrapped his arms around her waist and pulled her against his chest. "This could be a win-win situation."

"I'm not trying to make the papers for all the wrong reasons. Please try and understand that." She pressed her hands against his chest, but didn't pull away. It felt too good being in his arms.

"Wrong reasons? Connecting with another human is the wrong reason to make the newspapers?"

"Actress uses her body to get ahead is more like it," she said, still not leaving his embrace. "I could've been in many other movies, done a couple of shows on Broadway, had I been willing to sleep my way to the top. Not my style."

"I'm not offering you a role in a movie or on Broadway," he said, his voice husky and deep, sending shivers down her spine. "If we happen to get something started, what's the problem?"

Finally she pulled out of Raymond's embrace and sat on the edge of the bed. "Ray, I can't say that I want to get something started with you because that's not on my five-year plan."

"Five-year plan? You know plans were meant to be changed."

"And that's been my problem. I've allowed too many people to take me off course and that's why I'm here," she said, then slammed her hand against the bed. "As much as I want to get lost in those beautiful eyes of yours, I can't do that. My family has been against me acting from the start and I like to prove people wrong. I don't like the word no."

"Funny," he said. "You throw it around a lot."

Imani focused her stare on Raymond. She was beginning to think that Dana was right about her having a thing for arrogant men. Still, there was something about him that was drawing her into his orbit. Maybe he wasn't arrogant, just confident. "Raymond," she whispered, "let's stick to the plan."

"All right," he relented. "But plans were made to be changed. Keep that in mind." He turned toward the door and then looked over his shoulder at her. When Raymond winked at her before he headed out, Imani knew she was in trouble.

"Well, well," Lucy said when Raymond exited Imani's room. "I guess you like them fake and phony?"

"What are you talking about?"

"Well, I told you that she was here for the fame and the money, but every time I turn around, you're in Miss Actress's face," she said, then rolled her eyes.

"Lucy," Raymond said as he shook his head.

"What? I'm trying to offer you something real," she said as she took his hand in hers. "Tell me you don't feel this energy between us." Lucy closed her eyes and exhaled slowly. "I want you."

"That's nice," he said. "But all I want right now is a shower and a good night's sleep."

"I can help you with the shower and the sleep. I wash your back, you lick mine," she said with a seductive gleam in her eyes.

Raymond gave her a long once-over and decided that despite the fact that he'd never been hornier, he wasn't going to settle for a bed warmer when the one he really wanted was right across the hall. "Not tonight," he said, then gave her a soft pat on the shoulder.

"Your loss," she said with a snort, and then stomped away.

Raymond walked into his room and threw himself across the bed. His thoughts immediately turned to Imani. A woman he just met shouldn't have gotten to him in the way she had. Especially when she told him that she was only here to become a star. Maybe Lucy was right, he should run the other way and forget her. Forget the sweet taste of her kisses, the smoothness of her skin, and each and every curve on her body. How could he forget her when there was so much more to explore? Nope, he was going to have to break through that wall. Even if that breakthrough didn't happen until after the show. Imani was a woman he needed to be a part of his life.

But does she want a man or a prop? he thought as he locked his hands behind his head. *She made it really clear about her desire for fame. Men are always saying that women blindside us and introduce us to their representative before we get to see the real woman. Imani hasn't done that and I can't seem to get her off my mind. Damn it, this is not smart nor is it cool. But I have got to have that woman.*

Since he couldn't do anything about it tonight, Raymond decided to go to sleep and work on getting closer to Imani in the morning. As soon as he closed his eyes, though, her beauty invaded his sleep.

Sleep was not Imani's friend and when she heard a rumbling at her door, she had no desire to get up and open it. But the knocking continued, persistent and anxious. Part of her wished it was Raymond so that she could tell him off for keeping her up all night. Wait, those were just dreams. It was in her dreams—every time she closed her eyes—that he kissed her, sucking gently on her bottom lip and rubbing his palms slowly across her breasts until her nipples perked up, hard like diamonds. Each image of Raymond in her bed shook her to her core. Made her feel things that she'd never felt and think thoughts that she'd pushed out of her mind when she'd been propositioned by the casting director for the musical *Rent*. She may have wanted to play Mimi, a drug-addicted stripper, but there was no way she was going to put out to get the role. She'd always wondered if she'd been relegated to the chorus because she hadn't slept with that director. Both actresses who'd been selected to play Mimi, the understudy and the lead actress, were horrible and the reviews said so. Before she could give it another thought, the knocking continued. She knew she was supposed to do some sort of interview this morning, but why so early?

Flinging the covers back, Imani stalked to the door, filled with old anger and new disgust as she opened the door and placed her hand on her hips. "What?" she snapped.

"Imani, we need you in the interview room," the production assistant said. He grabbed her by the arm and ushered her out of the room. Dressed in a white cotton gown and no shoes, there was no way that she could be seen on camera. She ran a quick hand through her hair and tried to smooth it as much as possible. Imani imagined that she looked like a Troll doll. She stopped and glared at the PA. "Hey, I don't know how things work in TV land, but I need to get myself together before I go on camera."

"This is reality TV, not a movie set. If you don't want to follow the rules, then you can leave. And if you leave this soon, you forfeit any prize money that you may have earned." He tapped his wrist. "Time is wasting, let's go."

Imani rolled her eyes. "Fine," she mumbled as she followed the young man down the hall. She pulled her hair back behind her ears and exhaled. "Let's get this over with."

"Such the diva," the man mumbled as they walked into a small room. Imani took a seat in front of the camera and continued to fiddle with her hair.

A woman, who Imani assumed was the show's producer, appeared from behind a mirrored door. "Jason, thank you. You may go now," she said, then turned to Imani and extended her hand. "I'm Tres Ellis."

"Imani—but I'm sure you already knew that. Can I at least get a mirror and a brush before we start filming?"

She smiled. "Sorry," she said, then turned the camera on. "So, tell me a little about yourself. You're a B-movie actress, right? You did a film that wasn't very well received by critics or audiences."

"I'm not a B-movie actress and yes, *Fearless Diva* wasn't the best display of my acting talents, but I was working with what I had," Imani replied.

"Okay," Tres said. "So, I see that you are from New York. Do you know Raymond, who's also from New York?"

Imani hid her smile. "I wouldn't say that I know him, but he did save me from a speeding cab in Manhattan."

Tres wrote a note on her pad, then looked up at Imani. "How would you feel if America set him up with someone like Lucy? I noticed that you two clashed in the limo on the way over here."

"You all were filming that?" Imani asked, immediately wondering if every move she and Raymond had been making was filmed as well.

Tres nodded. "Mostly everything since you all arrived has been taped. We wanted to get some test shots and see who has the best chemistry and things like that. But back to my question. Raymond and Lucy—how would you feel about America bringing them together?"

"Well, I, umm . . . Lucy and Raymond wouldn't work. He's the kind of man who needs a woman who isn't clingy in his life. Lucy isn't that kind of woman."

"So, you are the kind of woman he needs?"

Imani cocked her head to the side and fingered her hair. "That's not for me to say. I think Raymond and America will make the right decision."

"So, you said that he saved your life in New York. Would you say that the two of you have a connection?" Tres asked.

A connection? Heat rose from the center of her being and settled on her cheeks. Hell yes, she had a connection with Raymond. Obviously, this woman hadn't paid attention to the footage that had been recorded. Squirming in her seat and praying that her face didn't reveal the true connection she wanted with Raymond, she was at a loss for words.

"Well?" Tres pressed. "Would you say something about your connection with Raymond?"

Imani shrugged and sighed. *Get it together, this is officially being filmed.* "Define connection," Imani said, channeling her Sharon Stone from *Basic Instinct.*

Tres raised her sculpted eyebrow at Imani as if she knew the actress was putting on a show. "Well, let's move on. Some of our other contestants have expressed doubt as to why you're actually here. They think you're just trying to show off your acting skills and that you're after the fame and the money."

"And I take it that you believe the rest of those women are not? Let's be real, finding love on TV is a pipe dream," she replied.

Tres stood up and extended her hand to Imani. "Thank you," she said.

Imani slowly rose to her feet and shook her hand. "Are you sure there aren't any more questions?"

"We're done for now," Tres said with a smile.

Nodding, she headed out the door and told herself that she had to be camera-ready at all times. She was not going to be caught looking like anything less than a star on camera again. Reality TV or not.

As she approached her room, she couldn't help but think of Raymond, and when she turned to glance at his door, Imani was shocked to see him opening it. Had he been waiting for her? Was he really seeing her standing there looking like this?! Sighing, she gripped her doorknob as he said, "Good morning." His smile was brighter than the sun, dazzling, made her heart skip a few beats. When she felt her nipples press against the flimsy material of her gown, she crossed her arms over her chest and returned his greeting. "Morning."

"You're up rather early this morning," he said.

She stared at him, drinking in his image. Shirtless, board shorts looking as if he was about to head out and conquer the ocean with his surf board. *Turn away, Imani!* she told herself as her eyes traveled his body in reverse. "Well, I was doing a cast interview, and now I'm going to get some breakfast from room service."

"That sounds like a horrible way to start your day. I have to do one of those too in a while. But why eat in your room when you can join me for breakfast on the beach?"

"I have to get dressed and . . ."

"You don't have the option to say no," he said

with another smile. "Breakfast is the most important meal of the day. Trust me, I'm a doctor."

Could she handle sitting on the beach with him while he looked so incredibly sexy? Was this what people meant when they said they had a hunger for someone? How could Imani hunger for something that she'd never had before? Why was her body responding to this man in ways that she'd never dreamed of in her life?

She told him she would join him for breakfast. "But first, I have to change into something more suitable for the beach."

Raymond winked at her. "See-though gowns are suitable for any occasion," he quipped.

"I'll see you in a few minutes," she said, before walking into her room. After closing the door, her breathing returned to normal. Looking down at her gown, Imani shook her head. "'See-through is suitable for any occasion. . . .' He is too much," she mumbled as she fished her pink and black bandeau bathing suit from her suitcase. The Chanel suit had been one of her gifts from the set of *Fearless Diva*. Had she known that the movie was going to ruin her career before it even had a chance to get started, she would've helped herself to more gifts.

After slipping into the strapless suit, Imani gave herself a once-over in the mirror and adjusted her breasts in the suit for the optimal amount of cleavage display. She would be turning heads today, though the only head she was worried about was Raymond's. She wanted to look tempting as opposed to slutty. Her skin was already beginning to show a sun-kissed glow, or was that the heat from seeing Raymond? Imani shrugged.

Why am I doing this? Focus. This breakfast is going to be filmed and you need to be less seductress and more America's sweetheart. Still, if he can show off his killer body, so can I. Let him see how it feels to see what you want, but can't have.

She pulled her hair back in a loose chignon, plucked an orchid from the bouquet on the night table, and stuck it on the left side of her head. Then she grabbed a bottle of sunscreen and tied her sheer black sarong around her waist before heading out the door. And she was right. Every man she passed turned his head to get a glimpse of the bathing beauty. Imani wasn't vain, but she couldn't help but smile at the attention. Hopefully they'd remember her when they saw her poster for her next film and go buy a ticket.

She happily skipped out of the hotel, thinking that she should try a drama for her next role. That was the surest path to an Oscar. But thoughts of scripts, award speeches, and movie roles flew out of her head when she spotted Raymond on the sand. He was serious about breakfast being important, and more appetizing on the beach than anything she could have dreamed up. She looked at the blanket he'd laid out, seeing fresh sliced pineapples, grapes, strawberries, and waffles. Her mouth watered at the sight of the food, at least that's what she told herself. Honestly, looking at Raymond, laid back propped up on his elbows and showing off every rippling inch of his abs, made her want to not only devour the pineapples, but get a taste of

Raymond as well. She sprinted to him, promising herself that she would stay in character. *America's sweetheart would not jump on that man and run her tongue down his six-pack,* she told herself.

"Wow," she said. "Everything looks so great."

"I'm glad you approve, because I had no idea what you wanted. So, I figured we couldn't go wrong with fruit and waffles. We can get coffee, iced if you'd like."

"I think some fruit juice would be a lot better," she said. "You can get coffee from any corner in New York. Orange and pineapple juice would set this breakfast off."

"But we can't get fresh Kona coffee in New York," he said. "We should try it."

"As long as I get the juice as well, I'll try it."

"I'll be right back," Raymond said, rising to his feet and turning to the hotel.

Imani watched his retreating figure and let out a low whistle as she focused on his muscular behind. It was shaped perfectly, and her hands itched to touch it. Shaking her head and reaching for a pineapple slice, Imani munched the fruit and wondered how she'd developed these hot lusty feelings for a man she barely knew. It wasn't just his body. She'd seen guys with tighter abs, broader shoulders and the like, but there was something else about Raymond. He wasn't like a lot of the men she'd met in the city. He seemed compassionate and cared about more than getting every pretty girl he saw into bed. *Focus,* her inner voice cried out. *You're not here to fall in love with Raymond, not here to do anything but perform for whatever director, producer, or playwright looking for a hot new actress.*

Leaning back on her elbows, Imani grabbed another slice of pineapple and sucked the juicy fruit while the sun beat down on her. Trying to gather her thoughts and what her next move should be, she didn't notice that Raymond had returned.

"I hope that smile on your lips is about me," he said, his voice deep and sensual. Imani lifted her sunglasses as he knelt down with a tray of Kona coffee, cream, sugar, and juice, careful not to spill anything. "They made a special juice blend for you, fresh squeezed orange juice and pineapple juice."

"Sounds good," she said as she reached for a glass.

"Slow down, woman," he said with a laugh. "You have to try the coffee first. It's delicious." Raymond poured the coffee into a mug and offered it to Imani.

"All right. I'm guessing you're one of those people who love coffee. I bet if I ever stood behind you in Starbucks in Manhattan, I'd get pissed because you'd have fifty thousand special requests," she said as she grabbed two packets of sugar.

Raymond drank his coffee hot and black, savoring the robust flavor. Imani sipped, then shook her head.

"What?" Raymond asked as he set his mug aside and picked up a strawberry.

Imani sipped her coffee again and scowled. "That's strong," she exclaimed.

Raymond handed her a glass of juice. "What are you, one of those caramel macchiato drinkers?"

"Yeah, I like a little coffee with my cream and

sugar," she said. "And I want it all with whipped cream on top."

"With whipped cream on top?" Raymond asked. "The things running through my mind right now . . ."

Imani reached for another slice of pineapple and smiled at Raymond before taking a bite of the sweet fruit. A line of juice dripped from her lip and traveled down her chin. Raymond leaned over and kissed the trail of juice. Imani shivered as his lips touched her skin. Her blood headed up like molten lava as his tongue flicked across her chin. When he wrapped his arm around her waist, her inner voice screamed for her to get away. It was too late as he brought his lips down on top of hers. His kiss tasted a lot better than the coffee, the juice, or the pineapples she'd been eating. His kiss tasted too damned good. This was not a part of the plan. Imani pressed her hand against his bare chest, counted to ten, then backed away from him.

"Maybe I shouldn't have done that," he said when he saw the confused and tense look on her face. "But it damned sure tasted good to me. I'd like some whipped cream on that."

"Raymond, I'm glad you find me attractive, and we've already established how much we like kissing each other. . . ."

"But you want to stay on script," he finished. "What if I can't do that?"

Imani inhaled sharply. What if she couldn't do that either? But despite how much she wanted him and how badly she wanted to feel those things that her girlfriends talked about after they'd had sex, she could not forget the reason why she was on this show and why she was sitting on the beach with him.

"You know . . ." she said, trying to fall into a character. A character from what movie? Shaking her head, Imani gazed up at Raymond, getting lost in his eyes and forgetting that this moment was being filmed. "I like you and that was so unexpected. But I don't want to be that girl on TV kissing the hot doctor and forgetting that when this is over, he has a real life and I have nothing—not even a callback for a community playhouse."

Raymond stroked Imani's cheek with his index finger. "Lady, you have what it takes to be a star, even if your first movie did stink."

Imani tossed a grape at him. "Maybe *Fearless* wasn't my best work. But I just need a chance to get my foot in the door and get a good script. It hasn't happened yet, but I take my work seriously."

"What about real emotions? Could it be that you take your work so seriously that you've forgotten that it's all right to have a life off stage and out of the camera's eye?"

She smirked. A life with no acting? That wasn't a life, that was a mess. That was proving to her family and everyone else that she had wasted her time and money by going to Juilliard and not getting a real job. She didn't have time to get distracted by a beautiful doctor who seemed to have a heart that was bigger than his . . . What if he was too big for her to handle? *Handle? There is no way in hell that I will lose my virginity on national TV.*

"Imani?" Raymond asked as a warm breeze blew

across them. The waves crashed in the distance, reminding her of a director's clapboard. She turned away from Raymond and picked up a strawberry, then offered it to him. He took it into his mouth; his lips gently grazed her fingertips. Shivers shot up and down spine, telling her this was not a movie scene, this was not a read through, and this was real. "Raymond, isn't it beautiful out here?" she said, sidestepping his question.

"It is," he said as he cut into a waffle and fed it to her. "What happens if America wants us to get married?"

Imani reached up and stroked his cheek. "Do you think a marriage between us would last? Marriage is supposed to be a serious matter, isn't it?"

Raymond shrugged his shoulders. "If it was so serious, there wouldn't be a show like this. People just want instant gratification. Microwave relationships, five minutes to matrimony. No one believes in the lost art of courting."

Imani flipped over on her stomach. "And you do?" she asked, stifling a laugh. "Tell me something, Ray, how many brokenhearted women are going to see you on this show and wonder why you never popped the question to them?"

He snorted, thinking of the one woman he had ever considered asking to marry him and the other ones who'd walked out of his life because he'd spent so much time in Harlem at the clinic. "Not a one."

Imani shook her head. "That I don't believe."

"Oh, really? Well, let me flip the question. How many brothers are going to wonder why you turned down their diamonds and now you're on this show?" He pulled her against his chest and Imani wrapped her arms around his waist.

"No one ever offered me a diamond," she replied. "My last relationship ended when I told him that there was no way I was going to be a number in his stable of women. And when he found out I wasn't a model, he lost interest." Imani sighed softly and snuggled closer to Raymond, silently willing herself to remember she was showing her range and to not get too comfortable in his strong arms.

Chapter 9

Doubts crept into Raymond's mind as he held her. Was Imani playing the game or could she be developing real feelings for him? Raymond stroked her arm, not wanting to know the answer to his questions. Part of him wanted to just live in the moment, enjoy her snuggled against him. Imani's hair was as soft as cotton and she felt so right in the curve of his arm. He had to stop himself from brushing his lips across her forehead.

"You're extremely quiet, all of a sudden," Imani said as she looked up at him.

Raymond forced a smile, then sighed. "I'm just thinking, and absorbing the beauty out here and in my arms."

She stroked his arm. "That was sweet. So, what's on your mind? Want to share?"

"No," he said, holding her just a little tighter. "Let's just enjoy the morning." Raymond buried his nose in her hair, his nostrils filled with the sweetness of the Hawaiian air and the jasmine scent of Imani's hair. If this was real, then it would be perfect. But Raymond couldn't tell if she was acting or not. He still felt as if she was holding something back. Maybe he wasn't getting to know the real Imani because she was so intent on acting on a reality show. He felt her relax and her breathing seemed to fall into sync with the ocean waves.

"It's beautiful here. No smog, no steaming sewers. It's paradise," she cooed.

"It wouldn't be the same without you," he said as he looked down into her eyes. "Imani." His voice was a husky whisper that turned Imani's insides into liquid desire. As he brought his lips closer to hers, she trembled with the anticipation of his kiss. Damn, she enjoyed kissing him and . . .

"Raymond, hi," a voice called out in the distance. He and Imani turned around to see Lucy bounding toward them. She was dressed in a red bikini that didn't leave much to the imagination. Her skin and ample breasts seemed to glow in the golden morning sun. Her hair was pulled up in a loose ponytail. "This beach is beautiful. I see why you spend so much time down here." She smiled and tightened her bikini top. Then Lucy shot Imani a cursory look. "Oh, Imani, I didn't notice you there," she said snidely. "Testing out your acting skills this morning?"

Raymond gently stroked Imani's arm as if he was trying to stop the brewing catfight between her and Lucy. Imani smiled at her rival as she eyed her in disgust. "You look like a video star this morning. Just letting it all hang out, huh? Should've hit the gym just a little harder before trying to pull this look off."

Lucy rolled her eyes, then turned to Raymond, deciding to ignore Imani's taunt. "How is everything going? Those cast interviews are something, right?"

"Everything is pretty good. I haven't done my interview yet," he replied. Raymond wanted this woman to disappear. She may have been sexy, but he didn't like women who couldn't show restraint. Didn't she see that he was lying on the beach wrapped up with another woman? Lucy was too hungry for a man and he was not going to be her matrimonial snack.

When she sat down as if she had been invited, Imani shifted in his arms and shot Lucy a look that was so cold it would've frozen lava. "We were in the middle of something," Imani said, her voice filled with attitude and displeasure.

"I'm sorry," Lucy said as she picked up the last piece of pineapple and licked it seductively. "Am I blocking your spotlight?"

"Ladies," Raymond said. "Really?"

Lucy smiled at Raymond as she bit into the juicy fruit. "Raymond, I sincerely apologize, but I just think it's rude to use people as props in hopes of getting an acting career."

Imani wanted to shove that pineapple down Lucy's throat. She moved Raymond's arm from around her and rose to her feet. "Raymond," she said, "let's take a walk."

Before Raymond could stand up, Lucy grabbed his arm. "Have you ever taken a swim in the ocean?" she asked him.

"Listen," he snapped, moving Lucy's manicured hand from his arm, "I'm not the gingerbread man. You two don't like each other, but I'm not going to be the prize in your little fight. Lucy, Imani and I are going to finish our breakfast alone."

She hopped up as if she'd been stung by a jelly-fish. Lucy glared at Imani as if she was the one who was telling her to back off. "It's a public beach. Maybe you should have had breakfast elsewhere."

"Or perhaps you should," Imani snapped, and then she stomped off from Raymond and Lucy.

Tres smiled as she watched the dust up on screen, then she pumped her fist as if she was Tiger Woods winning the Masters. "This is better than I could have ever scripted and Raymond hasn't even done his confessional yet," she said as she picked up the phone and called the network in New York.

When Elize Harrington answered, Tres said, "Elize, I just wanted to call and tell you that this show is going to be a runaway hit. The actress and the doctor steam up the cameras and there is a third party that is turning up the heat. It is like an erupting volcano!"

Tres could imagine her boss's demeanor in New York, could see Elize smiling and kicking her feet up on the desk. The reality dating shows were becoming trite and there was no star tied to the project. But Elize knew the right cast would make the show successful.

"We've got an amazing cast. Who cares if there's

no Ray J or a Flavor Flav when there is this developing love triangle with a sexy doctor, a wanna be actress, and a J.Lo stand in?"

"Well, well," Elize said. "I like what I'm hearing. Send me the dailies."

"They are on the way," she said. "Maybe we should release this show this summer. Or better yet, after the first episode, we should go live. Elize, if people don't like this show, then they just have no taste."

"I'll let you know after I see the dailies. That doctor is hot and I know every woman in America is going to want him. I'm not surprised that there's a fight brewing over him on the island. Make sure there's no violence between the women, though."

"Of course," Tres said. "And, when this show is the hit that I know it will be, do I get my chance to do a scripted show?"

"We'll see about that. Look, I have a meeting in five minutes. Get those dailies to me as soon as possible," she said.

Tres hung up the phone and looked at the screen. Raymond had torn off behind Imani down the beach, leaving Lucy standing on the blanket alone. Leaning into the screen, Tres watched the unfolding drama.

Raymond grabbed Imani's shoulder once he'd caught up to her. "Imani," he said.

"What?" she asked when she whirled around. "I thought you didn't want to be a prize in my fight with Lucy? I didn't invite her out there and the way she's always in your face, you must like the attention."

"Yeah, because I'm auditioning for a movie role, right?"

She narrowed her eyes into tight slits. "Don't pretend that I haven't been clear about why I'm here."

Raymond cocked his head to the side. "Maybe that's the problem."

"Excuse me?"

"All you want is the fame and you're not even—"

"You're just here for the money, remember," Imani interjected.

"You're not letting me get to know the real you. I don't know when you're acting or not. When you're being Imani and not some character that you think will get you a role in a movie."

She gritted her teeth, paused as if she wanted to say something to him. Instead, she glanced around as if she was looking for a cameraman.

Tres chewed her bottom lip and said if a cameraman showed up in this shot she was going to fire his ass. This was real, real emotion. Could it be that these two were falling for each other? "Come on," Tres muttered as Raymond closed the space between him and Imani. "Make some magic happen."

Raymond lifted Imani's chin and forced her to look into his eyes. "Let me see the real you," he whispered.

"This is me. Deal with it or go find Lucy," she replied.

"All right," he said as he dropped his hand and started to turn away.

Imani called after him and he stopped in his tracks. "I'm sorry," she said. "But there is just so much at stake for me right now. Back at home, I'm struggling. I don't know how—"

"But you're not home now. What about the here and now?"

"Raymond." She stamped her foot in the sand and looked up at him with an expression in her eyes that was hard for Tres to read. "There are certain aspects of my life that I don't want flashed on national TV."

"I get that. I feel the same way about that. But we knew what we were doing when we decided to come here. We signed away our privacy, me for money and you for fame."

Imani tugged at her hair. "And the damned show hasn't even aired yet."

"So, if you want this to develop and you want to be with me, then we should leave."

She backed away from him and eyed him as if he'd begun speaking German. "And how is that going to help me? You're a nice guy, very sexy, and I think we'd be great together. But how do I know that for sure? How is a relationship with you going to get my name in lights on Broadway?" Imani grimaced as her words hit her ears.

"So, it's like that? Everything comes second to your career?"

She reached out to touch his shoulder but Raymond jerked away. "I didn't mean it like that. Look, I've not had the best luck with love, so I avoid it. Men—at least the ones I've gotten involved with— always have a hidden agenda. I'm just trying to protect my heart, and maybe that's why I'm hiding behind my career."

Raymond was about to respond when a production assistant ran into the scene. Tres nearly fell out of her chair. *What in the blue hell?* Then she looked at her watch and the production schedule. It was time for Raymond's confessional. Damn. She scribbled a quick note never to interrupt Imani and Raymond again.

Chapter 10

Raymond stared into the camera, still thinking about what Imani had said to him on the beach. He was smart enough to know when to cut his losses, but there was something about that woman that had gotten under his skin and he wasn't willing to walk away—yet.

"Raymond?" Tres said.

"What?" he asked, then offered her a half smile. "I'm sorry. What was the question again?"

"You're quite popular. Do you often witness breakfast catfights over you?" she asked, crossing her legs and gripping the clipboard.

"You guys got that on tape?" Raymond asked.

She nodded and tapped her pen against the board. "Cameras are everywhere. Why do I have to keep telling you all this? Anyway, Imani and Lucy seem to like you a lot."

Raymond shrugged. "How in the world can you tell that by watching us on closed circuit TV?"

Tres laughed. "Because they were both in here

before you and all they could talk about was Dr. Thomas."

"Who knows what either of those women want."

"What do you want . . . in a woman, that is?"

Shaking his head, Raymond couldn't be honest and say what he wanted was wrapped up in the temperamental actress he'd left on the beach. Had he been honest with himself, he could admit that Imani had the major quality he wanted in a woman—honesty. She'd told him from the beginning why she came to Hawaii, and he didn't want to accept that now that he was falling head over heels for her. "I want a woman who knows what she wants, doesn't want to play games, and can have a life outside of me."

"Very specific. Who fits those standards more, Imani or Lucy?" Tres pressed, leaning forward with the camera.

"Who says either one of them is the woman for me?" he asked. "I honestly came here with one woman on my mind."

"Really?" Her nose crinkled as she looked at him. "I know you and Imani met in passing in New York, but—"

"Not her," he said. "Marion G. Palmer. The woman my clinic is named after."

Tres released a cleansing sigh, silently thanking God that this show was not going to have a stalker or murderer tied to it like some other reality shows. "That's right, you're a doctor with a huge heart. Do you have room in your heart to share it with a special woman?"

"Imani might be special enough," he said without thinking.

Tres folded her hands underneath her chin and grinned like a Cheshire cat. "Thank you, Raymond," she said as she shut the camera off.

He walked out of the room knowing that he'd said too much, but the hell with it. It was time for him to stake his claim on Imani. He wanted her and he would not be denied.

Imani stood on the beach for about an hour after Raymond left, wondering if she should just find someone that she didn't have feelings for to show off her acting skills with. This wasn't supposed to happen. She was not supposed to develop a genuine attraction to anyone on the show and here she was feeling her heart strings being tugged by Raymond Thomas.

She was supposed to use this show as a stepping stone, but why did Raymond have to be everything that she could ever want in a man? Considerate, sexy, and a damned good kisser? She took a step toward the raging waves of the ocean, allowing the salt water to splash over her. *When he finds out that you're a virgin, he's going to cool what's going on between you two,* her nagging conscience said. *He'll run off into Lucy's arms and bury his desire right between her thighs. How many men have left you because you wouldn't sleep with them? Do you honestly think Raymond is going to stick around?*

Imani pressed her hands over her ears as if she was trying to silence the voice of doubt. Raymond wasn't like any other man she'd ever dealt with and she had to trust that he wanted more than just a quick romp.

If that were the case, he could've hopped into bed or on the sand with Lucy's scandalous ass. She had everything on disgusting display and . . .

"Wait," Imani muttered. "Why am I acting as if I'm jealous? He's not my man and if he ever touches that warmed-over tramp he won't even be my friend." She wished Dana was close by so that they could get together, eat hot dogs, and she could lament about Raymond and how she thought he could be the one that she would give her virginity to. He did things to her that she'd never felt before, and she was so ready to explore those feelings—but not with a TV audience watching. No matter how much she wanted to be a star, Imani was not going to use her sexuality to become one. That wasn't the kind of fame that she wanted.

Truth be told, had she traded in her morals the first time she was propositioned on a director's casting couch, she might not be on reality TV. "And you wouldn't have any self-respect, either," she said to the wind as she headed back to the hotel. As she walked, she noticed Lucy standing at the door of the hotel with her arms wrapped around another contestant's waist.

"That didn't take long," Imani muttered as she passed them.

Lucy rolled her eyes and whispered something to the man she'd been cozied up with. The man looked at Imani and smiled, drawing a quick elbow to the gut from Lucy.

Imani couldn't help but put a little extra twist in her hips as she passed them. Laughing as she approached the elevator, when the doors opened she saw Raymond exiting the car. She stopped and locked eyes with him.

"I was looking for you," he said as he stepped back into the elevator and beckoned her inside. "We need to talk."

"We do," she said as she entered the elevator. "I know what I said—"

"Your career is important to you and I can't get upset about you wanting to use this opportunity."

"Right, but there is something else," she said.

"No," Raymond said, bringing his finger to Imani's lips. "I've given up a lot in the name of my career, but I'm not a prop."

"I don't think you are, Raymond. This is really scary to me," she said as he wrapped his arms around her waist and pulled her against his chest. "This isn't what I expected would happen when I came here and you . . ."

Raymond cut her off with a slow kiss that caused an eruption inside Imani. Heat radiated from the pit of her stomach and exploded throughout her entire body. As his hands gently stroked her back, Imani melted against him, losing herself in passion as his tongue slowly danced with hers. Feelings that were as foreign to her as Chinese arithmetic had her confused and filled with want, need, and longing. How was this even possible? He awakened a desire in her that she hadn't even known rested inside her. Raymond was cupping her bottom to bring her closer as the elevator came to a stop on the roof of the resort. They reluctantly broke their passionate kiss as the doors slid open.

"Where are we?" she asked him as he reached for her hand.

"Some place where we won't be interrupted," Raymond said. "We were having a discussion on the beach that I think we should finish."

"Raymond," she said as they stepped out on the roof, "you know, I—"

"I want you, Imani. And no isn't an option. You can stand there and try to hide behind your career, but that's not going to stop me." He stroked her forearm and Imani closed her eyes, then sighed.

"What if I'm not what you want?" she asked, staring into his bejeweled eyes.

"How can you tell me what I want?" he replied, cocking his head to the side and giving her a quizzical look.

"Raymond," she whispered.

He cupped her chin and fought the urge to kiss her. "Don't tell me you don't feel this energy between us. Don't tell me you don't want to see where it leads as much as I do," he said.

"I didn't say that," she replied. "But I know there is something that will—"

"Tonight, I want you to stay with me. I want to greet the morning with you in my arms."

Imani shook her head and took a step back from Raymond. "I can't do that."

He raised his eyebrow. "What's stopping you?"

"I—I have to go. Raymond, I can't do this. You're confusing me and I don't need this right now." She turned toward the elevator and pressed the button. Raymond grabbed her arm.

"Okay, so what is this—a game to you? Did I get you in the middle of a scene?" he asked as she pulled away.

"You know what?" she spat. "If you think I'm performing or that I'm always acting, then just leave me alone." The doors of the elevator opened and Imani dashed inside. Raymond shook his head as the doors closed. Just what in the hell was going on with this woman?

Turning his back to the elevator, he looked at the sun beating down on the island and decided that he wasn't going to force his way into her life anymore. Imani made her choice and he was going to accept it.

"This will never do!" Tres exclaimed as she watched the argument between Raymond and Imani. "Elliot."

"Yes?" her overworked assistant producer asked with an exasperated sigh. What could she possibly want now? More cameras on the doctor and the actress?

"Make sure we team Imani and Raymond up for the couples' tasks and let's get all the contestants on the beach in an hour to get started on those tasks."

"That's not scheduled until tomorrow morning," he replied as he looked at a production schedule.

"What did I say?"

He sighed again. "All right. I'll get it done."

"Thank you."

Imani flung herself across her bed the moment she entered her room. Why couldn't she have just told Raymond the truth? *I'm a virgin and I don't want to become famous for losing my virginity on a reality show.*

"He doesn't need to know I'm a virgin," she muttered. "Especially since he made it clear that he wanted sex. He wants me in his arms after a long night of sex." She pounded her pillow and rolled over on her back. There was no way Imani could stay on this show. Forget the money, forget the acting, she had to protect her heart and get away from Raymond Thomas. Just as she was about to reach for her cell phone, there was a knock at her room door. Thinking that it was Raymond, she decided to ignore it, but the knocking persisted.

Damn it, she thought as she padded to the door. Looking out the peephole, she saw that it was one of the show's producers.

"What now?" she asked when she opened the door.

"You need to be on the beach in an hour for the first couples' task," he said as he handed her a production note. Before Imani could tell him that she didn't want to do the show anymore, he was on to the next door.

Suck it up, Imani, her inner voice chided. *You want to be a star, here is your chance. Raymond is a distraction that you brought on yourself. Just do what you came here to do.*

Imani read the note, which stated that she needed to wear the wet suit that the show had provided for the activity on the beach. She grabbed her cell phone and started to call her agent, but when she dialed the number, a recording from her wireless company played in her ear.

"Your account has been suspended. Please call customer service to make a payment."

Imani tossed her phone across the room. "Damn," she muttered as she rose from the bed. She pulled the wet suit out of the closet and tossed the pink gear on the bed. She couldn't help but wonder what foolishness she and the other contestants were in store for. As she peeled her bathing suit off, she heard another knock on the door. She grabbed her robe and snatched the door open, thinking it was another representative from the show.

"What now?" she demanded, then looked into Raymond's eyes.

"Am I disturbing you?" he asked.

Imani clinched her robe tighter as he eyed her frame. "No, but I have to get ready and you do too."

"Ready for what?"

Imani motioned for Raymond to come in and then she handed him the production note she'd been given moments before. He read it over and laughed. "Wet suits?"

She nodded and chuckled. "I have to say, I'm surprised to see you at my door."

"There was something said on the roof that I wanted to clear up," he said.

"What's that? You made your intentions pretty clear and I'm not going to give you what you want. It's better that what was said on the roof is the end of it all." She knew the words were just lies, but she thought they sounded good.

Raymond folded his arms across his chest and cast his bejeweled stare upon her. "That almost sounded as if you meant it," he said, slowly walking toward her. Imani shivered with the anticipation of feeling Raymond's breath on her face, his hands on her body, knowing that she was naked underneath her robe. She imagined having him take her robe off and kissing every inch of her body until she couldn't take anymore and gave in to the desire of having sex. Would he be a gentle lover? A slow and tender teacher?

"Imani?" he asked, breaking into her intimate thoughts. "Are you listening to me?"

"What? What did you say?"

He placed his hands on her shoulders and she felt more fire building inside her. "I didn't catch what you said," she replied, then looked at his hands on her shoulders. "Raymond, maybe in another time and place we would've been perfect together and we would've been able to . . ."

"But we're here right now and I'm sorry if I came off judgmental about your career," he said. "Being an actress is important to you and I can't hold it against you because you want to get ahead. I just wish you felt as if you could be open with me and let me in more."

"Let you in where? In my bed?" she asked, nervously trembling because if he kissed her right now they would probably head right there—cameras be damned.

"Why do you keep bringing that up? You know I'm attracted to you and would like nothing more than to pull that robe off and take you right here. But I know you're scared. Maybe you're used to men using you, but I don't get down like that. When you want to join me in bed, you'll know where to find me."

"Huh?" she asked, taken aback by his statement. "I don't know who he is or what he did to you, but I'm not him and I'm not going to do what he did to make Imani the way she is now." Raymond stroked her cheek and smiled. "I'd better go and get ready. See you on the beach."

She blinked as he walked out of the room. Was he serious? If Imani had her way she'd drop her robe and head across the hall. *And do what? Lay there and give him the worst experience of his life? You wouldn't know what to do with that man and you're not doing this on TV. Stop letting this man pull at your heart strings when you know that nothing good is going to come from this.*

"But how can I keep ignoring what I really want? Maybe having someone like Raymond in my life is more important than being famous," she muttered as she dropped her robe and put the wet suit on.

Raymond pulled his production note off his hotel room door. He knew what it said and wasn't sure he wanted to play these games, especially when he thought that he was finally getting somewhere with Imani. The way she kept bringing up sex, the bed, and trying to discern his intentions with her let him know that someone had hurt her and she was hiding that pain.

Maybe he's an ex who didn't believe in her talent and that's why she was so hell-bent on becoming a superstar. *Nothing motivates a woman like revenge or heartbreak. I think Imani's been heartbroken,* he thought as he pulled on his wet suit. "She needs to get to know a good man, and here I am," he muttered as he reread the production note.

Chapter 11

The beach was filled with cameras, contestants dressed in pink and blue wet suits and curious tourists trying to figure out what was going on or get a look at the women in their supertight outfits. Tres glanced at her watch and then out at the assembled group and smiled. But her smile quickly turned into a scowl when she noticed her stars, Raymond and Imani, were nowhere to be found.

She grabbed Elliot as he walked by. "Where are they?"

"Who?" he asked.

"Raymond and Imani," she replied with a smack on his arm. "I know damned well they didn't leave the show."

Elliot rubbed his arm and pointed toward the hotel. "Here they come. We have fifteen minutes before we start filming. Will you calm down?"

"Calm down? Calm down? You do realize that after this we're going live? America is going to watch the drama between my favorite couple every night as it happens. Elize gave me the news after

I sent her what we'd already recorded and the network has already canceled that police drama. This is my chance to shine, Elliot. My chance to get a real show. Where I go, you go. So you make sure my stars are always front and center."

"What happens if the viewers like another couple?" Elliot asked. "I thought the purpose of the show was to allow America to vote for the couples."

"That was until I saw the magic these two have on camera," Tres said as she watched Imani and Raymond join the others. Elliot looked at the couple and shrugged. He didn't understand what was so special about them. All she did was whine about not wanting him and wanting to be a movie star. How were they supposed to be the stars of the show? And if Tres thought that Elize was going to give her a scripted show to produce, she was out of her mind.

"All right," Tres said as she walked over to the contestants. "Thank you all for doing the show. I have a few production notes before I turn the controls over to our host, Galen Edwards. People, we're going live, and today's taping will air next week. So, have fun and let's see who's going to get married."

The contestants cheered, everyone except Imani and Raymond. Galen Edwards walked over to the contestants with a camera crew in tow. Edwards, a once-upon-a-time teen idol with thinning sandy brown hair and a slight beer belly, smiled at the twenty-four players. Imani leaned over and whispered to Raymond, "He must think this is 1986."

"Play nice," he replied.

"Who wants to get married?" Edwards called out.

"The secret to any good marriage is being able to work together and that's what we're going to do out here today. We're looking for diamonds. There are four diamonds hidden on the beach and you and your partner have to find them. But first, you're going to need a partner."

Edwards waved over a bikini-clad woman carrying a box. "In here are the names of the couples. Of course, if you stay together, that is up to America."

Imani shook her head, then looked for the camera so that she could offer America a sparkling smile. *Channel your inner Gabrielle Union,* she thought as she spotted the camera. She smiled, then ran her fingers through her hair. Raymond glanced over at her as the host pulled the first name out of the box.

"Couple number one, Lucy and Murray," Edwards called out. Imani couldn't help but giggle when she saw Lucy was paired up with Murray, a short and slightly stocky man who didn't need to ever take his shirt off. The look of disgust on Lucy's face elicited a genuine smile from Imani. As Edwards continued reading off the names of the couples, Imani felt a hitch in her stomach. They were not going to team her up with Raymond, were they?

"And our final couple, Raymond and Imani," Edwards said. They stepped forward and took a shovel from the host.

Imani and Raymond exchanged heated glances, but didn't say anything as Edwards began going over the rules of the search.

"We're going to handcuff each pair together, give you a map, and you're going to have to navigate your course until you find the hidden treasure. Again, there are only four diamonds. Couples who find fool's gold will be up for elimination," Edwards said. "If you see another couple with a diamond, you have the option of getting it away from them. No violence, however. Are we ready to see who's going to be on the road to matrimony and who's just going to be on the road home?"

"Yes," everyone called out. The production assistants walked up to the couples and placed the handcuffs on their wrists.

"Good luck," Elliot said to Imani and Raymond as he locked them together.

"Thanks," Imani said, then rolled her eyes.

"It could be worse," Raymond said. "I'm left handed." He held his arm up. "So, if we have to dig, you're going to be in control, TV wife."

"I guess you're going to learn how to dig with your right hand today," she said as they headed to the box near the shore to grab a map.

As Imani reached for the map, Lucy snatched it from her grasp. "Enjoy your time with him now, because once the voting starts, you're going to be sent packing. Maybe you should do a sex tape."

"Maybe you should go to hell," Imani snapped, then grabbed the map from her. "Let's go." She started to run, but Raymond walked slowly and nearly caused her to fall.

"Raymond?" Imani asked, putting her free hand on her hip.

"If we're going to win this thing, we need a plan," he said, then took the map from her hand. "You know how to read a map?"

Sighing, she replied, "No, but if I didn't get away from Lucy, there might have been a fight."

"That would be a sight, but you're not a fighter in that way," he said.

"You're right and I refuse to be a stereotype on this show," she said as Raymond struggled to hold up the map. Imani grabbed the edge flapping in the wind. "Better?"

"Yes. Looks like we might make a good team, after all," he quipped.

She raised her right eyebrow but didn't say a word. Raymond pointed to a spot on the map. "We need to start moving in this direction, toward those rock formations."

"Why couldn't they just give us a GPS?" Imani asked as she and Raymond started toward the rocks.

"Where is the fun in that?" he asked as they walked. "Besides, women have built-in GPS when it comes to diamonds."

"That's true," Imani said. "But I'm not into the bling."

Raymond raised his eyebrow as if to say, "Yeah, right."

"I'm serious," she said. "I do flashy on the screen and on stage, but in real life, I'm just plain old Imani."

"So, how many diamonds have you turned down?"

"How many have you given away?" she tossed back at him.

"None," Raymond said. "When, and if, I ever decide to get down on one knee, it's only happening once."

"Unless you win the show," Imani quipped. "I

imagine that Lucy will expect you to go all out when you make her Mrs. Dr. Ray-Ray Thomas."

He laughed and shook his head. "Like that would happen." He held their shackled wrists. "Who knows, I could be linked to my spouse right now."

Imani shook her head. "Please, we'd never last. You'd never sign the prenup."

Raymond stopped in his tracks. "Prenup?"

"I'm going to be a star. If I get married, I'm going to have to protect what's mine."

Raymond chuckled and shook his head. "That's a hell of a way to go into a marriage. This is mine and this is yours. What happened to two becoming one?"

"Did you really just ask that question as we walk through the sand, handcuffed together looking for a diamond on a reality show about getting married?"

"Come on now," he said. "Neither one of us is here to get married, and I still believe in that old-school thing that my parents had."

Imani rolled her eyes and slowed her gait. "My parents showed me one thing about marriage."

"What's that?" Raymond asked.

"If you want to be happy, don't get married."

"Seriously?"

Imani nodded. "Maybe that's why I jumped into acting. When I was ten, my parents decided to separate. When they stopped living together, everything changed. My mother became the best attorney at her firm and my dad went back to school and started an interior design firm in Georgia. The only thing they agree on is that I'm wasting my time trying to be an actress."

"You don't like being told you can't do something, huh?"

She shook her head and pointed to a half-buried box. "What's that over there?"

Raymond looked down at the map, surprised that he and Imani had made so much headway, then said, "That might be the diamond."

"Get ready to dig, doc," she joked as she handed him the shovel.

"Remember what I said about us making a good team?" he asked. "I was wrong." As Raymond dug around the box, Imani looked to see if any other couples were coming their way and she saw Lucy and her stocky partner barreling toward them.

"Knock the box open and let's get out of here, the gremlin and the witch are coming our way," she said. Lucy locked eyes with Imani and tried to run, but Murray fell in the sand.

"Bend down here and help me with this," Raymond said after digging more than half of the box out of the soft sand.

"Okay," she said, dropping to her knees beside him. With her unshackled hand, Imani unsnapped the closure on the box. There wasn't a diamond inside, but a key. "What the . . ."

Raymond grabbed the key and stuck it in the lock on the handcuffs. They popped open. "Come on, let's go to the next box and see if we can get the diamond."

"I have an idea," she said. Then she shouted, "Yes! We got it." Imani looked toward Lucy and

Murray. Turning to Raymond, Imani kissed him slowly and deeply.

She meant the kiss to be a swipe at Lucy, but when Raymond pulled her closer to his chest and deepened his kiss, Lucy wasn't even a thought in the back of Imani's mind. Her tongue tangoed with his, her spine tingled like a sparkler. *Pull back, pull back,* her inner voice yelled. She ignored it as Raymond cupped her bottom and pressed her against his erection.

"That's not a convincing act!" Lucy yelled out, causing the couple to break off the kiss.

"I don't know what I did to deserve that," Raymond whispered, "but I liked it and expect another kiss just like that when we find the next box."

She smiled nervously. "Let's go," Imani said. They took off, not looking at the map. They had run for about a half mile when Imani tripped over another box.

"Are you all right?" he asked, dropping down beside her. He took Imani's leg into his hands and looked over her ankle, making sure she wasn't bleeding. "Do you feel any pain?"

"No, just my ego's a little bruised," she replied. "Look on the bright side. Me being clumsy may have found that diamond."

Raymond looked at the box, which didn't appear to have been found by another team, so he nodded in agreement, then started digging. "Crack it open," Raymond said after uncovering the top of the box.

Imani opened the box and expelled a deep

breath when she saw the diamond in the box. "This can't be real," she said as she picked up the rock.

"Damn," he said, taking a look at what had to be a huge piece of glass or the Hope Diamond. "I'm guessing we don't get to keep this. If we sold this, you could buy performance space and the clinic would be in the black for years."

"It's so not real," Imani said as she held it up. "There would be no need to finish the show. Let's get back to the host and see what we win."

"Sure you can walk?" Raymond held his hand out to help her up. Imani stood up and did a little dance.

"I think I can make it."

"But," he said, "you owe me something." Raymond wrapped his arms around her waist, drawing her against his chest, and brushed his lips across hers. He felt her tremble in his arms and leaned in for the kiss, but Imani's next move, running her tongue across his lips, made him shiver in the sunlight. She captured his lips with a quick move and drew his tongue deep into her mouth. Imani moaned softly as he licked the inside of her mouth, seemingly touching the depths of her soul and heating her body like an oven. Raymond lifted her leg and wrapped it around his waist. It was as if they'd both forgotten about the cameras, the task at hand and that fact that they were in the middle of a competition. The diamond tumbled from Imani's hand as she was lost herself in the taste of Raymond's mouth. Feelings that she'd never experienced flowed through her body like a raging river. She could feel the wetness between her thighs, she could feel her heart beating like a drum playing a song that she'd never heard before.

"Look!" a male voice yelled out. "The diamond." As much as they would've loved to stay lost in their kiss, Imani and Raymond pulled themselves apart, grabbed the diamond, and took off toward the finish line.

"This is not fun," Imani said as she ran.

"Just think," Raymond said, "you can kiss me again when we cross the finish line."

"You can kiss me," she teased. *And just what are you going to do when he wants to do more than kiss?* her conscience nagged. Imani sighed and forced herself to remember why she was on this show anyway. But all she could focus on as they crossed the finish line was how good his ass looked in that wet suit.

Tres couldn't have scripted a better ending to the first day of taping. Imani and Raymond were moving from sizzling to just burning up every time they were on the screen. And those kisses. Hot. They'd have to be edited, of course. "Elliot," she said to her overworked and bewildered assistant, "do you see why I need a camera on them at all times? Do you see that?"

"Yes, I see it," he said. "But what if America doesn't like them together? Did you hear how she whined about her parents? All she wants to do is be famous, and I don't think the viewers are going to connect with that."

"I don't give a damn about the viewers," Tres said as she leapt from her seat. "I just want to see these two drive up my ratings with all of that sex appeal and those kisses. They are almost too hot for TV, but Raymond and Imani are the key to my future."

Elliot rolled his eyes as Tres headed outside to smoke a cigarette.

Chapter 12

Since Imani and Raymond had found the largest diamond on the beach, they were treated to a spa treatment and private—yet filmed for the show—dinner on the beach. When he saw Imani walking toward him as the chef set their salads on the table, Raymond's body had never been more aware and thankful to be a man. She was dressed in a strapless pink dress that kissed her curves and skimmed her knees. In the flickering light of the candles, she looked like an angel. He rose from his seat, mouthing, "Wow," as he crossed over to her. He wished they were simply having a real date in Hawaii without the cameras and without America watching at home.

Come on now, he thought, *You're here to win money for the clinic and she's here to get discovered.* But the moment she smiled at him, those thoughts disappeared from his mind.

"You look amazing," he said, his eyes devouring her body.

Imani brushed her hand across his soft cotton

shirt. "You don't look bad yourself," she replied. "I'm guessing this is going to be an interesting dinner. If my knowledge of reality shows is right."

"Dinner got interesting when you showed up in that dress," he said as he took her hand in his.

"This old thing," she joked.

Raymond couldn't tear his eyes from Imani, though he wondered if she was falling into a character or if they would have another real conversation like they had when they'd been searching for the diamond on the beach. Raymond reluctantly let go of her hand as they took their seats.

"So," she said as the wait staff began mulling around, "any idea what we're about to eat?"

Raymond paused, looked at her with a slight smile on his lips, then he licked them. "I know what I'm craving isn't on the menu." Even underneath the blanket of darkness that covered the beach, he saw the blush on her cheeks.

"See," she said, her quiet voice masking the burning of desire, anger, and need in the pit of her stomach. "I thought you were different."

"What?"

"You've got one thing on your mind. And if you think I'm just going to rip my clothes off and let you have your way with me, guess again."

"Have I ever made it a secret that I want you, Imani? You come out here looking sexier than the law should allow. Did you expect me not to notice?"

Imani fingered her hair and glowered at him. "Whatever."

"You know that you're beautiful and I'm going to notice it. What are you afraid of?"

"Nothing," she said coolly. "Certainly not you. And if you think we're getting into bed together for the world to see, you're as wrong as two left shoes."

"Sounds like we're married already," he quipped. "Imani, I told you that if that day ever comes, it will be your choice. I know you want me and you are afraid to give in to what you want. I'm just trying to make it easier for you."

"I'm not giving in to you," she said as she crossed her legs. "Sex complicates everything." *As if you have a clue?* "I've spent my career trying to be more than a set of tits and an ass."

"That's admirable," he said genuinely.

"That's one reason why I don't work. Talent means nothing in the Kardashian era. But I don't want to be that actress who just gets by on her looks and figure. I have real talent."

"What does that have to do with you finding real love?" Raymond asked. "I'm not trying to lure you on the casting couch. I want to get to know you, every part of you. I want to be sitting on the front row when you star in your first Broadway play. I want you to be mine and not just on this show."

Imani sucked her bottom lip in. His words sounded so sincere; he had no reason to put on an act. "Are you serious?" she asked quietly.

He took her hand in his and brought it to his lips. "Yes," he said, then kissed her hand. "When I see the real you, I like what I see."

She closed her eyes and wished that she could just tell him everything, that she was afraid of real emotions, afraid to give herself to a man because she was a virgin and maybe she couldn't please him. "That's a nice thing to say, but you make it seem as if I have multiple personalities or something," she said.

"Isn't that what makes a good actress?" he teased. "One day, when we're away from the cameras, you can continue to show me the real Imani."

"What if you find out that you don't like the real Imani?" she asked.

"Why wouldn't I?"

Imani propped her elbows up on the table and stared into Raymond's eyes. Even in the lighting, they were brilliant. In her mind, she wasn't on a movie set acting, she was with a man that she could fall in love with, sharing dinner and about to make love for the first time.

But you're on a reality show and the last thing you want to do is let the world know you've never been touched that way by a man. Who's going to buy you in a sexy role then? What is the purpose of all of those hours in the gym to keep your body ready? she thought.

"Imani?" he probed.

"There are a lot of things I wish I could say to you, but we have too many prying eyes around right now. But I can say this, and I'm not acting. I really do want to see where this thing could go and how we could be together. But I'm still scared."

"I wish you would tell me why."

Before Imani could say another word, the chef came over with a camera crew.

"Good evening, lucky couple," he said. His eyes shifted to the table, where Imani's and Raymond's salads and appetizers were untouched. He pursed his lips and stamped his foot like a petulant child. "Are you two too good to eat my food?"

Raymond looked up at the man and shook his head. "No disrespect to your food, but have you taken a look at my dinner companion?"

The chef snorted and stomped off as the cameramen laughed uncontrollably.

Imani blushed and turned away from Raymond as she chuckled herself. Inside, she wanted nothing more than to go back to her room with Raymond and give every part of herself to him. Never had she been around a man who understood and appreciated her dreams. He was more supportive in the short time that she'd known him than her family had ever been. Could he be the one she'd been saving herself for? Was Raymond the one? "Oh my God," she whispered.

"What?" Raymond asked. "Is something wrong?"

"I—I can't . . . I'm not hungry and I'm really tired. I have to go." She leapt to her feet and ran toward the hotel.

"No, no, no!" Tres exploded as Imani ran away. "What is that chick doing? I thought they had a real connection and she just runs off like a little child." She turned to Elliot. "Imani is hiding something and you need to find out what it is. You know what? Get Lucy down there. Let's create some more drama."

"Why are you playing puppet master with these three people?" Elliot asked. "There are other couples on this show."

"But this story arch has a sizzle and I'm going to

exploit it for the ratings as long as I can. Do what I said, all right?"

Elliot picked up the phone and dialed Lucy's room. When she answered, he instructed her to go down to the beach for an uninterrupted chance to dine with Raymond.

"And that Imani clown isn't going to be there?"

"No," Elliot sighed. "He's all alone with a candlelit dinner." The next sound he heard was the dial tone in his ear.

Raymond downed his glass of wine, refusing to chase after Imani. Part of him wondered what she was running from or if this was just another emotion that she wanted to show to the movie directors she hoped were watching the show. *Cut your losses and move the hell on,* he thought as he poured himself another glass of wine.

"Is this a private celebration or is that second glass meant for me?" Lucy said from behind him. Turning around slowly, Raymond wondered why she was there, but as he downed his wine, it didn't matter. He was tired of trying to understand what was going on in Imani's mind. Sure, she made it clear what she was doing on the show, but she gave just as well as she took. She initiated plenty of kisses between the two of them. She never turned away when he pulled her into his arms and he could feel her body heat up like an oven every time he touched her.

Glancing at Lucy, he thought about simply burying his utter frustration and aggravation between her shapely thighs. But that wasn't fair to Lucy nor would it be fair to Imani or himself. Raymond knew what he wanted, but he still nodded for Lucy to sit down.

"Thanks for that glowing invite," she quipped. "Where's your little 'wife'?"

"I'm not married," he replied as he filled her glass with wine before refilling his.

"You know who I'm talking about," Lucy said as she took a dainty sip of wine. "I guess you've finally seen what the actress is all about, huh?"

Raymond sighed, suddenly feeling sober. "You know what," he said, rising to his feet. "I need to find out everything about her. You enjoy the wine and dinner."

Lucy hopped up and put her hand on Raymond's chest. "Come on, Raymond. That girl is not worth all of this energy." She smoothed her hand across his chest. "Everything you could ever need is right here. I'm all the woman you can handle and Imani is just a flighty actress trying to make a name for herself."

"You may be a lot more than I can handle," he said. "But I know what I want."

"Your loss, playboy," she said. "This could be your last chance unless America has the good sense to put you and me together."

Raymond patted her on the shoulder. "I've got to go." He tore off toward that hotel and went immediately to Imani's room. Tonight the cat and mouse game would end. If she wanted to build something with him, then she was going to have to make a decision about it tonight.

As he approached her room door, he sighed. Was she worth it or was this going to be just another performance? He knocked on the door and waited. It seemed to take forever for Imani to open the door. But when she did, looking fresh faced and innocent with her hair pulled back in a ponytail and dressed in a terry cloth romper, Raymond didn't stop himself from pulling her into his arms and kissing her deeply.

Imani could barely gather her thoughts with Raymond's lips pressed against hers. She went with the kiss, telling herself that as soon as they stopped kissing, she was going to tell him why she was hot and cold. She would tell him that she was too afraid to open every part of herself to him or any man because she didn't want to get her heart broken. She dealt with too much rejection in her professional life and she couldn't take it in her personal life.

But did she want the audience of *Let's Get Married* to know that? Pulling back, she inhaled deeply. "Raymond," she said breathlessly.

"Look, we need to talk—seriously."

"I know," she replied. "But, I just can't right now. Not with all of the cameras and—"

"To hell with the cameras and this show. Imani, I want something real with you," he said, taking her face in his hands.

She closed her eyes, hoping to hold back the real tears stinging her eyes. "Everything we say and we do is being filmed right now," she said. "I want to tell you . . . Let's go out on the beach."

"I don't think you want to do that. Lucy's out there," he said.

Imani rolled her eyes. "I really don't want to run into her. But we need to go somewhere we can be alone and as far away from the cameras as possible."

Tres pointed to Elliot. "Make sure a camera crew is on these two at all times. Roll someone with a hand camera to Imani's room right now. If she reveals this secret, I want to make sure we find out what it is and I want it on screen moments after she utters the words."

Elliot shook his head. "How do you know she has some juicy secret?"

Tres pulled out her package of clove cigarettes and took one out of the box. "She's probably a lesbian," she said as she dangled the slim stick between her fingers. "That's why she runs away every time she kisses him. That will ruin this show. Please don't let that be her secret."

"What if she has some fatal disease?" Elliot asked.

"That's ratings," Tres said, slipping the cigarette between her lips. "If I don't find out what this secret is, you're fired."

"This is really a new low for you, Tres. I know you've done some shows that hovered over the bottom of the barrel, but this is scraping it."

"How so? They all knew what they were getting into when they signed up for this show. I don't feel bad for wanting to know her secret, especially since Imani hasn't hidden the fact that she's using this show to get noticed by movie directors. And you know what? I'm sure she's getting noticed. Call her agent in the morning and find out. His name is

Funderburke or something. Make yourself useful and find out," Tres said, waving him off as she headed outside to smoke—again.

Elliot thought what he and Tres were doing was nothing but exploitation, like those old black movies from the late seventies, but he wasn't going to make too much of a fuss about it because he needed to work. Still, he had to do something to help Imani hold on to some of her dignity. No matter how much of a diva he thought she was, she didn't need to be exploited on national TV, unless that was what she wanted.

Raymond took Imani's hand as they headed down the hall. She looked over her shoulder and gave him a thumbs-up signal. He turned to his left and nodded. "Let's go," he said. They took off running like two school children sneaking away from their parents, only to run into a lone cameraman. While he didn't say a word to them, his intentions were pretty clear. He was going to follow them wherever they went.

"This sucks," Imani said under her breath. "Had I just stuck to my plan, this wouldn't even be happening."

"Hey," a quiet voice called out. "You two, come over here."

Raymond and Imani looked at each other and shrugged. "Who is that?" he asked.

"I don't know," Imani said.

The man stepped out of the shadows so that they

could see his face. "Look, I can help you guys, but you have to come over here and be quick about it."

They recognized him as one of the show's producers and they followed him. "Listen," he said. "I'm Elliot Reynolds, one of the producers, and I have to tell you something. Tres, the executive producer, thinks that you two are the stars of this show and she has assigned a camera crew to follow you everywhere."

"Isn't that happening with everybody?" Raymond asked.

"Not to the extent of what's going on with you two," he replied. "We know about your secret, Imani."

"What?"

Elliot shrugged. "There are cameras and microphones everywhere. Tres wants you two to be the stars of this show. Now, I can't guarantee that your image won't get captured, but if you go around the north side of the hotel, there are no mics and you should be able to say what you need to say."

"Why should we trust you?" Imani asked. "If she's trying to get that deep in our business, how do we know you aren't?"

"First of all," he said, "I am not even supposed to be talking to you all and I'm risking my job. This is because I don't want *you* to be exploited."

Imani inhaled sharply. "So, you all have been . . ."

Elliot clasped his hands together. "Look, I'm trying to help and I've done what I can. Get over there before the cameraman catches up with you two again." He started down the hall and Imani touched his elbow.

"Thanks," she said.

He nodded and kept walking.

Raymond slipped his arm around Imani's waist. "Let's get moving," he said. "That was really righteous of the dude to tell us about this. But, Imani, if you don't want to tell me this secret, then you don't have to."

"But I need to," she said. "It's only fair."

They peeked around the corner looking for the cameraman. Seeing that the coast was clear, Imani and Raymond tore down the hall and out of the hotel. When they made it to the side of the hotel Elliot told them about, they found a small bench behind a few potted plants.

"So," Raymond said as they took their seat. "What do you have to tell me?"

Imani inhaled deeply. *Just say it,* she told herself as she stared into his eyes. "I've never felt what I'm feeling when I'm around you before."

"All right," he said. "I think I'm there too."

"You don't understand," she replied as he took her hand in his. "Raymond, when I'm close to you like this and when I kiss you, I want to do things that I've *never* done before, and it's exciting and scary at the same time."

"I get that. This isn't the ideal setting to . . ."

Imani groaned because he obviously wasn't picking up on her hints. "I've never been intimate with a man before," she whispered.

Raymond's mouth dropped open and everything he was going to say died on his tongue. Immediately he thought she didn't look like a virgin. *But what does a virgin look like?* She definitely didn't kiss like a virgin. Then again, he hadn't kissed a virgin in over twenty years. Though he couldn't believe the words that had come out of Imani's mouth, he felt a swell of pride as he looked at her. He'd been right when he thought there was something different about her. "Wow," he said. Imani averted eye contact with him. "I had no idea." He turned her face toward his.

"It's not something that I advertise," she said in a low tone. Raymond held her hand, stroking it reassuringly. Finally, she met his gaze. "I'm not ashamed or anything. I just haven't met someone who I wanted to share that part of myself with. Most of the men I meet are in the business and I probably could have been in many more movies if I had spent some time on the casting couch. I just have more respect for myself than that. If you don't want to waste any more time . . ."

Raymond placed his finger to her sexy lips. "I never feel like any time I spend with you is a waste. Imani, I'm not going to lie and say that I'm not taken aback. But I applaud you. That being said, when I look at you, I still see a sexy and beautiful woman I'm still going to kiss, touch, and yearn for."

Skepticism made her purse her lips and raised her right eyebrow as if she was asking, "What?"

Raymond pulled her closer to him, bringing her face inches from his. "It's your body, as beautiful as it is. And you respect it. Anyone who only wants you for your body doesn't deserve you. Anyone who doesn't respect you enough to wait until you want to share your gift with him is wasting your time."

A lone tear dropped from Imani's eye. "Really?"

"Hell, yes. And there is no way that you should or

will lose your virginity on national TV," he said, then kissed her tear-stained cheek.

"Raymond," she whispered as her lips moved toward his. He brushed his lips across hers and kissed Imani, slowly, tenderly, gently. And she trembled because she realized that this was no show-mance. She was falling head over heels in love with Raymond Thomas.

Chapter 13

Tres banged on her desk until everything but the monitor itself fell off while Elliot smirked behind her. "Why is there no sound?" she demanded as she watched Imani and Raymond kiss.

"That's one of the resort's dead spots," Elliot said. "At least you have the video."

"Not good enough. We have to get them in the confessional chair tomorrow first thing," she said as she started picking up the files that crashed to the floor. "Why would they go there?"

Elliot shrugged and started helping Tres clean up. "Her secret," Tres said, "was going to be the focus of tomorrow's show. What am I going to do now?" She turned back to the monitor and saw Imani and Raymond kissing deeply. "They're going to have sex! Elliot, make sure the night cameras are set in both of their rooms."

Elliot nodded, but didn't move. There was no telling what Imani's secret was and maybe they needed some time alone to continue talking, he thought, but Elliot had to at least go through the motions and pretend that he was going to make sure the video Tres wanted would be available. "Did you reach out to Imani's agent?" Elliot asked.

"I did and she should be excited. Because of the buzz from this show and the dailies that Elize has been shopping around, Imani's agent said he's been getting a lot of calls about her. Make sure we share that with Raymond in the morning."

Elliot nodded and made his notes. For some reason, he wanted to see Imani and Raymond make it without all of the reality show drama. Looking at them he could see that there was something bubbling underneath the surface. *Wait a minute,* he told himself. He couldn't develop a soft spot for them. But he didn't have to help exploit them either. As he watched them return to the inside of the hotel, he hoped this show wouldn't be the runaway smash hit Tres was hoping for and those two could have a real chance to be together. Damn, he did have a soft spot for them.

Raymond held Imani's hand as they walked back to their rooms. Her admission put so many things into perspective and made him realize one thing—he wanted to be the first and the last man she ever shared her body with. He wanted to be the one to teach her what making love was all about, wanted to be the one who she shared her first orgasm with. It was his job to uncover all of her erogenous zones, then stroke, kiss, and lick each one of them until she quivered with desire and screamed his name.

He felt a tug at his hand and his thoughts moved

from making love to Imani to what she was saying at that moment.

"Yes?" he asked.

"Where did you go?"

"What do you mean?"

"I was asking you if you wanted to come in and order some room service, but you were out in space somewhere," she said, facing him and cocking her head to the side. "What's going on in your head?" Dread started to spread through Imani's system. Had Raymond really meant what he said? Or had he just said what he'd thought she wanted to hear? Did this mean that Lucy would actually have a chance with Raymond since she was willing to do what Imani wasn't?

"I was just thinking about our conversation," he replied honestly.

Imani frowned, thinking that what she'd feared was right. "Look," she said, her voice low and melancholy. "If this is too much for you to deal with, then let me know."

"Not at all," he said as he twirled her around to face him. "Imani, I meant everything I said to you. Nothing about how I feel for you has changed, or the fact that I find you to be the most beautiful woman I've met in a long time."

"But . . ."

Raymond shook his head and held his hand up. "But nothing. Imani, if I simply wanted to sleep around, then I have had plenty of opportunity to do that here and in New York. You're special and—"

"Don't think of me as a project or some—"

"Imani, there's no way in hell that I could think of you in that way," Raymond said.

"Good," she said with a sigh of relief. "So, want to order room service or what?"

"Let me check in with Keith and then we can order something with a lot of pineapples and wine," he said, then turned toward his room. When he noticed that Imani looked as if she was going to head to her room, he shook his head. "You're coming with me. This phone call is going to take about five minutes."

She smiled and Raymond felt as if she lit the entire hallway. How could he fall any deeper for this woman? Damn the show and to hell with the money. If he could walk away with Imani and make love to her, then he'd be a winner.

"If you need to talk on the phone in private, I understand," she said.

Raymond rolled his eyes. "You know what I think. I think you want things to change so that it will confirm whatever it is you think about men."

"Oh, now you know what I'm thinking?" she asked.

"Yes."

She slapped her hand on her hip and rolled her eyes. "Maybe I'm trying to make it easy on you. You have your needs," Imani said as Raymond opened his room door.

"I know what I need," he replied as they walked into the room and he closed the door. "And you're it."

"How can you be sure?"

Raymond pulled Imani against his chest and held her tightly as they settled on the bed. "Because

I know. I've never met a woman who has challenged me as much as you have and who knows what she wants and will hold out for it."

"Really?"

"Yes. We've all dated the wrong people in New York and I've had my share of women who thought 'doctor' meant a lot of money and when they found out I didn't have as much as they wanted, the relationship ended. But that doesn't mean I think all New York sisters are gold diggers. I'm sure you've met some jackasses, but don't lump me in that group."

"All right, I'm sorry," she said as she tossed her head back and shook her hair. "But . . ."

Raymond placed his finger to Imani's soft lips. "No buts, no ifs or ands," he said, then leaned into her and kissed her lips softly. She moaned quietly as his tongue flicked across her bottom lip.

"If you kiss me like that again," she said, "I might forget that there are cameras watching our every move."

"Is that so?" he asked, then brushed his lips against hers. "Then I guess I'm going to have to control myself, huh?"

"And why would you do that?" She leaned over and kissed Raymond, but there was nothing gentle about her wanton kiss as she darted her tongue between his lips. He pressed his body against hers and Imani immediately felt his arousal and this time, she didn't back away. She allowed her body to melt with his and relished in the tumble of emotions flowing through her. Desire, passion, and lust now took on new meaning for Imani as their kiss took an even more sensual turn with Raymond slipping his hand between her thighs.

He pulled back from her as his palm brushed across her mound of untold sexuality. "Tell me to stop at any time," he moaned as he felt a trickle of wetness when he slipped his hand inside her silky panties.

"I—I," she stammered as Raymond slipped his forefinger between her wet folds of flesh and touched her in a spot that made her knees quiver. She'd forgotten about hidden cameras and what this would look like immortalized on video. "My God," she exclaimed as he teased her clitoris with his finger, making small circles and giving her a feeling that she'd never experienced. Was this an orgasm, she wondered as she felt a hot explosion from deep inside.

Raymond stared at Imani as he felt her come. She had a look of satisfaction and surprise on her face. As much as he wanted to strip her down and make love to her—especially after licking her essence from his finger—he put his want on ice and asked, "How do you feel?"

"Amazing," she replied breathlessly. "I've never. Felt anything. Like that."

"That's just a taste, baby," he whispered as he leaned into her, his lips inches from her ear. "One day soon, I'm going to make you feel even more amazing, if you want me too."

She smiled and tingles danced up and down his spine. Raymond had to let her go because if he didn't, he'd be tempted to spread her legs and bury his face in her sweetness. "All right," he said, rising from the bed and taking a deep breath. "I have to call Keith."

"And I'll order our food," she replied once her breathing returned to normal. As he headed for the balcony with his cell phone, Raymond watched Imani flip through the menu.

"What's up?" his friend greeted. "Tell me you're not calling because you've gotten kicked off the show already."

"I'm still here," Raymond said. "And so is the most intriguing woman I've ever met."

Keith chuckled. "I should've known a woman was involved. Before you tell me about her, I got to tell you this. *Let's Get Married* has a big buzz around the city. A crew from New York One came by here today to do a profile on the clinic and the bachelor doctor on the reality show."

"Really?" Raymond asked. "Please tell me you didn't make me sound—"

"No worries, man. I told the reporter you were desperate for a wife but you're so ugly this was the only way you could find someone to give you the time of day."

"Dude!"

"Kidding," Keith replied. "I told the reporter about the clinic and our struggles with finances. Then we talked about what Marion G. Palmer means to the community and how you're taking one for the team so that we can keep our doors open. Then, the phones started ringing off the hook. In the last two days, we've had about ten-thousand dollars in donations."

"Are you serious? That's great."

"And, of course, there have been about fifteen marriage proposals since the billboard went up in Times Square with your face on it."

"What?"

"But forget your ugly mug. I want to know if you have had a chance to get to know that sexy actress? She was in a horrible movie, something about a diva, but damn! She is wearing that pink wet suit in the ad."

"That's Imani and I know her," Raymond replied, smiling as if he was sitting across from his friend.

"If you tell me that's the woman you were going to rave about, I'm hanging up the phone. No way in hell you should be that lucky," he quipped.

"Then I'll holla at you when I come back to New York."

"Lucky bastard," Keith exclaimed. "So, what makes her so amazing?"

Before Raymond could say anything, he heard a commotion in the background on Keith's end, followed by a string of profanities. "Ray, I got to call you back, slight emergency."

"What's wrong?"

"A water pipe just burst. I'll call you back. Make sure you win some money before riding off into the sunset with the sexy actress."

Raymond laughed, pressing the End button on his cell phone. Then he heard the balcony door open and Imani walked out, pushing the room service cart.

"I ordered pineapple slices, *haupia* and a Yalumba Antique Tawny. The room service attendant said this Tawny is the best wine to go with this coconut pudding," she said.

Smiling, Raymond wanted to tell her that he knew what would go best with the pudding and the fruit and it wasn't found on the room service menu or on that cart. Instead, he nodded and replied, "Let's give it a taste." Raymond took the bottle and filled the empty glasses as Imani stuck her finger in the pudding to sneak a taste.

"This is delicious," she said as she swiped some more.

Raymond set the wine aside and gripped Imani's wrist. "Let me try that," he said, then slowly and methodically licked the thick pudding from Imani's index finger. Even though the treat was gone, he still sucked her finger as if she was made of the coconut dessert.

"Oh, stop," she moaned.

"Sorry," Raymond said with a sly smirk. "But it just tasted so good, I couldn't help it. Every part of you is delicious and sweeter than sugarcane."

"Umm, you're something else," Imani said, grabbing a spoon and dipping it into the pudding. She held it out to Raymond and he dipped his finger in the heaping mound, then brushed it across her lips. He leaned into her and kissed the pudding away, using his tongue to lick the corners of her mouth. She shivered, her body flinching with delight as he wrapped his arms around her waist and held her close. Imani wished they were just together on vacation or celebrating their honeymoon privately. Then she could allow him to peel her clothes off and teach him how to make him feel as good as he'd made her feel earlier in the room. She could share her body with him in the privacy of their honeymoon suite and scream his name. Sucking her bottom lip in as they broke their kiss, Imani wondered if this show was really worth it. Should she just take a real chance on love and leave?

Just because you decide to leave, it doesn't mean that Raymond would follow you. He's here to make money for his clinic, not chase the last virgin in New York.

"Are you all right?" Raymond asked.

"I was just thinking about being here and how different it would be if we weren't being watched."

He picked up his wineglass and took a sip. "I guess we have to deal with it, since we're both here for reasons other than falling for each other."

"I wonder, though, will this show actually help my career? Hell, if Juilliard didn't, how can a reality show?"

"Well, maybe the billboard in Times Square might," he replied after another sip of wine. "This is good."

"The what?" she asked, excitement brimming in her voice.

"When I was talking to Keith, he told me that the show has a billboard with you on it in Times Square," he said.

Imani clasped her hands together and bounced happily. "That is amazing. Do you know how many people are going to see my face?"

Raymond stopped short of telling her that it wasn't her face that would grab the most attention.

"I need a favor," Imani said. "May I use your cell phone for a minute? I need to call my agent."

He handed her the phone, then took another sip of wine. His old thoughts of Imani using him for her career resurfaced in his head. He couldn't begrudge her for wanting to take advantage of the opportunity to be a star, but he wanted more from her. He couldn't help but wonder if everything would always be second to her quest for stardom.

"Funderburke," Edward said when he answered.

"Edward, it's Imani," she said.

"Imani," he said excitedly. "I've been trying to reach you but your cell phone is disconnected."

"I know," she said. "I heard that I'm in Times Square."

"Yes, you are, and that's not where the good news ends," he said. "I have three scripts on my desk with your name on them. Didn't I tell you this show was going to be a great shot in the arm for your career?"

"Yes, you did. Three scripts! I can't believe it."

"Two are really good, one is so-so. And I got a call from Alex Timbers. He wants to work with you."

"Are you serious?"

"My dear, you are on your way. Whatever you're doing on that show, keep doing it, because you're making an impact."

A smile spread across her face. "Remember all of that stuff I said about being too good for reality TV? I take it back. Is there any way you can get those scripts to me?"

"Sure, just give me the hotel's address and I'll have them overnighted to you," Edward said. "This is just what you needed, Imani. Oh, and New York One did a feature on you and the show. Since it aired, I've been getting calls about you. Of course, some of them are just men who love your picture in Times Square. Someone even mailed an engagement ring and said if you came back to New York, he'd marry you."

"Well, if it wasn't Kelsey Grammer or Denzel, then there is no need for me to leave," she said, looking directly at Raymond. "Whoever sent the ring can't compare to the man that's meant for me."

Raymond smiled and shook his head.

"Well," Edward said, "I'm sure hearts will be breaking all over New York when that gets out. Give me that address and I'll have my assistant send these to you. Oh, and one more thing. Can I get that apology in writing?"

Imani laughed, then rattled off the address of the hotel and told her agent good-bye. "Thanks," she told Raymond as she handed him his cell phone back.

"I take it that things are looking good for your career," he said.

Imani nodded happily. "Scripts are rolling in, I'm getting press, and one of Broadway's hottest directors wants to meet with me." Imani picked up her wineglass and clinked it against Raymond's glass, not noticing that he didn't seem to be reveling in her excitement. "Now, I'll get a chance to make up for *Fearless Diva*."

"This is what you wanted, right?" he said. *But when you get it, what is that going to mean for us?* Raymond thought as he sipped his wine and watched Imani seemingly glow underneath her good news.

Chapter 14

After Imani and Raymond finished their mid-night snack, he walked her to her room. He wasn't surprised that she hadn't noticed his change in mood because all she could talk about were the scripts that would be waiting for her to go over in the morning. As much as he wanted to share in her excitement, he couldn't help but think everything would change now. When the show went live, he was certain that Imani would be on, acting every chance she got, and he wouldn't be able to tell the difference between what was real and what was part of her audition for America.

"I had a great time with you tonight," she said, then kissed him on the cheek. "And thank you for letting me borrow your phone."

"Anytime," he replied. "Sweet dreams, Imani." Somehow, he knew the man in her dreams wouldn't be him, but a thirteen-and-a-half-inch golden statue named Oscar. He returned to his room and thought about calling Keith back, but he kicked back in the bed and looked up at the ceiling, willing himself to believe that Imani wouldn't change because her career was on the uptick.

But what if she does? he thought. *What if she decides that she's gotten everything she needed and wanted from me and this show and leaves to do one of those movies or a Broadway show? Then what? She made it clear from the start that she was here to become famous and she's well on her way to that. Still, if that was her main objective, why would she have shared her secret with me?* Raymond hopped out of bed and decided to take a walk on the beach. As he headed out the door, he ran into Lucy.

"Well, hello there," she said with a slick smile. "All alone tonight?"

"What's up, Lucy?" he asked flatly.

She looked him up and down and licked her lips. "That's a question I'd like the answer to. Where are you heading at this hour? Sneaking over to the little actress's room for—"

Raymond held up his hand to cut her off. "Don't do that."

"What?"

"Every time I see you, you're trashing Imani and you don't even know her."

"I really don't give a damn about her. It's you I'm trying to get to know, but she's always in the way." She took two steps closer to him. "Why don't you give me a chance?"

"It would never work."

She slipped her hands around his waist and stood on her tiptoes. Just as she was about to kiss him, Imani's door swung open and the cold and heartbroken look on her face nearly ripped his heart to shreds. He pushed Lucy aside and started toward Imani, but she forcefully slammed the door in his face.

Tres was nearly asleep at her desk, then she saw Lucy and Raymond meet in the hallway. It was golden when Imani walked out of her room and Tres couldn't help but cheer a little. The evening had been horrible because for whatever reason, the video feed from Imani's and Raymond's room was off-line. If Elliot didn't tighten up, he was going to be looking for a new job. But this—the hallway confrontation—would be the clip of the day. Still, she needed to know what Imani's secret was and how she could use it to increase the show's ratings. Elize had already told her about the buzz the show had in New York, a billboard in Times Square, a feature on NY1 and CBS. There was even talk about a feature on *The Early Show* and *Today*.

"If you keep Raymond and Imani in the forefront of this show," Elize had said, "you're going to be on your way to getting your drama series produced."

"I'm looking forward to it," she'd replied. Things were looking really good for her getting that show now if all she had to do was keep Raymond and Imani in front of the camera.

Tres picked up the phone and called Elliot. "Yeah?" he said.

"Have you checked the equipment? We can't lose footage of Raymond and Imani anymore."

"The engineers are looking into it right now," he said with a sigh.

"Make sure it's taken care of," she said, then slammed the phone down. Tres needed to see what was going on in Imani's room after she caught Lucy and Raymond together.

Imani pounded her pillow and vowed not to cry. Raymond was no different than any other man she'd been around. As soon as she turned her back, there he was pressed against that tramp Lucy. *I guess he wanted instant sexual gratification, and he's not getting that from me.*

This should've been one of the happiest days of her life and because she couldn't sleep, she'd wanted to ask Raymond to join her for a walk on the beach. Seeing him in Lucy's grasp made her heart break and her stomach churn with anger and disgust. Why did she think that a man like Raymond would wait for her to decide that she wanted to give him the most intimate part of herself? Especially when Lucy was offering it up on a platter?

Damn it, she was crying. Her cheeks were damp with disappointed tears and when she heard a knock at the door, she made no effort to move.

"Imani, open the door," Raymond called out after the banging continued.

"Don't you have somewhere to go with Lucy?" she yelled.

"Not this again. Will you open the door so that we can talk like adults?"

Despite wanting to curse him out and tell him

that he should go bang Lucy since it was obvious that that's what he wanted to do, she bounced from the bed and opened the door, glaring at him. "What in the hell do you want?"

"First of all, it wasn't what it looked like," Raymond said.

"Then what was it and why does it happen so often? She's always around you and we both know what she wants."

He closed the space between them and placed his hands on her shoulders. Though Imani wanted to push him away, take a step back and get out of his reach, she stayed rooted in place.

"I really don't give a damn what she wants, because I know what I want and that's you. Why don't you believe that? What have I done to make you think that I have any interest in that woman or that I want anyone but you?"

"Raymond, just be serious with yourself," she said. "You want to—"

"Now you're reading my mind?"

"I don't have to read your mind. If you didn't want anything to do with that woman, then she wouldn't always be around you!"

He shook his head and shrugged his shoulders. "What more can I do? If you want to make me pay for what someone else did to you, fine. Have a good night."

Watching him walk away, Imani wondered if she'd messed up, made a mistake thinking that Raymond was just like the losers who'd hurt her and made her hold on to her virginity as if it were a security blanket. If she didn't have sex, she wouldn't get hurt. If she didn't give her heart away, she wouldn't be hurt. Wouldn't be like her mother, who never got over the end of her marriage to Imani's father.

Love was about as practical to Imani's mother as an acting career. Though Imani planned to prove her mother wrong about the acting, she might have taken her view on love to heart.

You're here to make a name for yourself and it seems to be working. Let this thing with Raymond go, she thought. "But how can I let it go when I'm falling for this man so hard?"

Imani sat on the edge of the bed and dropped her head. Why did everything have to be so damned complicated?

The next morning, Imani was awakened with a knock on the door. Yawning, she kicked out of the covers and padded toward the door without putting her robe on. But then she remembered the last time that she opened the door in just her gown, so she grabbed her bathrobe and snatched it on before opening the door.

Just as she suspected, it was a production assistant from the show. "Yes?" Imani asked with her hand on her hip.

"You're needed in the confessional and I'll wait for you to change," he said with an exasperated tone in his voice.

Imani fluffed her hair and shrugged. "I'll go like this. The sooner we do this interview, the sooner it's over."

"All right. But you're actually going to be doing your interview with someone else today." He looked down at the clipboard. "Raymond Thomas. Are you sure you don't want to put some clothes on?"

Imani grabbed her room key card and stuffed it in her robe pocket. "Let's go."

The last thing she wanted to do was see Raymond this morning. Part of her wanted to believe that he spent the night with Lucy and had sex with her. She wanted to believe that seeing him this morning wouldn't bring back the memories of his hand between her thighs and the sweet feeling of an orgasm. Closing her eyes as she and the production assistant waited for the elevator, she listened to the sound of Raymond's voice. His presence ramped up her emotions and caused her to shiver inwardly. How could she keep up the pretense of being angry, disappointed, or done with him?

"Good morning, Imani," he said.

Pull it together, pull it together, she thought as she opened her eyes and looked at him. Imani inhaled sharply as she took in his image, shirtless, loose pajama pants and no shoes. How was it that he could look this delicious this early in the morning?

"Morning," she replied calmly.

Raymond stepped closer to her and whispered, "Over your temper tantrum?"

"Excuse me?"

"Last night, I left you alone so that you could get your head together and think about not only what I said but what we did. I'm not going to keep fighting with your ghosts, but I'm also not giving up on you because I know who and what I want."

She faced him and chewed on her bottom lip. "So, you didn't spend the night with Lucy?"

"No. When do you plan to let that go? I don't want Lucy."

Before she could reply, the doors to the elevator opened. *Please let him be telling the truth. Don't let me set myself up for failure.* Raymond took Imani's hand in his and kissed it as they stepped on the elevator. He pressed the Close button before the production assistant got on. Once the doors shut, he pulled the emergency stop button.

"What are you doing?" Imani asked.

"Clearing something up with you. Don't ever think that I'm not a man of my word. And since you want me to be honest with myself . . ." he said as he backed her against the wall. "I want you more than I want my next breath, and no other woman will ever stand a chance with me as long as you're a part of my life. But you're going to have to stop jumping to the conclusion that I'm incapable of waiting for you."

"Raymond, I'm scared. I don't want to wake up and be played for a fool. This whole situation here is so surreal. What happens when we return to the real world?"

"You're going to have to give us a chance to see what happens then. Stop trying to end it before we have a chance to really get started. And by the way, you look absolutely beautiful."

She self-consciously fingered her hair and smiled. Standing on her toes, she kissed him on the tip of his nose. "Raymond," she said, "you know just what to say to make a woman feel special."

"I'm telling you the truth. And the reason why you feel special is because you're more than simply special to me," he said, then pulled her into his arms. "I could see myself falling deeply in love with every part of you." Raymond brushed his lips against Imani's before capturing her mouth in a sultry kiss that melted any thoughts she had of leaving him. The elevator jolted to a start as they broke off their kiss.

"Guess they figured there was no emergency," Raymond said as he gently patted Imani's backside.

"Yes, the emergency is over," Imani replied as she leaned her head against his chest.

The doors opened and Tres met them. "What happened? Why was the elevator stopped?" she asked. "Come on, we have to do this interview. And Imani"—Tres held out a thick envelope—"I'm guessing things are looking up for your career. These came from New York for you."

Imani took the envelope and inspected the seal. Satisfied that it hadn't been opened, she told Tres, "Thank you."

"All right," she said. "Our winning couple, we need to do this interview. Now that our couples are forming, the interviews will be done together."

Raymond smiled as he and Imani followed Tres. He liked the idea of being a couple. Liked the idea of having Imani as his, and not just on TV. As they waited for Tres to set up the cameras, Raymond couldn't think about anything but going back to New York with Imani on his arm. Showing her his clinic and introducing her to his friends, especially Keith and Celeste. He imagined that Celeste and

Imani would lament together about how much time he and Keith spent at the clinic as they shopped at Macy's or attended a Broadway show. He would love walking the red carpet with Imani at one of her movie premieres or her first Broadway show.

He glanced at her as she opened her envelope. "Oh my God," she gasped.

"What?"

"Yes," Tres said, reminding them both that she was in the room and the camera was rolling.

"This script is from Gina Prince-Bythewood. I love her," Imani exclaimed.

"Then I guess you've accomplished what you came here for," Tres probed. "I spoke with your agent and you're becoming quite the hot commodity in New York these days. How does that make you feel?"

Imani ran her hand through her hair and cocked her head to the side. "Of course I'm excited about it. I'm an actress, I want to be in demand for roles. That's why I'm here. If producers and directors like what they see now, wait until I get the right script."

The hairs on the back of Raymond's neck stood on end. Tres seemed to notice the look on his face and turned the camera on him. "How does that make you feel, Raymond? Especially after our last talk?"

"I'm happy for her. She hasn't hidden the fact that she wants to be a successful actress, as I haven't hidden the fact that the prize money from this show will help my clinic."

"But," Tres said, "everyone can see that there is

something between you two. You worked really well together during the challenge and you spend a lot of time together."

Imani and Raymond glanced at each other. "He's fun to be with," Imani replied. "I enjoy our time together."

"And kissing him?" Tres asked.

"Raymond's a great kisser," Imani said, then laughed.

"As are you," he replied.

Tres smiled. "So, love connection? Do you think America will want you two to stay together? Especially when there is chemistry with Raymond and Lucy?"

"There is no chemistry with me and Lucy," he interjected.

"Is that so?" Tres asked, then turned a monitor around to Imani and Raymond. "Care to explain this?" The screen was filled with the previous night's dinner, showing Raymond and Lucy sharing a glass of wine. "She looks really into you."

Imani seethed as she watched Raymond pour Lucy a glass of wine. "What is this?"

"Remember when you left?" he said.

"So, you just called her over?"

"No, Lucy showed up. She ended up alone because I went looking for you."

Imani turned back to the screen and saw Raymond getting up to leave and her defenses fell. She remembered what happened when he found her and how he made her feel with his special touch.

"Are you all right, seeing this?" Tres asked Imani.

"Why wouldn't I be? I know what Raymond wants

and it isn't Lucy," she replied confidently, and took Raymond's hand in hers.

"All right, thanks guys," Tres said. "The next task starts this afternoon."

Imani and Raymond rose from their seats and left the room. "So," she said once they were in the hallway, "they want to see me, you, and Lucy have drama, huh?"

"That's what it looks like, but you do know that—"

She placed her finger to his lips. "I know that when I left that dinner and you found me, neither one of us were thinking about Lucy. Before we have to do whatever task they have set up for us, I have to go look through these scripts. Gina Prince-Bythewood—can you believe it?"

Raymond smiled, trying to be happy for her. But he had to wonder if she was going to focus more on her career goal than their budding relationship.

Chapter 15

As the filming continued, more scripts and offers for Broadway shows rolled in for Imani—as well as advances for endorsement deals. Imani was happy that she was able to pay her cell phone bill and have contact with the outside world. But she hadn't even bothered to use it.

She and Raymond had been spending so much time together that she hadn't called Dana. She sporadically checked in with Edward, happy to learn that the deals were still rolling in as well as quality scripts. Gina Prince-Bythewood was a big fan and couldn't wait for Imani to come in for a screen test for her latest project.

Of course, America loved her and Raymond as a couple. According to Tres, they received the most votes after every show. Imani hoped the fans she and Raymond had attracted would translate into movie sales. She could not wait to start shooting a movie when she returned to New York.

I wonder if I should do something to rock the boat, something to get kicked off so that I can get my career started, she thought, then looked over at Raymond's sleeping frame. Imani shook that thought out of mind because she didn't want to be away from him. Over the last three weeks, Imani and Raymond had spent every free moment together. He even helped her decide what scripts she should give serious consideration to.

Having a man in her life who actually encouraged her dream made Imani feel so warm and special. So special that she'd nearly forgotten that they were being filmed the night before.

"Stay with me tonight," Raymond had asked as he pulled her into his arms when they'd returned from an evening stroll on the beach. For the first time since they'd been officially matched by America's votes, they had lost a challenge. Lucy and her partner had bested the couple in a relay race. It hadn't bothered Imani that she and Raymond had lost to the couple because they'd had immunity on the challenge anyway. Besides, they had spent much of the race—accidentally on purpose—falling against each other and sneaking kisses.

"Umm, tempting," she'd replied as she felt heat rising to her cheeks.

"Come on," he'd whispered, his lips close to her ear and his breath making her hotter as he spoke.

She'd leaned her head against his chest. "Okay," she had replied as Raymond twirled her around.

He'd held her out at arm's length, drinking in her body, the way her tan strapless dress clung to her curves. She was beautiful. The island sun had bronzed her skin to golden brown perfection. Red hues framed her face from where the sun had lightened her hair. Raymond wasn't used to what he was feeling. He felt as if he was holding a goddess. Better yet, a living doll. He would have never believed it if someone other than Imani told him that she was a virgin. How could a woman that kissed the way she did and had so much sex appeal be a virgin? He kissed her hand and led her into the bedroom.

Imani held her breath as Raymond had closed the door behind them. She had no idea what was going to happen once they'd entered the room. She'd felt as if she wanted him and wanted to experience the passion that was silently promised to her every time they'd kissed. She'd wanted to lose herself and her virginity as soon as they'd laid down on the bed. She wanted him more than she had ever wanted a man. Raymond had awakened something inside her, something that she didn't know existed. When he touched her, her body came alive. Desire burned inside her and flowed through her bloodstream. When he kissed her, she felt as if she was melting.

But Imani hadn't wanted to share her first lovemaking experience with a national audience. She'd always dreamed that her first time would be in a fancy hotel room, with the lights low and roses surrounding her. She didn't want cameras everywhere, though. But as she'd looked at Raymond as he'd taken his shirt off, the cameras had been the last thing on her mind. Her mouth had watered at the sight of his bare chest and washboard abs. A shirtless Raymond had become a normal sight, but that night had enforced what sexual desire meant to her with an exclamation point and a wetness between her thighs. Would he be a gentle lover? she'd won-

dered as she'd sat on the edge of the bed nervously
biting her bottom lip. Damn, he was a beautiful man
with skin like sunshine and caramel. She forced herself to turn away as he dropped his slacks, revealing
a pair of black and white boxer briefs.

Imani had slowly risen from the bed and unzipped her dress, but she didn't take it off, couldn't
take it off. She hadn't wanted to show herself to the
camera. She'd wanted to save that for a time when
she and Raymond were alone. When he'd glanced
at her, he smiled and opened his bottom drawer,
then handed her a T-shirt. It had been like he'd felt
how apprehensive she'd been about getting naked
in the room.

"Thank you," she'd whispered as she'd taken the
shirt. The moment their fingers had touched, Imani
had felt a surge of electricity shoot through her
bloodstream. She'd been on fire from the slight contact and Raymond seemed to feel it as well as they'd
stood near the bed, locked in each other's gaze.

Imani inhaled, hoping to quell the fire burning
in her stomach. Raymond's lips came toward hers.
She braced herself for the richness of his kiss, the
sweetness of his lips and tongue, and before she
knew it, she'd been the one to initiate the kiss.
He'd held her close as their lips remained locked
together. His fingers danced across her skin, making
her wet, hot, and filled with wanton desire. She'd
pressed her body against him, feeling his erection
against her thighs.

Do it. Let him make love to you, had played in her
head as his kiss went deeper.

Raymond had pulled back from her and looked

deep into her eyes before brushing a light kiss across her lips. "I know we'd better stop," Raymond had said, "because one more kiss . . ."

She placed her finger to his lips and he instinctively licked it. Imani shivered and took a step back. "I want you," she'd said. "But you know . . ."

He nodded and cupped her face in his hands. "I know. All we can have at this point is you falling asleep in my arms. That's all I want."

"Is that enough for you?"

"For now, yes," he'd replied. "Baby, I can wait for you. Because I know that it will be amazing for both of us. But we both have to be ready."

"And away from these cameras."

"You got it," he said as he twirled her around and they fell back on the bed, with Imani landing on top of him. Instantly, Raymond had gotten hard, wanting to just melt with her. When she'd felt his erection, Imani rolled over on her side. Raymond had locked his arms around Imani's waist and she rested against his chest. Then they'd both drifted off to sleep.

When the sunlight poured into the room and Imani stirred against Raymond's body, she smiled. He'd been the perfect gentleman as they'd slept, despite the fact that she knew he wanted to make love and she did as well.

She stroked his strong arm, which was draped across her, and Raymond grabbed her hand and kissed it. "Morning," he said, his voice deepened by sleep.

"Morning," she said, then kissed his chin. "Sleep well?"

"Anytime you're in my arms, I sleep well."

Imani stretched and smiled. "I feel the same way. Can you believe that we're one of the final four couples? I think I actually want to win now."

"Umm, I really don't care about being here, just being with you," he said as he wrapped his arms around her waist. "What I'm looking forward to is waking up with you in my arms in Harlem."

"Yes. No cameras, no Lucy and"—Imani was interrupted by a knock on the door—"no production assistants ruining our morning." Neither of them made an effort to move.

"But I do expect breakfast in bed," she teased him.

"Really?" Raymond said. "So that means you're going to spend the night often?" The knocking persisted.

"You'd better get that," she said.

"Why me? You're closer to the door," he quipped.

"Your room and I don't have any pants on. Unless you want me show the world my booty."

"Absolutely not," he replied as he released her and swung his legs over the side of the bed. "That's a sight that is only mine."

"What if a movie role calls for nudity?" she asked as she sat up and wrapped the sheet around her. "It got Halle an Oscar."

"You're a better actress than that," Raymond said as he opened the door. "Yeah?"

The frazzled production assistant nearly dropped her clipboard as she looked at Raymond's bare chest. "D-Dr. Thomas, Tres needs to see you. Something happened in New York."

"What? What happened?"

The girl shook her head, causing her kinky twists to swing like branches in a windstorm. "I—I don't know."

"I'll be right there," Raymond said as he shuffled back into the room and grabbed a T-shirt and a pair of shorts.

"What's wrong?" Imani asked. "Did that lady say something happened in New York?"

"Yes. It sounded pretty ominous," he said as he pulled his clothes on.

Imani grabbed her dress from the night before and pulled it on. "I'm going with you."

"Imani, you don't have to," he said.

"If it's something really bad, you're going to need me. That's what couples do. I'm supporting you," she said. "Discussion closed."

"Yes, ma'am," he said as he opened the door and held it for Imani.

As they walked to the elevator, Imani gripped Raymond's hand. "Everything is going to be all right," she murmured.

"I hope you're right," he said as he pressed the button. They stepped on the elevator as the doors opened and rode to the production area in silence. Raymond wondered what was going on in New York. Had the water pipe burst been more serious than Keith let on? What if the clinic had suffered a serious setback while he was in Hawaii falling in love with Imani? The whole point of doing the show had been to get money for the struggling clinic, and if something terrible had happened at the clinic, then shouldn't he leave and go fix that?

But can I leave Imani? Can I ask her to leave when this show is setting up her career for success? he thought as he glanced at her when the elevator came to a stop.

"Are you okay?" she asked, catching his pensive look.

"Yeah, just wondering what in the hell is going on."

"I'm hoping it's not serious," she said. "We only have about two weeks left and you need this money."

"Especially if something bad happened. I keep thinking about all of our patients who will have nowhere else to go for their health care. Damn it, I should've been there. We should've found a better way to fund the clinic."

His words stabbed Imani in the heart as she thought about how she wouldn't have met him had he not come on the show. Would he blame her if something terrible happened to the clinic?

Raymond tapped on the production door and waited briefly for Tres to open it. When she did, neither Raymond nor Imani liked the somber look on her face.

"Please, come in," she said in a low tone.

"What's going on?" Raymond asked.

"Please sit," Tres said, nodding toward a chair.

"Just tell me what's going on," Raymond said gruffly.

Tres sighed and pulled a mini bottle of Malibu Rum out of her desk drawer and offered it to Raymond. "Normally, I wouldn't even give you this news, but there's no way I can keep this from you."

"Will you just spit it out!" Raymond bellowed.

"We got a call from New York about your partner, Keith." Imani placed her hand on Raymond's shoulder when she saw his hand trembling.

"What about Keith?" he asked tentatively.

"There was an accident," Tres said. "And according to Celeste, Keith is in really bad shape. He is in a coma and he has several internal injuries."

Raymond dropped down in the chair across from Tres, his face tight with sadness. Imani stroked his shoulders, at a loss for words. If it had been Dana, she'd be inconsolable.

"I—I have to get back to New York," he muttered.

"That's fine and your choice. But you're so close to winning the—"

Raymond slammed his hand against Tres's desk so forcefully that the bottle of rum tumbled over and Imani yelped. "Do you think I give a damn about some money right now when my best friend is in the hospital in New York? Why didn't Celeste call me on my cell phone?"

"Well," Tres said, looking a little shaken up, "Elize decided that we should block all incoming and outgoing cell phone activity until the end of the show."

Raymond cocked his head to the side and glared at Tres. "You and Elize can go to hell. Keith is like family to me and if he needs me, he should've been able to get in contact with me. I shouldn't have to hear from you that his girlfriend called about an accident."

"I'm sorry. I understand that you want to be

there for your friend. But if you leave now, you're going to lose your chance at a million dollars."

Raymond gripped the arm of the chair so tightly that Imani thought he was going to break it in half. "Raymond," Imani whispered in his ear, "let's go back to your room and get things in order for you to return to New York." Her voice seemed to calm him and he loosened his grip on the chair and bolted out of the room.

Before Imani could reach the door and catch up with him, Tres grabbed her shoulder. "Imani, I know you and Raymond are close. But if you leave the show, do you know what the fallout for your career will be?"

"Are you serious right now? And are we talking my career or yours? If Raymond and I are being used in as many ad spots as we are, then we must be the show. If you have a dedicated cameraman following our every move as you do, then we must be good ratings."

"That may be the case and you may think this is just a reality show, but no one is going to want to work with a quitter. That's what you're going to look like to Hollywood if you leave this show. Sure, you may want to jump the good doctor's bones, but you and I both know that you want the fame. You enjoy the fact that the scripts are pouring in and when you get back to New York, you won't have to go back to waiting tables or whatever you were doing just to scrape by."

"You don't know a damned thing about me. I have talent and leaving this show isn't going to undermine or change that."

Tres folded her arms across her chest. "If you really believe that, then you don't know a damned thing about this industry and it's no wonder you thought *Fearless Diva* was a good project to attach yourself to."

Imani glared at her. "Are you supposed to be better than me? Any high school dropout with an iPhone can produce a reality show."

"But I have enough of a reputation to put your fledgling career on an even further downward spiral."

"Go to hell," Imani snapped, then stormed out of the room. *Heartless bitch! Does she think I'm going to let her idle threats keep me on this island when Raymond needs me?*

As much as she wanted to pretend that she was going to be able to shrug off Tres's words, she couldn't help but wonder if leaving the show would cool the hot streak her career had been on. Scripts were still coming in, Edward had already booked a guest appearance for her on *How I Met Your Mother* and *Modern Family.* Could she really give all of that up?

What means more to you? Fame or Raymond?

She rode the elevator back to his room with conflicting thoughts fighting inside her head. When the elevator stopped on her floor, she rushed to Raymond's door and knocked loudly.

He snatched the door open and Imani saw that he had begun packing. "What can I do to help?" she asked as she walked into the room. He shook his head and crossed over to the bed, perching on the edge. Raymond dropped his head as if it weighed a ton. "I can't believe this," he said in a near whisper.

Imani joined him on the bed and wrapped her arms around his waist. "I can't imagine what you're going through. Have you had a chance to talk to Keith's girlfriend?"

He nodded. "Celeste sounds so scared and so alone. Both she and Keith are only children and his parents are in North Carolina. They're on the way to New York, but right now, she's alone. No one should have to go through this alone."

She hugged him tighter. "Baby," she whispered. Imani wished she knew what to say and how to ease his pain for a moment. Instead, she silently stroked the back of his neck, realizing that Raymond couldn't face his friend's accident alone either.

Yes, her career was important, but seeing him look so broken and so hurt, Imani knew the most vital thing was being the shoulder Raymond could lean on. "When are we leaving?" she asked.

"What?" he asked, turning to face her.

"You just said no one should face this alone, and I'm not going to allow you to be alone when your friend and his girlfriend need you. Who's going to be there for you?" Imani questioned.

He looked deep into her eyes. "You don't have to do this," Raymond said. "I know you're here for your career and this has been going well for you."

She held his face in her hands. "That doesn't matter right now," Imani said, even though she heard Tres's voice in her head telling her that leaving the show would be the nail in the coffin of her career.

"I can't let you do this," he said. "Imani, this isn't your problem. This show is going to help your career. I can't ask—"

She placed her finger to his lips. "You're not asking me to do anything. You mean more to me than a movie role and if you're going home, I'm going with you."

Raymond opened his mouth to protest. Imani shook her head. "Don't argue with me," she said as she dropped her hands and rose from the bed. "I'm going to my room to pack."

"Imani," he called after her as she headed for the door. She turned around, expecting another protest from Raymond. Instead, he smiled wryly and said, "Thank you. I really do need you."

She sighed, realizing that she needed him as well. Nodding, she headed out the door. Watching Imani leave the room, Raymond realized right then that she was the woman he'd spend the rest of his life with.

Chapter 16

Imani packed hastily when she arrived in her room, but stopped for a brief second when she realized that she didn't know how she was going to pay for her ticket back to New York. *I really can't ask Raymond to do it. I'm supposed to be supporting him, not draining his bank account.* Reaching for the phone on the nightstand, since cell phone service was nonexistent and she hadn't paid her bill, she called Edward.

"Ed Funderburkc," he said when he answered the phone. Imani could tell that he didn't recognize the number because he sounded über-professional.

"Edward, it's Imani," she said.

"I've been meaning to call you," he said in a fatherly tone before saying, "Have you lost your damned mind?"

"What? Edward, what are you talking about?"

"Tres Ellis called me. You're leaving the show and you are about to be in the finals? Again, have you lost your mind? All of this for a man? Is that the reputation that you want to have in Hollywood? Imani, you're getting there but you aren't well-known enough to be a diva and leave the show that's giving you the foundation for the career we've been trying to build for years. Do you know how much money we're about to start making?"

"I also know that there are some things that are more important than money and movie roles, which I haven't gotten yet."

"Wait, wait, wait. Who are you and what have you done with the Imani Gilliam who would've cut off her left arm for a taste of fame? You've gotten it, baby, you're on your way, and you're willing to throw it away for a man? I mean, help me understand this. A few months ago, you were in my office insisting you were not the type who lost herself in a man, unless he was Will Smith?"

"This is different," she said. "Look, I need a plane ticket back to New York."

"I don't think I should do this," Edward said.

"Whether you help me or not," she said pointedly, "I'm getting on a plane and going back to New York with Raymond."

"That corny doctor?" he asked, and chuckled. "I guess you weren't acting."

"Edward!"

"All right, Imani. I will make the travel arrangements for you. But keep in mind, Tres may simply be a reality show producer today, but if your paths cross again, she's not going to forget this."

"Edward, I really don't give a damn."

"I tell you what, since your purpose for coming back to New York is to help the good doctor, get me the particulars about his return ticket and I'll make sure I get you two on the same flight."

"I'll call you back," she said, then hung up the phone. After finishing her packing, she headed back to Raymond's room to find out when he was leaving for New York. She was about to knock on the door when she heard a female voice from behind her. It was Lucy. Imani was not in the mood.

"You just can't let that man breathe for one minute without running up on him. Insecure much?" Lucy taunted.

"Haven't you humiliated yourself enough? He doesn't want you, could've had you and decided to go with someone much better. I don't have time to argue with you," she said.

"Whatever," Lucy snapped. "There is still time for—"

Imani padded over to Lucy and pushed her against the wall. "Look, I said I don't have time for this and if you gave a damn about Raymond or were a friend to him, then you would know what's going on and what he needs. Since you don't, take your husband-hungry ass somewhere and find someone else to stalk. Raymond and I are leaving."

Lucy, surprised by Imani's forcefulness and the news that she and Raymond were leaving, pushed back against Imani. "What? Why are you leaving now when the show is so popular? Didn't you say that you were coming here to be famous? Everyone wants me around because they like to see us fight."

"Lucy, get over yourself!" Imani turned away from her and knocked on Raymond's door. He opened it and shook his head as he saw Lucy standing there with Imani.

"Raymond, is it true?" Lucy asked. "You've let her talk you into leaving the show because she thinks she's some kind of star now?"

"Lucy, can you just leave," Raymond said, not attempting to hide the annoyance in his voice.

"Damn, I thought you were smarter than that," Lucy muttered as she turned toward the elevator. "If you're so gullible, then . . ."

"Lucy!" Imani bellowed. "You are the stupidest, most coldhearted bitch I've ever met."

"Imani," Raymond said, placing his hand on her shoulder and beckoning her inside the room, "I'm sure you didn't knock on my door for this."

Turning away from Lucy, she nodded. "I need your flight information," she said calmly. "I called my agent and he's making my travel arrangements."

"Well, call him back and tell him that Tres obviously grew a heart because the show is paying for our return to the city."

"What's the catch?" Imani asked. "This doesn't mean we have to take a camera crew with us?"

"No, not at all," he said, pulling her against his chest and kissing her forehead. "She said that you opened her eyes to what's really important."

Imani raised her eyebrow quizzically. "She said that?" Her mind returned to their conversation and she wondered what game Tres was playing or if she had indeed changed her mind. It didn't matter, she and Raymond were going to leave together so that he could check on what was important to him—his friend and his clinic. She pushed thoughts of her career out of her head and decided to focus on her man and the pain he was dealing with.

"Are you packed?" he asked, breaking into Imani's thoughts. "Tres said we can leave within the hour."

"I'm ready when you are."

"All right. I'll grab my bags and come get yours," he said. "Then we can head back to New York."

"Have you checked on Keith?"

"I just spoke with Celeste and there hasn't been much change," he said. "I want to get back to New York and find out firsthand from his doctors what's going on and what if anything I can do to help."

Imani squeezed his hand. "The first thing you're going to have to do is stop thinking the worst."

"It's hard," he said. "Very hard."

She searched her mind for words, for something comforting to say. But this wasn't a movie where the lines were written out and she could just pronounce words to save the day. Instead, she just hugged him tightly and gently kissed him on his cheek.

Raymond held her, burying his face in her neck. "Thank you for doing this. But I want you to know that you can stay here. You don't have to give up your chance to be a star and get your name out there." His words were more for her benefit than his. Raymond couldn't deny that this was one of the most stressful moments in his life.

Imani scowled at him. "You're not getting rid of me that easily," she replied in a terse whisper. "I'll be back with my bags and we can go."

He cupped her face in his hands. "Imani, you don't know how much this means to me. I know what you're giving up."

"And I know that I love you," she said. "I'm not giving that up." Imani dropped her head, not sure why she made her confession of love, but she did love Raymond, and the last thing she wanted was for him to think that leaving this show was a huge sacrifice for her.

Would she lose some roles? Probably. But did that mean as much to her now as it did when she first joined the cast of *Let's Get Married*? Not at all.

"Imani, thank you," he said. Not exactly what she'd expected to hear after telling him that she loved him. Rather than start a discussion about what he did or didn't say, Imani just headed to her room and grabbed her bags. She couldn't help but wonder if she'd made a mistake confessing her love to him when he was in crisis.

When she returned to Raymond's room with her bags in tow, he took them from her hand and kissed her with a slow and deep passion that made her shiver with anticipation.

Pulling back from her, he looked into her glossy eyes and said, "I love you, too."

"Raymond, just because—"

"With everything that's going on in my world right now, I don't have time to bullshit you or play any games. I meant what I said and I didn't say it because I felt as if I owed you something."

"Ray," she said. "I'm glad you . . . Let's get out of here."

He nodded, telling her that they could talk about it later, and lifted their bags onto the rolling luggage cart.

They headed to the elevator in silence. Imani

didn't know what to say and Raymond was deep in thought, hoping over and over that Keith would survive his injuries and he'd have a chance to see his friend before anything happened.

When they arrived in the lobby, Tres was waiting there for them with the tickets in her hand. "Imani, I guess you haven't changed your mind," she said.

"Why would I?" she replied when she snatched the tickets from her outstretched hand.

"Because," Tres said in a low voice, "you're the one who's going to lose a career. He's going to be the toast of the town while you're serving coffee at Starbucks."

Imani smiled and glanced over her shoulder at the camera crew preparing to film Tres handing the plane tickets off to the couple. "I'm not going to argue with you. You want me to make an ass of myself and I'm not going to do that. You should be proud," Imani said. "This show was about two people falling in love, right? Well, that's what happened."

"Well," Tres said. "I hope you love your mediocre acting career as well."

"Tres," one of the cameramen called out. "We're ready."

She nodded at the cameraman and snatched the tickets back from Imani.

Raymond crossed over to them with their luggage. "Thanks for doing this," he said to Tres.

She smiled brightly and handed Raymond an envelope, since Imani already had the tickets. "I hate to see you and Imani go, but I know your partner and friend is important to you. There's a car waiting for you two out front," she said as she stepped aside to let them walk to the door.

Imani flashed her an appreciative look, but she didn't say anything to Tres. Elliot stood in the background and waved to Imani and Raymond. Imani mouthed, "Thank you," as she and Raymond headed outside.

They got into the black Town Car and waited for the driver to pull off. Imani held Raymond's hand as the driver started the car, and the film crew zoomed in on the car as it pulled away.

"Do you think we're finally off camera?" Raymond asked as he pulled Imani against his chest.

"I hope so," she replied. "The next time I'm on camera, I want to be somebody else."

He laughed and kissed her forehead. "I don't know what's more disturbing about that statement, the fact that you said it or the fact that I understand it."

His laughter was music to her ears since she knew what had been on his mind all morning. As she glanced at him, she realized that she had to help him find peace as they headed back to New York. She knew he would be worried about his friend, but Imani couldn't allow Raymond to worry himself sick and watch him end up in a hospital bed beside his friend.

She smiled inwardly as she thought about the first time they met. She was extremely rude to him, in total diva mode, yet he still turned around and saved her from a runaway car on the street. She wouldn't have admitted it at the time, but Raymond was a knight in shining armor and she didn't think those men existed anymore. She stroked his arm gently. No man had ever gotten this close to her, made her care about his feelings and what he was going through. But Raymond's tenderness and respect made Imani care more that she'd ever thought possible. He hadn't run away when she told him that she was a virgin and he hadn't pressured her to have sex with him when she knew good and well he'd wanted to. He'd respected her wishes not to lose her virginity on television so that Tres could exploit it.

He was real. He was caring. Imani didn't usually consider other people's feelings. It was her fatal character flaw, but she ached for Raymond and silently prayed that Keith would be all right.

Did that mean he was her soul mate? That thought shook Imani to her core. Yes, she loved him, but could she imagine her life without Raymond? Not after the time they had spent together and getting to know each other.

He looked at her and smiled weakly. "Thank you for doing this," he said. "I know what a sacrifice this is for you. Tres really wanted you to stay on the show, didn't she?"

"That doesn't matter," Imani replied as she snuggled against him. "I'm here with you because you need me. I already know you would do it for me if the shoe was on the other foot."

Though he wouldn't say it aloud, that little voice in the back of his head that kept telling him that Imani was in it for the fame asked, Was her departure from the show about the scripts she'd received? *Stop it,* he thought as he kissed her cheek.

"Are you all right?" she asked, noting his silence.

Immediately, she felt silly for asking that question. Of course he wasn't all right. "I know you have a lot on your mind," she added.

"Keith is like a brother to me. You know, we started the clinic because we wanted to give back. When we went to school in Atlanta, a lot of the people we attended school with from New York decided to stay in the south. The money was better, the weather was a lot better, and a lot of us had things that we could only dream about in New York. And the women were lovely."

Imani smacked her lips and rolled her eyes. "They have nothing on you, though," he added. "But Keith and I wanted to do something for Harlem. Despite the bad things that went on in our neighborhood, we had a lot of people who were in our corner. Mrs. Palmer had a bigger impact on us than we realized. Then she passed away our freshman year of college."

"And she's who you named the clinic after?" Imani said.

"We did that for two reasons," Raymond said. "When she retired and got sick, it was so hard for her to find somewhere to go and get treatment. She didn't have a car, so she would have to take the train into Manhattan, and doing that when you're sick is no picnic. Keith and I didn't want the other women in our neighborhood to face what Mrs. Palmer went through, especially since she had done so much for generations of children in Harlem. She taught first grade, and failure was never an option when it came to the kids she worked with. Cs were not acceptable and if she decided that you were one of her kids, she followed you for life. It was better to mess up and have your mother find out about it, rather than Mrs. Palmer finding out. Back in the day, kids listened to all adults. She was fierce."

"Sounds like you guys had a great mentor," Imani said.

Raymond nodded. "That's why we wanted to honor her and make sure that people remembered her. I couldn't do this without Keith. That's why he has to pull through." Tears threatened to spill from Raymond's eyes, and Imani felt powerless, wanting to do something or say something to ease his distress. Words failed her, though. They rode the rest of the way in pensive silence.

Once they arrived at the airport, the couple was escorted to a charter plane, which was a surprise to them both, since they'd expected to fly commercial. There was no long security line and Raymond seemed to breathe a sigh of relief as they were seated on the plane and he could make a call before takeoff.

"Celeste," he said. "How is he?" Imani watched the worry lines grow on his face. "I'm on the plane now and when I get there and take a look at his chart, I'll be able to explain things to you. Have his parents gotten there yet? Celeste, don't worry yourself sick, understand me? He's going to pull through this." Emotions choked him up and he swallowed hard. "Keith can't leave us. I'll call you when we land. Yes, we. When I get there, we can talk all about it."

When he hung up the phone, Imani leaned against Raymond's shoulder. "How is everything?"

"Celeste is going out of her mind because she doesn't understand, so she says, what the doctors are telling her about Keith's condition. She's crying at the drop of a hat. But she did say that Keith is in stable condition, he just hasn't open his eyes yet."

"Maybe he's waiting on his best friend to get there," she said as the plane took off. Raymond nodded and closed his eyes, while Imani stared out the window, watching as Maui began to shrink away from view.

Raymond drifted off to sleep pretty quickly, leaving Imani alone with her thoughts and worries. She knew that Edward didn't think it was a good idea for her to leave the show with her career being on an uptick. She wondered, though, if the offers that Edward had sent to her were real and would mean that her return to New York would lead to doing real work.

But what about Raymond? He's still going to need me in his corner, especially if his friend isn't getting any better. How am I going to do both?

Imani prayed that Keith would recover, not because she wanted to freely explore her options with the different roles offered to her, but because Raymond was in such pain. She hated seeing him this way because he'd always seemed so strong. Imani hoped that she could be strong enough for him because that's what people did when they were in love. And, she thought as she looked down at his sleeping face, she loved this man. She couldn't wrap her mind around how she fell for him so hard and so fast. Raymond awakened something inside her, not only desire and lust, but love and devotion also. She thought about all the other men she had discarded in her life, superficial brothers who were after one thing and made it clear that if she wasn't sleeping with them, then there was no need for things to continue.

No one else had ever caused her heart to flutter and butterflies to dance in her stomach. She gently stroked his cheek and his eyes opened.

"Are you all right?" she asked.

He nodded. "How about you? You having second thoughts about returning to New York?"

Imani cupped his face in her hands and stared into his beautiful eyes. Was she having second thoughts? Of course. But she wasn't going to tell him that now. "Not at all," she replied. "Raymond, we don't know what is waiting in New York and I know if it were my best friend, I would need someone to support me."

"Yeah, but . . ."

"No buts, Raymond. Why don't you just face the fact that you are stuck with me?" She smiled and Raymond couldn't help but laugh himself.

"Stuck, huh? I kind of like the sound of that," he said as he pulled her into his arms.

Imani held his hand and leaned back in her seat. Within minutes she had drifted off to sleep.

Raymond watched Imani intently as she slept, paying attention to the ebb and flow of her breathing, enthralled by the rise and fall of her breasts. She was so beautiful and her presence was calming. Had she not been on the plane with him, he would have been going out of his head. Her touch and her voice were better than any drug he could have taken to sleep on the plane.

Keith, you have to be all right so that you can meet the woman who stole my heart, he thought. Raymond gently pushed a strand of hair back from Imani's forehead. She looked like an angel. He knew she was going be a star. Hell, Halle Berry didn't have anything on his chocolate drop. She hadn't been that bad in *Fearless Diva.* And she had more sex appeal than a *Playboy* centerfold. Raymond leaned in and took a whiff of her scent. She smelled like a woman, sheer femininity. He ran his finger down her arm. Her skin felt like silk. He wanted to sleep buried inside her essence. Raymond put his arm around her shoulders and closed his eyes. Six hours later, Imani and Raymond were waking up as the plane landed at JFK International Airport.

Chapter 17

After getting their luggage from baggage claim, Imani and Raymond hopped into a taxi and headed to Beth Israel Medical Center. In the back of the cab, Imani held Raymond's hand tightly as she silently prayed for Keith. After hearing how close he and Raymond were, all Imani hoped for was walking into the hospital and finding Keith on the road to recovery.

Though what she wouldn't share with Raymond was that walking into the hospital was going to be hard for her because she hated hospitals. It seemed as if death was on every corner and sadness hung in the corridors like thick drapes.

"You're quiet over there," Raymond said. "Are you all right?"

"I should be asking you that," Imani replied. "I was just saying a prayer for your friend."

Raymond tenderly kissed her forehead. "Thank you."

Before she could reply, her cell phone rang, surprising her because she hadn't paid the bill. Imani concluded that Edward took care of it and was the caller.

"Answer it, if you need to, it's okay," Raymond said as Imani pulled her phone from her pocket.

"Sorry," she mouthed to him before saying hello.

"Imani," her agent said. "You decided to leave, huh?"

"Edward, this really isn't the best time," she replied tersely.

"I'm calling with good news," he said. "The show's producers are trying to spin this story to make you look like a real heroine, and I think you should run with it. How would you feel about doing *The Early Show*?"

Imani glanced at Raymond as she considered what Edward was saying. Did she want to do *The Early Show*? Hell yes, but she couldn't and wouldn't use Raymond's friend's accident as a stepping stone to fame.

"Can I call you back?" she asked.

"Are you nuts? Imani, more national exposure, a chance to show people looking to work with you that you're not a quitter . . . He's with you, isn't he?"

"Yes. But, I don't have a good feeling about . . ."

"Imani, we're on the cusp. You're getting quality roles, your face is all over Times Square for a show you're no longer a part of. If we don't strike while the iron is hot, you're going to find yourself right back where you were six months ago," Edward stated. "Is that what you want?"

"I'll call you back," she groaned as the cab

stopped in front of the hospital. Imani ended the call and turned to Raymond. "Sorry about that."

He didn't respond as he opened the door, held it for Imani and then paid the cab fare and retrieved their bags from the trunk of the taxi. She dropped her phone in her purse as she waited for Raymond on the curb. Imani could feel a change in his attitude. He seemed distant and she knew it was because he'd heard what Edward was saying.

"Raymond," she said, touching his arm. "I won't do it."

"Imani, do whatever you want. I knew this was all about the fame for you, but I was hoping that this was something deeper," he said. "If you want to go on *The Early Show* or *Today* and talk about how you put your acting aside to come and be with me, go ahead. Just don't expect me to be waiting in the wings after you and your people spin it," he said.

"My agent is just doing his job, but that doesn't mean I have to do the shows. This is private and I'm not . . ."

Raymond threw his hands up. "Imani, I'm going in here to see my friend. I don't have time for this."

Taking a step back, Imani reached out for her luggage and shook her head. "You know what, take care of your friend. I'm going back to Brooklyn." She stomped off, heading for the subway. Raymond started to run toward her when he heard Celeste call his name.

"Raymond," she said, running into his arms. "I'm so glad you're here."

He hugged her tightly, hoping that he and Imani

could connect later. He knew that he owed her an apology because she was right. She hadn't committed to doing the show her agent had been trying to sell her on. Still, right now, he needed to focus.

"Was that the other part of 'us' running for the subway? Keith told me you were really falling for her. Now, how did you mess it up?" Celeste asked.

"Don't worry about that. How is Keith?" he asked, still cutting his eyes in the direction Imani ran off in.

"You should really check your messages," she replied happily. "He woke up. He's going to be all right. Come on."

"What happened, Celeste?" he asked as she half dragged him through the entry of the hospital.

"Well," she said after pressing the Up button on the elevator, "he finally asked me to marry him. And he did it typical Keith fashion."

Raymond laughed. "Over slices?"

Celeste nodded and then tears spilled from her eyes. "It was shaping up to be the happiest night of my life. But when he got down on one knee and reached into his pocket, he didn't have the ring. The big oaf had left it in the examination room. I told him we could get it later and I got the point. But you know Keith. He said, 'Baby, I've made you wait too long for this and I want to put this ring on your finger so when we walk out of here, everyone will know you're taken.'

"He rushed to the car and didn't get three blocks before a car came out of nowhere and plowed into him. That man," she spat disgustedly, "was drunk. Twice the legal limit and walked away without a scratch." Tears silently poured down her cheeks as the doors to the elevator opened. Raymond wrapped his arm around her shoulder.

"Come on, now. You can stop crying. Keith had to stick around so that he can marry the best woman he's ever known."

"Glad you said that. You know what's funny? While we were watching you and that girl on TV, Keith said he didn't have to go to Hawaii to find love like you did."

"What?"

"Everyone could tell you were falling for her. We just hoped she wasn't acting," Celeste said. "But if she came back to the city with you, then it's obvious that she wasn't."

Before he could reply, the elevator came to a stop and Celeste led him into Keith's room. Raymond's breath caught in his chest as he looked at his friend, hooked up to machines, legs in traction, his head bandaged and his eyes slightly opened.

"Look who I found," Celeste said as she crossed over to Keith and kissed his cheek gently.

Keith pressed the button to raise the back of the bed and nodded in Raymond's direction. "You left paradise for me?" Keith asked hoarsely.

"They made it sound like you were near death. I'm glad that's not the case." Raymond walked to the end of the bed and picked up Keith's chart: ruptured spleen, fractured hip, and two broken legs. The chart said that the surgery to repair his spleen had been successful. "Looking good. Glad to see you're on the mend, brother."

"Where's your TV wife?" he asked, then broke into a fit of laughter that became a cough. Celeste quickly poured him a cup of water. Once his cough subsided, he turned back to Raymond. "Well, where is she? Don't tell me she stayed in Hawaii?"

"No, she's on a train to Brooklyn," he replied with a sigh. "We had a misunderstanding."

Celeste shook her head. "I'm not one to pry. . . ."

"Since when?" Raymond and Keith asked in concert.

"Whatever," she said with a dismissive wave of her hand. "But, if she came back here to be with you, then you need to fix what's wrong between you two. If I've learned anything from this accident, it's that life is too short. I could see when you looked at her on TV that you were really falling for her, Raymond. What happens if that train crashes or she's killed walking to her house?"

"Damn, Celeste, you have the guilt trip down cold," Keith said. "I see I won't be winning many arguments."

She tilted her head and smiled. "Don't start none, won't be none," she replied.

"Ouch," Raymond said as he sat down and watched Celeste check Keith's bandage. "Guess we know who will be wearing the pants in this marriage."

"Come on, now," Keith said. "I'm giving her a pass because I'm in the hospital."

"Anyway," Celeste said, "you two should really get over yourselves." She readjusted Keith's pillow and kissed his cheek. "And you know I've been running things."

"That's right, baby."

She rose to her feet and started for the door. "I'm going to get some coffee, Ray, you want anything?"

What he wanted wasn't in the hospital's cafeteria, but somewhere in Brooklyn. He wanted and needed Imani. He had to tell her that he was wrong and that he appreciated what she gave up returning to New York with him.

"Raymond?" Celeste said again, breaking into his thoughts.

"No, I'm fine. Thanks."

When the men were alone, Keith asked Raymond what happened to Imani. "I wanted to see if she was as fine in person as she is on TV and on that billboard. You've messed it up already, huh?"

Raymond folded his arms and leaned back in the chair. "I did."

Keith wagged his forefinger at his friend. "She came back with you when the world knows she was on that show to become famous and not fall in love. That says a lot."

"But as soon as we got in the cab, her agent called her about going on all of these talk shows to talk about her return," he said.

"That's what actresses do."

"It made me feel some kind of way . . . like she was still using me as a prop and now she was pulling your accident into it."

Keith shook his head. "Really?"

"Well, she didn't agree to do any of the shows."

"What's the problem? I appreciate you coming

back to check on me. I would've done the same thing. But you have to realize she never made it a secret that she wanted to be famous. Didn't stop her from falling in love with you, though."

"And you figured that out from watching us on TV?"

"I don't wear glasses and the fact that she's in New York proves you're not a prop."

Before Raymond could reply, Keith's parents, Lydia and Benjamin, walked into the room. "Thank you, Jesus," Lydia exclaimed as she rushed to her son's bedside. She kissed his cheeks. "I heard you talking down the hall."

Benjamin shook hands with Raymond. "I thought you were on that TV show. When did you get back?"

"Today," he replied. "I couldn't stay there not knowing what was going on with Keith."

Benjamin nodded and smiled. "You two have always been like brothers. I'm glad things turned out better. For a day or two I thought we were going to lose him."

"I never thought that," Lydia said, looking back at Raymond and her husband. "Raymond, you'd better get over here and give me a hug. Where is your girlfriend, or was that just made for TV?"

"Too hot for TV is more like it," Benjamin mumbled.

Lydia shot him a look that was icier than a New York January. Benjamin shrugged but didn't say another word.

"She had to go back to Brooklyn," Raymond said noncommittally.

"Roses always say I'm sorry pretty nicely," Lydia

said. "You two may be brilliant doctors, but when it comes to women, both of you are lost. This one took forever to ask Celeste to marry him, and you, Mr. Picky, had to go on TV to find a good woman. What happened to that stuck-up little girl from the Bronx that you used to date? That was a good breakup."

Raymond shook his head and hid his smile. Lydia was right about Mena; he'd made the best decision when he ended that relationship. Now, he had to save what he and Imani had. "Now that I see you're in good hands, I'm going to make a run to Brooklyn," he said. He walked over to Lydia and hugged her.

"I hope she's good for you," Lydia said. "You two would make pretty babies. Almost as pretty as Keith and Celeste's."

"Thanks," he said over Keith's groan. Raymond turned to his friend, "Buddy, I'll see you tomorrow."

"All right," Keith said.

Imani slammed into her house, dropped her luggage at the door, and kicked her sandals off. Her eyes were red and raw from crying all the way from the hospital to Brooklyn. Raymond had a damned nerve. He had every right to be upset about his friend being in the hospital, but what had she done to deserve his anger? Imani dropped down on the sofa and thought about calling Edward and telling him to book her on every show that wanted her. Then she recalled the look on Raymond's face after he heard her agent on the phone. This wasn't what she thought was going to happen when they returned to New York. What about all of the promises he'd made in Hawaii about teaching her pleasures that she'd never experienced?

Men, she thought, *they just think about themselves. Do I get any credit for dropping everything and coming back here with him? I wanted to be there for him. I wanted to be his shoulder and he gave me his ass to kiss. So, to hell with him!* Imani fished her cell phone out of her purse and dialed Dana's number.

"What's up, superstar?" her friend said when she answered the phone. "I'm really proud of you."

"Why?" Imani asked.

"First of all, you didn't go on TV and act like a stereotype. Secondly, you put your heart above your career. You and Raymond are an adorable couple."

"We're not a couple!" Imani snapped.

"What?"

"Why don't you let me buy you dinner and I can tell you all about it."

"But you left the show with him after his friend got in the accident. That episode just went off."

Imani rolled her eyes. "When did you start believing everything that you see on TV? Especially reality TV, which is edited to death?"

"I know you, and I know the looks you and Raymond were exchanging were real. You couldn't edit those in or out. What happened?"

"Can I shower and we'll talk about it over coconut shrimp at Red Bamboo?" Imani asked.

"All right. I'll meet you at your place in an hour."

After hanging up with Dana, Imani headed for the bathroom and took a hot shower. Being back in Brooklyn felt different, felt lonely. She missed Raymond already. It wasn't as if he was across the hall from her anymore. How would she see him again? They hadn't even exchanged numbers and addresses.

Just kisses, she thought as the water beat down on her, seeping into her scalp. *Is it really over?* Imani shut the water off, stepped out of the shower, and grabbed a towel. As she dried her body, her cell phone rang. She rushed into the living room to grab the call, but by the time she reached her phone, she'd already missed the call. She looked at the number and rolled her eyes. It wasn't familiar and she didn't feel like dealing with any bill collectors today.

What if it's about a movie or a Broadway role? she thought as she redialed the number.

"Imani?" Raymond's voice echoed in her ear.

"How—who is this?" she stammered, trying to play cool.

She heard him chuckle. "It's Raymond."

"How did you get this number?"

"You called your agent from my cell phone, so I called him back and begged him for your number. I think he's going to book us on *The Early Show* now."

"Oh, you can joke about that now?" she snapped.

"I was wrong and I owe you the biggest of apologies. Can I make it up to you?"

Can he make it up to me? "I don't know, Raymond," she replied, still trying to play cool, but she was wavering in her cool manner. This was not the time to act as if she didn't care and didn't want to see him. Not when she'd spent an hour crying because she thought she would never see him again. "How's your friend?"

"Keith is doing much better. He has quite a few broken bones and he's going to need a lot of physical therapy."

"I'm glad to hear he's all right."

"But are we all right?"

"I don't know," she said. "You still seem to have issues with what I do. You just don't get that being an actress is only part of who I am."

"I was an ass, Imani. You know, I've been in relationships where my career was an issue and I should've been more understanding. I know that you coming back here was a sacrifice and you did that because you care about me, not because you wanted to use this as a way to make your star rise."

"Finally, he gets it."

"What are you doing?"

"About to go have dinner," she said.

"Don't tell me I've been replaced already."

"I hate to inflate that ego of yours, but you're pretty irreplaceable."

"After dinner, do you have plans?"

"No."

"I'm sending a car for you. I'm not going to be able to sleep without you in my arms tonight. Where are you having dinner?"

"Red Bamboo," she replied. "Dana and I are going in about an hour."

"Well, you enjoy your dinner and I'll take care of dessert. And again, I'm sorry about being an asshole earlier."

"Umm, I'll think about accepting your apology."

"I think I can convince you to accept it," he said before telling her good-bye. Imani smiled and held her cell phone to her chest when the call ended. She couldn't wait to see Raymond and have her first private moment with him.

Chapter 18

When Dana arrived at Imani's, her friend had experienced a complete one-eighty from the way she sounded on the phone.

"Okay, what is going on?" Dana asked when a smiling Imani, dressed in a pink and yellow sundress and a pair of gold gladiator sandals, met her at the door. "I thought you were in a funk."

"Oh, I was. Raymond called."

Dana nodded, catching Imani's smiling bug. "And?"

"Well, he apologized, which I wasn't expecting. But you know how he found me? He called Edward."

"So, what happens next?"

Imani shrugged. "After dinner, he's sending a car to pick me up and then he wants me to spend the night with him. Dana, I think he's really the one."

"Tell me something that America and I don't know already. The vibe between you two was undeniable. I can't wait to meet the guy."

"Let's go," she said.

They hopped into Dana's car and headed for the

Red Bamboo. "I'm glad you're still camera-ready, because I imagine the paparazzi might be out. And I heard, the last time I was in Edward's office, that you're up for a role in Gina Prince-Bythewood's new movie."

"Yes. I read the script and it's fresh and smart. I hope I get a chance to play Courtney. She's the kind of character that I can identify with—smart, but not taken seriously because of her looks. I can rock that role."

"That sounds like you," Dana said. "I can't believe this reality show was the shot in the arm your career needed. I should've brought my camera so that I could've taken a picture of you eating and sold it to a tabloid."

"You wouldn't dare."

"Of course not. But when you become famous and start ignoring me, I do have a bunch of test shots that someone would pay top dollar for."

Imani pinched her friend on the shoulder. "I will hurt you."

"Just remember, I know where the bodies are buried. Do you think your reality show beau will let me shoot you two?"

"Umm, I don't know. Raymond is really private."

Dana pulled into a parking lot about two blocks from the restaurant. "How is that going to work? Your career isn't exactly stockbrokering. When you start doing these movies and Broadway shows, you're always going to be on the cover of a magazine, on Page Six and in the papers. Will he be able to deal with that?"

"I don't know, but I have to get those roles first."

"You're going to get them," Dana assured. "You showed plenty of range and realism on that show. But would you put your dream on hold for love?"

Imani shrugged. "Why can't I have both?"

"You can, I guess. Just depends on the good doctor."

When they arrived at the restaurant, Imani was surprised to see Raymond waiting at the entrance with a dozen roses in his hand.

"Raymond," she said as she quickly crossed over to him. "What are you doing here?"

"I couldn't wait until after dinner to see you and a wise woman told me that an apology isn't complete without roses." He handed Imani the long-stemmed red roses and then pulled her into his arms and kissed her until she was breathless. A few passersby who recognized them snapped pictures of the couple as they kissed.

"Ahem," Dana said, reminding her friend that she was there. Imani and Raymond broke their kiss and turned to face her. "I knew I should've brought my camera," Dana quipped

"Dana, this is Raymond. Raymond, my best friend, Dana," Imani said.

He extended his hand to Dana. "I hope you don't mind me intruding on your dinner," he said as they shook hands.

"Not at all. This gives me a chance to interrogate you," Dana replied with a laugh.

"All right, let's do it," he said as he opened the door for the women.

Imani was surprised that so many people recognized her and Raymond as they walked in and waited for the host to seat them. Any other night, she would've loved being the center of attention. She'd craved this type of reaction for years, but tonight all she wanted was to sit in a quiet corner and share dinner with her man and her best friend.

Her man? Yes, he was her man. Now that the show was over—at least for them—she didn't have to share him with Tres, Lucy, or the millions of viewers. Would tonight be the night that she shared everything with him? She glanced up at him, catching his eyes and the gleam in them. Imani felt as if dessert was going to start in his bed in Harlem and she could not wait.

After they were led to their table and stopped to pose for photos for a few fans of the show, Dana, Imani, and Raymond fell into a comfortable conversation. Imani reached for Raymond's hand underneath the table and Dana smiled at them.

"Raymond, what are your intentions with my friend over here?" Dana asked.

He lifted Imani's hand to his lips and kissed it gently. "Strictly honorable," he said. "I've never met a woman like Imani before in my life."

"And you never will again," Imani said.

"Then I guess I'd better hold on to you," he replied, nuzzling her neck.

Dana feigned disgust at her friend's display of public affection, but she was happy to see a real smile on Imani's face. When her phone buzzed with a text message, Dana decided to pretend it was an important call about an assignment.

"Imani, we'll get together soon. I forgot about this shoot at my studio," Dana said, then turned to Raymond. "It was so nice to meet you, Dr. Raymond." He rose to his feet and gave her a brotherly hug. "Raymond, Imani's a handful, but she's my best friend and if you hurt her, I'm going to hurt you," she whispered in his ear.

"That you don't have to worry about," he replied.

Dana stepped back and waved to the couple, then she left.

"She's not slick," Imani said when Raymond sat down. "She didn't forget anything."

"Dana is one tough chick, huh?"

"You could say that. We started this journey together and have been the presidents of each other's fan clubs since forever," Imani said.

"Can I join the Imani fan club? As a matter of fact, I want to be the CEO."

Imani placed her hand on his chest. "Let's clear something up first."

"All right."

"You hurt me earlier. Yes, I want to be famous and I want to conquer Broadway, Hollywood, hell even Bollywood, but I would never use you to do that. I—I . . ."

Raymond cut her off with a slow, deep kiss that heated her body like a forest fire. As she wrapped her arms around him, the clicking sound of cell phone cameras echoed in front of them and beside them. Breaking the kiss, Raymond whispered to Imani, "We don't have to do this in front of cameras anymore."

"That's right," she said as they slipped out of the booth. "But what about dinner?"

"We have food in Harlem."

Imani nodded and they rushed out of the restaurant under a hail of flashing camera lights. Raymond called for the car as they stood on the curb. "What do you have a taste for?" he asked.

Imani looked him directly in the eye and flashed him a sensual smile that cause a tightening in his pants. "You."

He inhaled and released a low whistle. "Are you sure about that? Because, I've had that same hunger and need since I saw you standing there in that dress."

Imani twirled around and laughed. "I'm sure," she said. "I want to feel all of those things you told me about in Hawaii."

"And what else, Imani, what else do you want?" Raymond drew her into his arms, brushing his lips across her forehead. He felt her shiver with desire as he held her.

"Everything," she said. "I want everything."

"Then that's what I'm going to give you," he said, his voice deep and raw. He couldn't hide the fact that he wanted to peel her clothes off and kiss her all over. Where was that car? Tonight, his fantasy was going to come true. He'd get to taste her sweetness, her passion, and teach her how he made love to his woman. Because Imani was going to be his forever, and tonight, he was going to brand her with his love. Pulling her into his arms, he held her tightly and nibbled on her ear, before whispering, "I've been dreaming about holding you like this and taking you back to my place."

"Tell me more," she said as the car pulled up.

"Mmm, I'd rather show you," Raymond replied as he led her to the car and opened the door.

The trip to Raymond's brownstone in Harlem seemed excruciatingly long, especially when Imani crossed her leg over his. The heat rising from her body nearly caused him to combust. He ran his finger across her thigh and her skin felt like silk. Imani moaned softly and moved closer into his touch as Raymond massaged her thigh. He could smell her desire rising as he leaned in and kissed her softly on the neck. The intense shiver that ran up and down her spine jolted her like a shock of pure electricity. She backed against the seat and stared at Raymond.

"I guess I found your hot spot," he said as he stroked her cheek.

"Is that so? Where's yours?"

Raymond smiled. "You're going to have to find mine just like I found yours."

"Is that so?" she asked with a grin. "Do I get to use my hands or my lips?" Before he could answer, Imani was in his lap and running her tongue up and down the column of his neck. His body tingled as if a package of firecrackers exploded inside him. Groaning and fighting back a squeal, he said, "All right, all right. You found one."

She pulled back from him and smiled. "Good, now we're even," she quipped as the car came to a stop. Imani glanced out the window and let out a low whistle when she saw the restored brownstones. "Harlem is beautiful."

"Better than Brooklyn?" he asked.

"Never," she replied. "But almost."

"Come on. You feel the history here, the soul of Zora, the creativity of Richard Wright and jazz." Raymond hopped out of the car and extended his hand for Imani. She slowly climbed out of the car and allowed Raymond to spin her around as if they could hear Duke Ellington playing. She wrapped her arms around Raymond's waist as they swayed to their own tune. "Let's go inside before someone shows up with a camera," Imani said.

Raymond didn't have to be told twice as he turned toward his brownstone with Imani wrapped around him. Once they entered his home, Imani drank in the rich earth tones and supple leather furniture in the living room. He had a breathtaking view of the East Harlem River. She stood in the center of the room and marveled at the view. But she was fully aware of Raymond's presence behind her. His hands roamed underneath her dress, kneading her shoulders, sliding down her back and finally resting on her bottom. A feeling of anticipation, fear, and excitement rushed through her system as his lips brushed her neck.

"You are so beautiful," he whispered.

Imani turned around and faced him. They locked hands and she sighed. She was ready to give him every part of herself, ready to allow him to make love to her. But she was still afraid. Would she be able to handle making love to Raymond? What if she couldn't satisfy him? If she disappointed him, would that be the end for their relationship? *What we have is deeper than sex, isn't it?*

Raymond stroked her cheek. "Are you all right?"

"Yes," she said breathlessly.

"We don't have to do anything you're not ready for," he said as he held her face and stared into her eyes.

"I want you, but . . ."

"No buts. I want you and I want you to feel good about what we're going to do. Anytime you want me to stop, say so and I will. No questions."

Imani nodded, slowly feeling the tension easing from her shoulders. Raymond pushed the straps of her dress down her shoulders, kissing the skin he exposed. Imani shivered with desire as his tongue eased down the back of her neck. With his free hand, he unzipped her dress and it fell off her body, pooling at her feet. Raymond spun her around and drank in her image. She was clad in a pink lace strapless bra that held her breasts the way he wanted to and a pair of matching lace panties that clung to her hips and behind. Raymond ran his hand down the center of her chest, stopping at the waistband of her panties.

"May I?" he asked.

She nodded nervously. He pulled her panties around her ankles, then slipped his hand between her thighs. Imani was wet, hot, and waiting. "I want to taste you," he said, salivating at the thought of wrapping his lips around her bud. Raymond scooped her up in his arms and carried her into the bedroom. He could feel Imani's heart beating in overdrive. "Are you all right?" he asked again.

"I can't lie, I'm a little nervous," she said as he laid her in the center of his king-sized bed.

"We can stop."

"We haven't even started," she said.

"If you're ready, I know how I want to start," he said as he slowly spread her thighs apart. With the palm of his hand, he stroked her wetness back and forth. Imani squirmed under his touch. Her body seemed to take on a life of its own, responding to Raymond's touch in ways she never imagined that it could. Easing between her thighs, he parted her wet lips with his fingertips, then gently licked the folds of flesh until Imani's moans turned into screams of passion. "Raymond, Raymond," she cried as he sucked her throbbing bud of desire. She was so sweet, so delicious. Better than he'd dreamed she would be. He licked and sucked until she trembled and exploded in his mouth. Propping up on his elbows, he looked into Imani's sated face. "How do you feel?" he asked.

"Amazing," she breathlessly replied. Raymond massaged her thighs gently. "I've never felt anything like that before."

"There's more where that came from. When you're ready. But first you need something to eat because you're going to need all of your energy this evening."

"All right," she said, her body still buzzing from her first full-on orgasm. Imani couldn't wait for what came next. She was about to get out of bed, but Raymond stopped her.

"Don't move. Let me cater to your every need, including bringing you dinner in bed. Because if I recall, someone told me that she liked this kind of thing."

"Ha, ha," she said. "But if you want to give me the star treatment, I'm not going to stop you." Imani locked her hands behind her head and crossed her legs. Raymond let out a low whistle as he took in the sexiness on his bed.

"Chinese good for you?" he asked once he found his voice.

"That's fine."

Raymond called in their dinner order and then he sat on the edge of the bed, kissing Imani and stroking her breasts because he just couldn't get enough of her, couldn't resist touching her supple body, tasting her lips, and for the first time, taking her diamond hard nipples into his mouth. Imani held the back of his head as he sucked her nipples. "Ooh," she cried out as his tongue flicked across one nipple and his finger teased the other. As he was about to slip his hand between her thighs to stroke her clitoris, the doorbell rang.

"Forget it," she moaned. "I need you."

"That's dinner and we have to eat, even though I could feast on this body for the rest of my life," he said as he reluctantly pulled himself away from her. When Raymond headed for the door to get their meal, Imani released a sigh. She'd never felt so sexy, so wanted, and so cared for. She couldn't wait to make love to Raymond. She felt safe enough to push thoughts about satisfying him out of her head because she could've sworn that he enjoyed bringing her to climax as much as she enjoyed reaching it.

"Penny for your thoughts," Raymond said from the doorway.

"I was thinking about everything you did to me," she said with a smile. "And how much I liked it."

"I aim to please," he said as he set the bags of

fried rice, shrimp and broccoli, and egg rolls on the nightstand beside the bed. She smiled at him as he pulled his shirt off and stripped down to his boxers. When Imani saw the size of his erection, she froze in place. Though she didn't have anything to compare him to, she wondered if she'd be able to handle what Raymond had to offer. She couldn't tear her eyes away from his manhood.

"Imani?" he asked as he slipped into bed with her. "Did you hear me?"

"What? I didn't hear you."

"I said open your mouth." He held out a fork full of fried rice. Imani accepted the food, telling herself to relax. After they ate their fill of dinner, the couple lay in each other's arms, quietly watching the stars twinkle.

"This feels so right," Imani whispered.

"That's because it is. I love you, Imani," he said. "I could see us spending many nights and mornings this way."

She turned over on her stomach and faced him. "Seriously?"

"Yes. What about you? What do you want from this? Where do you see us?"

"Walking down the red carpet together at the Oscars," she said. "And once we get inside, you kissing me when they announce my name for the best actress award."

"I like that," he said, then he kissed her deeply, his tongue dancing with hers. Instinctively, Imani spread her legs, and Raymond eased between them, never breaking off the kiss. She locked her legs around his waist as the kiss deepened and Imani felt a now familiar feeling between her thighs. She was wet, and she wanted to take that next step and feel him deep inside her valley. Breaking the kiss, Imani moaned, "Make love to me."

"Are you sure you're ready?" he asked. She nodded and wrapped her arms around his neck. Imani drank in his lean and beautiful body as he ground against her without entering her wetness. Though she'd seen his body several times in Hawaii, she hadn't felt it like this. Flesh against flesh, nerves on end and a surreal anticipation.

"I have to protect us," he said as he pulled back and reached into the nightstand drawer, pulling out a gold condom package. He ripped it open and slid the sheath in place after kicking out of his boxers. Imani watched him intently, her eyes focused on his dangling erection as he turned to her.

"We're going to take it slow," he said as he pulled her into his arms. Imani kissed him slow and deep. Raymond eased her back against the pillows and lowered himself on top of her. Imani eased down his body until she felt the tip of his manhood against her wetness. She quivered as he held her hips and gently pressed into her. Her body tingled; the sensation was new and exciting and different from feeling his lips and tongue down there.

Raymond planted himself inside her, diving in slowly to her tight valley. Imani shuddered in a brief moment of pain, then she felt bliss like nothing she'd ever imagined or felt in her life. He ground against her at a pace that took into account her inexperience. The slower he pressed against her, the wetter and hotter she grew, catching the natural rhythm of his hips.

Imani felt comfortable enough after a few more strokes from Raymond to match his moves and intensity. She shifted her hips, taking him deeper and deeper inside her untouched femininity. "Oh, Raymond," she groaned as she felt the waves of an orgasm wash over her body. "Thi-this feels so good. Don't stop."

"I have no plans to. You feel so damned good, baby," he moaned as he felt her coming.

Raymond gripped her hips, flipping her over so that she could be on top of him. Imani ground slowly against him as he held on to her waist. What she felt was indescribable. He filled her womanhood and touched places that she didn't even know existed. And when he took her breasts into his mouth, alternating between licking and gently biting her erect nipples, Imani howled in delight. She shivered and inadvertently tightened herself around him, making Raymond call out her name as he began to climax. He hugged her against his chest as he exploded inside her hot and tight valley. She shivered and quivered as she experienced her third orgasm.

"You feel so good," he whispered in her ear. The heat from his breath sent chills down her spine. Imani gently kissed his collarbone and held him tightly, pressing her breasts against him. "Are you all right?" he asked her as she snuggled against him.

She nodded. "So this is what it feels like. I never in my wildest dreams thought making love would feel like this."

"Me either," Raymond said.

Imani pushed off his chest and looked at him. "What do you mean?" she asked.

"I love you and this was the best feeling I've ever had. It's like we connected, mind, body, and soul. It doesn't get any better than that." What he didn't tell her was that he could never allow another man to ever touch what was his and she would be his forever.

Chapter 19

Imani woke up with a start and a slight soreness between her legs. Raymond's strong arms held her this morning just as they had last night. After they'd made love for the third time, Raymond had told Imani that they needed to stop and she should soak in his garden tub. At the time, she hadn't wanted to do anything but make love to him again. She'd wanted to test out her new skills of riding. Imani and Raymond had discovered that she enjoyed being on top. Which had been why Raymond suggested a soak in the bathtub. Raymond had enjoyed watching Imani ride him as well. What she'd lacked in experience, she'd definitely made up for in enthusiasm. Her strokes had been long, deep, and slow. Raymond had matched her pace, allowing Imani to explore her burgeoning sexuality and find out what she liked and what worked for her to get pleasure. By the time they'd had their fill of desire, the sun was coming up over the horizon.

She brushed her lips against his. "Good morning, darling," she said.

"Morning, babe," he replied. Imani loved the deep and gruff sound of his voice when he first woke up. It turned her on and now that she knew what to do with that feeling, she pressed her hand against his chest and mounted him. Smiling, Raymond said, "You're insatiable."

"That's only because you make me feel so good. But I can move," she said.

Raymond held her thigh with one hand and reached for a condom with the other. "Don't you move yet," he said.

Imani took the condom from his hand. "Can I give it a try?" she asked. Imani already felt his erection and knew he was ready. Raymond nodded as Imani slid down his legs and opened the condom wrapper. Before she slid the sheath in place, she stroked his hardness back and forth making him groan low and long as her hand moved faster and faster. "Oh, damn, baby. You're killing me. Need. You. To. Stop."

Smiling, she did what he'd asked, then slipped the condom on, silently hoping that she'd done it right. Raymond guided her to his erection, slipping inside her wetness and grinding inside her as she gyrated against him. Easing into a seated position, Raymond held her against his chest, diving deeper inside her. He covered her neck with his mouth and immediately felt her shiver and shake. She was about to come and so was he. Their bodies were in tune, moving with one purpose, one need, one desire. Their mutual explosion caused them to scream out in pleasure and satisfaction.

Sweaty, happy, and a bit drowsy, Raymond wished

he could spend his morning buried inside his woman, but he had to go to the clinic, visit Keith and . . . Looking at Imani, he thought, *I can wait another hour.* He wrapped his arms around her and kissed her neck, knowing that it would drive her wild.

"Umm," she moaned. "I know we can't do this all day. Don't you have to go to the hospital to see your friend?"

His reply was to run his tongue down the length of her neck. "Oh, Raymond," she groaned as he reversed his position. "What about you—your clinic?"

"Just another few minutes and then we will return to the real world. But right now," he said as he gently turned her over on her stomach and spread her legs from behind, "I want to make love to my woman again."

And for the next three hours, Raymond introduced Imani to untold pleasures, showed her different positions that gave him direct access to her throbbing bud of desire. By the time Raymond got up to shower and get ready for work, Imani could barely move, but she'd never hurt so good before in her life.

What comes next? she wondered as she listened to Raymond in the shower. *Is this where I get cab fare back to Brooklyn and wait for his call by the phone? Is he really happy with what has happened? Did I satisfy him?* Imani was so deep in thought that she hadn't noticed Raymond standing by the bed, damp with a towel wrapped around his waist.

"Imani?" he asked, his voice dripping with concern. "Are you all right?"

"Yeah, I was just thinking."

"About?"

"Us, everything that happened, and what comes next." She sat up and brought her knees to her chest.

"Let me tell you what comes next. After I go and check on the clinic, we're going to Brooklyn so that you can change your clothes. After that, we're going to see Keith. Hopefully, you're going to have an overnight bag so that we won't have to go back to Brooklyn tomorrow morning."

She smiled and fingered her hair. "Raymond."

He brought his finger to her lips. "Don't tell me you were sitting in here thinking that we were done or that this was about sex. Imani, I didn't say I loved you to get you into my bed. I said it because I mean it."

She leapt forward and kissed him with a relieved passion because he'd erased all the fears and doubts that had been floating in her head.

When they broke their kiss, Imani said, "Why don't I fix you a quick breakfast before you leave?"

"Can you cook, woman?" he quipped. "If you can, I may never allow you to return to Brooklyn."

"Well, if toasting a bagel and spreading cream cheese or lox on it counts as cooking, then I'm a regular Rachael Ray," Imani joked.

"We're going to have to work on that, because I don't like my bagels toasted."

"That's why Brooklyn is so much better. Everybody likes their bagels toasted," she replied. Raymond pulled his polo shirt over his head and then leaned in to kiss Imani.

"I don't know if the bagels in the cupboard are any good, but there is coffee," he said as he reached for a pair of boxers and navy blue slacks. Imani rose from the bed, walked over to his closet and pulled out a white dress shirt. Raymond turned around and watched her cover her body in his shirt. She'd never looked sexier, with her bed hair, skin glowing from satisfaction, and the way the sunlight lit her brown eyes. The only thing Raymond wanted to do with the slacks he'd just slipped into was kick them off and take his woman back to bed.

"What?" Imani asked as she caught his eye. "Should I have asked first?"

Raymond crossed over to her and pressed her against his body. "You're making it so hard for me to go to work right now. That shirt has never looked better. Tonight, wear this to bed so I can show you just what you did to me." He glanced at his watch, groaned, and gave her a quick kiss on the forehead. "I have to go."

"Have a great day," she said, hating to see him go to work. But Imani knew how important that clinic was to Raymond and she would never stand in the way of his work, no matter how badly she wanted to make love to him again. What had he called her— insatiable? Up until he awakened desire and passion in her, she'd thought it was just a song by Prince.

Before she got to the kitchen to make herself a cup of coffee, her cell phone rang. She sprinted to her purse in the living room and grabbed the phone.

"This is Imani," she said.

"Imani, where are you?" Edward asked frantically.

"In Harlem. What's wrong?"

"You will not believe who wants to meet you in an hour," he said.

"Who?" she asked.

"Brock Harrison."

Imani's knees went weak and she nearly dropped the phone before screaming at the top of her lungs. Once she realized that she wasn't dancing around her place in Brooklyn, where her neighbors had grown accustomed to her outbursts, she calmed down. "Edward, how did you swing that?"

"I didn't swing anything. Brock called me last night and I tried to reach you. What is the use of you having a cell phone if you're not going to answer it? But I digress. He's a fan of reality TV and when he saw you leave the show with the doctor, that touched him, he said. So, he's about to start the casting process for Will Smith's new project and he thinks you have what it takes to play Smith's leading lady."

"Stop!"

"So, whatever you're doing uptown, wrap it up and meet me in my office by twelve-thirty," Edward ordered. "Don't be late."

"Got it!" Imani hung up with her agent, scribbled a quick note for Raymond, and then put on her dress, leaving his shirt on the sofa and dashing out the door. She couldn't believe that this opportunity had fallen in her lap like this. *Dear God,* she thought as she headed down the subway entrance, *please let me win this role.*

* * *

"Superstar," Maria said when Raymond walked into the empty clinic. "Welcome back."

He smiled slightly as he looked around the clinic. "What's going on here? Where are our patients?"

"Well," she said, "it's hard to treat people when the doctors aren't here. But if you go into the break room, there are several pies and cakes for Keith and his speedy recovery. I saw him yesterday and he looks a lot better than I expected." She shook her head. "I was so scared for him and Celeste."

"I know. I guess it is a good thing that I won a little money on that show. Where's the appointment book? I need to make some calls and let our patients know I'm back. Especially Mrs. Hanover. We need to schedule her A1C test because her sugar levels were high before I left."

Maria picked up the book and clutched it to her chest. "I hope you didn't think you were going to come in here and just get back to work without telling me all about Imani. Did you two get married yet? Oh, and you made the blogs. Perez Hilton!"

"Who?"

Maria motioned for him to come behind the desk, and she pointed to an image on her computer screen. It was of Imani and Raymond kissing outside the Red Bamboo.

"'Love from a reality show? Doubt it,'" Raymond read. "Who the hell is Perez Hilton?"

"A gossip blogger and when you make it on his site, you're pretty much famous. Although, it may benefit Imani more than you, Dr. Hot-Body Thomas of Harlem," Maria said, quoting the Web site. "So, is what you two have real or is this part of her act?"

Raymond tried to downplay the smile spreading across his face. "Give me the appointment book."

"Oooh," Maria said. "Both of my doctors are in love. So, when is Ms. Fearless Flop Diva going to come see what you do?"

"Hey, don't ever call her that," Raymond said.

"Perez's words, not mine. I actually liked that movie."

Raymond laughed as he flipped through the book, checking which patients he needed to call immediately. "Make sure you share that with Imani," he said. As Raymond began to make his calls to the patients, a camera crew and three reporters burst through the door.

"Dr. Thomas," a woman called out, "since you've become a reality TV star, are you going to continue practicing medicine here?"

"Do you and Imani Gilliam have a real relationship?" another reporter asked.

"Hey," Maria bellowed, standing up behind her desk. "This is a doctor's office. Now I need you to get the hell out of here and call his publicist."

"Why do you need a publicist?" the last reporter asked.

"Enough, people," Raymond said. "I have a clinic to run and patients to see. I need you to get out before you scare them off."

"Can we get a statement, just one?" the first reporter asked.

"All right," Raymond said. "My relationship with Imani is real and private. That's it, good-bye."

As he ushered the reporters out, they continued asking questions. "Will you two get married?"

"How will her acting career and your medical career impact the relationship?"

"Good-bye," he said as he closed the door behind them. Raymond turned to Maria and shook his head.

"They've been coming around here for a week," she said exasperatedly. "Keith ate up the attention."

Raymond chuckled under his breath. "Of course he would. All right, I'm getting to these calls. Keep the reporters out." Back in the office he and Keith shared, Raymond felt empty, missing his friend and partner. But he was happy to see that all of the clinic's bills were paid for the month and they had enough money in the account to take care of things for at least a year. Things were finally looking up and Raymond couldn't help but smile as he dove into his work.

Imani hated cabs because every time she took one, she got stuck in traffic, just like today. She looked at the street sign and decided even in three-inch red pumps, she'd have a better chance on foot of making it to Edward's office on time for her meeting.

"Just let me out here," she said, stuffing two twenty-dollar bills in the driver's hand and jumping out of the car. Imani knew she overpaid for her cab ride and it actually felt good to be able to do that. She ran down the sidewalk, sidestepping Starbucks-sipping stockbrokers, tourists who were gawking at the sites, and New Yorkers who were just in a hurry to get to the subway. She loved this city. But what she loved more than anything else was the way Raymond made her feel, not just in bed, but when he'd told her how beautiful she looked with her hair matted to her head and dressed in his shirt. She never knew that love was this easy, this blissful and dynamic.

Now, if she could get her career going. It was funny to her that now she didn't just want success in her career, she wanted to make things work with Raymond. Maybe she could do something to have a fund-raiser for his clinic. As she walked into Edward's office building, she decided that she would suggest that some of his more successful clients could take part in a telethon or some kind of benefit for the Marion G. Palmer Clinic.

Knocking on his office door, Imani was all smiles when she entered. "Here I am," she said, looking from him to Brock.

"Well, hello," Brock said as he rose from his seat and shook Imani's hand, then kissed it. "You're even more stunning in person than you are on TV or in Times Square."

"Right on time," Edward said, then muttered under his breath, "Thank God."

"Mr. Harrison, it is a great honor to meet you," she said after taking her hand out of his grasp. Imani prayed that he was serious about casting her for this role and not just angling to get her on the casting couch. She'd been here before and wasn't ever going to deal with sleazy types again. But with the reputation Brock Harrison had, Imani should've been more confident. However, she didn't want to get her hopes up.

"I have to tell you, you have screen presence and

I want you to screen test with Will Smith in Los Angeles."

"Really?" she asked, urging herself to calm down, but she smiled widely. "When?"

"I'm leaving for the Left Coast in three days and I can fly you out there. We've been looking for the right actress to play Will's leading lady. Even though *Fearless Diva* was the worst piece of cinema I've seen in years, you have the physical ability that role requires." He reached into his messenger bag and pulled out the script. "I think you will be perfect for LeAnna. Read the script and if you like it, the ticket to LA is there for you to use." Imani saw the first-class ticket and smiled. This was for real.

"Wow," she said quietly.

"My card is in there and I need you to call me tomorrow and let me know if you're interested in the role. I think you're going to love her. She's sexy, strong, and she has a heart. It's going to be almost like playing yourself," Brock said. "You were the highlight of that show. It was hard to tell when you were acting and when you were being serious. I just want to know, what was the secret you told the doctor?"

Imani folded her arms across her chest and smirked at Brock. "Now, if I tell you that, then it won't be a secret."

He clasped his hands together. "I love it! You are LeAnna. That was something she would say."

Edward cleared his throat. "You're taking care of travel, but what about accommodations for my client? Willing to pay for loss of wages?"

Brock faced Edward and folded his arms across his chest. "Accommodations, sure. But you're asking too much with the lost wages, especially since I think Ms. Imani is going to win the role."

Imani beamed, as she'd never seen Edward work before. She had definitely underestimated her agent and she owed him a huge apology.

"We're going to go over the script and you should hear from us tomorrow, Brock," Edward said as he shook hands with the casting director. "I've heard that this project is a star maker, and I'm certain Imani is the next big star."

Brock winked at her as he and Edward headed for the door. "I'm with you there."

When Imani heard the elevator chime, she broke out into her version of the happy dance.

"Whatever you do, don't do that at the screen test," Edward said with a laugh when he returned to his office.

Imani rushed into his arms and hugged him. "Can you believe this?"

"Actually," he said, "I can. I knew you had this level of talent. Now admit that I was right about doing the reality show."

She closed her eyes as images of naked Raymond danced in her head. "Yes," she said when she opened her eyes. "You were right."

"How's the good doctor and what do you think his reaction to your movie role will be? And don't be one of those women who gives up on acting because she's in love."

"First of all, I've worked too hard to get here. And Raymond has already given me his support. He knows what acting means to me."

"So, is this the real deal between you two?" Edward asked.

Imani smiled. "Yes."

"I'm happy for you," he said. "But don't get distracted. Read that script and get back to me. Brock likes you and since you already think you're a star, I know you won't be tongue-tied when you read with Will Smith."

"Not at all. He should be in awe of me," Imani said as she turned toward the door. She looked back at Edward. "What about the Gina Prince-Bythewood movie?"

He shook his head. "Haven't heard back yet, but you do realize this is bigger, right?"

"It's not always about bigger," she said. "I just want options."

"You will have plenty."

Imani waved to him and headed out the door. She called Raymond and told him she was on her way to the clinic. Rather than waste more money on a cab, she hopped on the subway and headed to the clinic. As she rode the train, Imani found herself taken in by the script. Brock was right, LeAnna was her kind of character. Tough, chic, and more than anything else, smart. When the train stopped at 125th Street, Imani had finished reading the script and couldn't wait to land this part. She smiled all the way across the platform, ready to share her good news with Raymond.

Chapter 20

Finding the clinic had been easy, after the way Raymond had talked about how the community depended on it. The building, on 125th Street, was unassuming, but the artwork on the door captured what Imani imagined was the spirit of Marion Palmer. A tall brown-skinned woman with a thick black afro and a halo was painted on the front of the office building. When Imani walked in, all eyes focused on her.

"Oh my gosh," one of the little old ladies at the desk said. "It's her." A murmur rippled through the waiting room and the nurse behind the desk crossed over to Imani with a smile on her face.

"Hi. Dr. Thomas is in with a patient, but you can either wait for him in the waiting room," she said while shaking her head, "or I can take you to the break room and let him know you're here."

"I'll wait out here," Imani said.

The nurse shook her head again. "I don't think you want to do that. Those old ladies are going to grill you. I know two of them have tried to set him up with a granddaughter or a daughter."

"Good thing they failed," Imani quipped.

"By the way, I'm Maria Emerson and I loved *Fearless Diva*."

"That's sweet, but you don't have to say that," Imani said, still finding it hard to believe that people actually liked that movie.

"Oh, if I didn't like it, I would've—"

"All right, Maria, who's . . ." Raymond stopped talking when he saw his nurse and his woman laughing. "Imani." He crossed over to her and kissed her cheek. The women in the waiting room watched them intently, as if they were still viewing the couple on TV. "Hold up one second," Raymond said as he headed into the waiting room. "Now, ladies," he said to his group of patients, "why is it that when you have appointments with me, I can't get you here. But today, none of you have appointments and here you are."

One older lady stood up and walked over to Raymond. "Well, maybe we missed you," she said.

Raymond gave the woman a hug. "I missed you too, Mrs. Wentworth," he said.

"And," Mrs. Wentworth said, "we wanted to see if you two were still together. Because if she had broken your heart, we were going to get her."

"That's right," another lady called out. "Because Leslie is still available."

Imani looked from Raymond to his patients trying to decide how she felt about the little old ladies.

He held his hands up. "Imani and I are together

and she's the best thing—other than you ladies—that has ever happened to me."

Imani beamed and said, "And he's the best man I've ever met."

The women clapped and then Mrs. Wentworth turned to Imani and pointed her finger at her. "Don't make us come get you. We love this man like he's our son. He takes such good care of us and you're going to have to take care of him."

"I plan on taking very good care of him," Imani said. Raymond winked at her.

Mrs. Wentworth nodded and gave Imani a slight smile. "Got my eye on you, girl."

"Ladies," Raymond said. "Since none of you has an appointment, serious illnesses, or needs refills on your prescriptions"—he reached into his pocket and handed Mrs. Wentworth a prescription for cholesterol medicine—"I'm going to take my lady to lunch."

"You just make sure we all get invitations to the wedding," Mrs. Wentworth said. "Come on, ladies, let's go."

The women left the clinic and Imani turned to Raymond. "Okay, I see why you love your job. You have ten grandmothers," she joked.

"Yes. But they're hardheaded when they want to be," he said.

"They love you, though, and that's special. Where are we going for lunch because I have some news?"

"Let's go see Keith and then we can go eat," Raymond said. "You can tell me your news on the way."

"All right," Imani said, smiling happily.

Raymond cupped her face and kissed her petal-soft lips. "I don't know what's putting this smile on your face, but I'm about to be jealous," he said.

"I have a chance to screen test for a role in Will Smith's new movie," she said as they walked to the curb to hail a cab.

"Congratulations, baby," he said excitedly. "When did this happen?"

"Today, right after you left, Edward called me and told me that Brock Harrison wanted to meet me. *Me!*"

"Okay," Raymond said. "Who is Brock Harrison?"

"One of Hollywood's premiere casting directors," she said. "And the script he gave me was wonderful. LeAnna is the right fit for me. She's smart, she kicks ass and she gets to go toe to toe with Will Smith!"

"That's great, baby."

"I'm going to LA to do a screen test this week."

"What? Wow, this moves fast. So, what happens after the screen test?"

Imani shrugged. "Hopefully I will blow them away and they will offer me the role and I'll be on my way to being the leading lady that I deserve to be."

"Then we celebrate tonight. My lady, the superstar." Although Raymond was happy for Imani's chance to star in a movie, he didn't want her across the country. Not when he was getting used to having her in his arms when he went to sleep and woke up.

"I've been waiting for a role like this since *Fearless Diva* wrapped." Imani tilted her head to the side. "I guess I have to thank you for this."

Raymond raised his eyebrow. "How so?"

"Because you tested the full range of my emotions when we first met on the show and then you accepted me for who I am and I got to be real with you. Who really knew that someone like Brock Harrison was watching? But more than anything else, you have my back and you're rooting for me."

"You're right about that," he replied as he kissed her on the cheek. A cab finally stopped for them. "When are you going to Los Angeles?"

Imani slipped in the car as Raymond held the door for her. "Possibly, in two days." He nodded as he climbed into the car. "Come on," she said. "You still have to be excited for me."

"I am, but it doesn't mean that I have to like not having you in my arms when I go to sleep in three days."

Imani leaned against his shoulder. "I'm going to miss that as well."

"Then we're going to have to make some great memories tonight," he said, then told the driver to take them to Beth Israel Medical Center. They rode to the hospital in a comfortable silence, holding each other close. She felt so right in his arms and so blessed to have Raymond in her life.

When they arrived at the hospital, they headed straight for the fourth floor. "Keith is doing a lot better, but he looks a lot worse for the wear," Raymond said as they stepped off the elevator.

Raymond slowly opened the door to Keith's room and saw Celeste sitting in the chair beside the bed with her head resting on the edge of the bed.

Raymond looked at Keith, happy to see that the bandages had been removed from his head and some of the machines that had been helping him breathe were gone.

Keith glanced at Imani as she slipped quietly into the room. "Please tell me you're my new nurse," he joked.

Imani smiled nervously. "No, I'm here with Raymond."

Celeste began to stir on the bed and sat up at the sound of voices. She looked around the room and smiled when she saw Raymond. "Ray, I'm glad you're here," she said as she sat up.

Raymond walked over to her and hugged his friend. "Are you getting enough rest? You know you don't have to stay here twenty-four hours a day. They're not going to toss this bum out yet," he joked.

Celeste nodded and placed her hand on Keith's shoulder. "Thank God the doctors are expecting him to make a full recovery," she said. "I just can't go home. You never know what's going to happen." Celeste smiled as she locked eyes with Imani. "Well, hello. Glad to see you."

"Hi," Imani replied.

Celeste smirked at Raymond. "I see you made up for being an ass."

"Ouch!" Raymond said, clutching his chest. "That's just mean."

Imani laughed, immediately deciding that she liked Celeste.

Keith laughed as well. "Get him, baby," he said.

Celeste turned to Imani. "Welcome to our wacky family," she said. "We watched the two of you falling in love on that show and this one was miserable the other day when he came in here without you."

Imani smiled. They were in love and she had no idea that everyone could see it. "That won't happen again. He's got his act together now."

"Oh, do I?" he questioned as he squeezed her bottom. "Guess who's going to meet with Will Smith this week?"

"Not you," Keith said. "Congrats, Imani. Now we can all say we knew you when."

"So, are you auditioning for a movie?" Celeste asked.

"Yes, and I'm so excited. But it's bittersweet," Imani said as she cast a glance at Raymond. "I don't want to leave this guy."

"Aww," Celeste exclaimed. "This is so sweet. Raymond, she's a keeper."

"You think?" he joked as he kissed Imani's cheek. Then he turned to Keith. "What have they said about when you're getting out of here?"

"More good news. I'm probably getting out of here tomorrow and will be able to go home and get waited on hand and foot by my fiancée and my mother."

Raymond shook his head. "You'd better watch how you act before you end up like that dude in *Misery*."

"Thank you, Raymond!" Celeste said.

"I got something that will end this argument," Raymond said as he reached in his pocket and pulled out a blue Tiffany box. For a split second,

Imani thought the ring was hers and covered her mouth with her hand. She felt a twinge of disappointment when Raymond handed the box to Keith.

Imani, stop being silly. Raymond isn't trying to get married, she chided herself as she watched Keith struggle to open the box. Beaming, he showed the pear-shaped diamond ring to Celeste.

"Keith, it's beautiful," she said as she slipped the ring on her finger.

Keith pointed at Raymond and Imani. "You two are next," he said. "America is waiting for your wedding."

Raymond laughed nervously, and Imani said, "It may be a little too soon to talk about that." She squeezed Raymond's hand as if she was telling him that he was off the hook and she understood that this was Keith and Celeste's moment. Imani felt as if she had to say that, but she did want to marry Raymond, when the time was right. In that moment, she wanted his wedding band as much as she wanted an Academy Award. But she didn't want to seem desperate like Lucy. They hadn't known each other long, but how could you put a time table on love?

"Is that so?" Keith asked, "Because . . ."

Celeste placed her hand over her fiancé's mouth. "Imani, ignore him," she said.

Raymond wrapped his arm around Imani's waist and brought his lips to her ear. "We're going to have to talk about that," he whispered. Then Raymond turned to Celeste and Keith. "All right, guys, we're gonna bounce. Try not to piss your fiancée off, Keith."

"Come on," Keith said as Imani and Raymond

headed out the door. "If I behave, how will she know that I'm ready to go home?"

Raymond wished he could read minds as he and Imani walked out of the hospital. What did she mean by saying it was too early to talk about marriage? He was sure she was the woman he wanted to marry and he would ask her tomorrow if he knew that was what she wanted. Raymond was certain no other woman would ever touch him as deeply as Imani had. There was something about her that got under his skin. She was the perfect mix of minx and pussycat. She was sexy, innocent, and beautiful. He glanced at her as they walked to the corner to hail a cab.

Imani caught his gaze and raised her sculpted eyebrow. "What's wrong?" she asked. "You've been quiet since we left Keith's room."

"Nothing," he replied. Raymond waved his arm at the yellow cab that approached them.

"Don't say nothing when it's something. I know you better than that," she said. "Keith is on the mend, I'm going to read for a plumb role in LA and we get to spend the night together."

The cab stopped in front of them and they climbed into the car. "I wonder," Raymond said, "you going to Los Angeles and doing this screen test . . . Does this change what we have? Are you back to the Imani I met at the airport?"

"What? How can you even ask me that? You think that I can't have my career and be with you too?" Imani asked as Raymond closed the door and gave the driver the address where they were going.

He turned to Imani and placed his hand on her

knee. "Look, you were the one who just gave a little speech about not being ready for marriage. I knew from the start that you've had a singular focus. I can deal with that, but be honest with me and yourself. I won't stand in the way of your career, because I wouldn't let you interfere with mine."

Imani sighed and rolled her eyes. This argument was old and she was tired of it. "Driver, will you pull over up here, please?"

Confused, Raymond asked Imani what was going on. She glared at him. "Since you want me to focus on my career so much, that's what I'm going to do. My agent's office is down the block. I'm going to go tell him that I'm ready to go to LA tonight." Imani opened the door and hopped out before the taxi had even come to a complete stop. As she stalked down the sidewalk, she cursed under her breath. Was this his way of letting himself off the hook? But why? He'd just proclaimed his love for her in front of all of his patients. Hell, maybe Raymond should be the one reading for roles in LA and not her.

"Imani, stop, wait," he called out as he reached out and grabbed her arm. "What is your problem?"

"Why do you keep throwing my career in my face? Do you think I choose to be with you as a publicity stunt? Damn it, I love you," she said. Then she quickly covered her mouth with her hands.

"And I love you too. But I can't read your mind. I want to marry you. So, when you say things like you said in Keith's room, I don't know what to think."

"You what?" she asked, her mouth dropping open.

"I said I want to marry you, but a marriage takes

two people. I don't want you to do something that you don't want to do. If you think it's too soon for us to talk about marriage and you want to focus on this movie, then fine."

Imani stood on her tiptoes and kissed him slowly. "I said that for your benefit," she said when they broke their kiss. "Watching Keith and Celeste, I knew I wanted that, but I didn't want you to think that I was trying to force you into something that you weren't ready for."

"Let me tell you something. I'm never going to let you go. And you are going to be my wife."

Tears welled up in her eyes. "You don't have to say that," she replied, blinking back the tears.

Raymond stroked her cheek. "I don't say things I don't mean, especially when it comes to the woman I love." Raymond pulled Imani in his arms and kissed her with a furious passion. She held him tightly, accepting his kiss. His tongue entered her mouth, probing the crevices, branding her as his. Imani melted against him, falling deeper and deeper into his kiss. Onlookers on the busy street hollered and whistled at them as Raymond's hands roamed her back.

He broke off the kiss and stroked her cheek gently. "Let's get out of here. These people have seen enough of you and me kissing to last a lifetime."

"Yes," she said breathlessly. Desire was building between them like a campfire. They rushed back to the cab, which hadn't pulled off yet.

"Where to now?" the driver asked as they got in. "The meter is still running."

"That's a surprise," Imani said in a whisper. Raymond gave the driver his address and moments later, they were arriving at his Harlem brownstone.

Walking inside, Raymond led Imani to the sofa and pulled her skintight leggings off. Then he slipped his finger inside her barely there thong. "Can I tell you that I love your underwear?" he said as he teased her throbbing clitoris with the tip of his index finger. "First rule of our future marriage, you can never wear those horrible granny panties." He pushed the crotch of her panties to the side and replaced his finger with his lips and tongue.

Imani inhaled sharply as he licked and sucked her pleasure zone as if she were the sweetest piece of chocolate he'd ever tasted. She held the back of his head, pushing him deeper into her wetness. "Yes, yes, yes," she cried as his tongue lashed her.

He looked up at her, their eyes locking in a lustful stare. Raymond entered her with his finger as she tugged at his shirt. "How do you feel, baby?" he asked as his finger went in and out, round and round.

"G-good," she stammered as she felt an explosion spill down her thighs. Pulling out of her wetness, Raymond peeled his shirt off and tossed it across the room. Then he scooped Imani into his arms. He nearly ran into the bedroom and laid Imani in the center of the bed. He pulled her sleeveless tunic off her body and climbed into the bed beside her. He closed his mouth down on her neck, licking and kissing the spots that he knew drove her crazy. With his free hand, he unsnapped her bra and then stroked her breasts until her nipples hardened at his touch.

He placed the flat of his hand on her chest and eased down her body, yearning for another taste of her sweetness. He held her hips tightly as he slowly kissed her puckering lips, then in a swift motion, he darted his tongue between those lips. Imani shivered as he repeated the motion two times and then he sucked gently on her throbbing bud. Moaning, she arched her back and gave Raymond full access to her passion. Using his fingers and his tongue, Raymond sent ripples of pleasure throughout her body. He lapped up the sticky sweet nectar that poured from her body. "Ooh," Imani moaned as Raymond pressed his tongue deeper inside her. She clasped her thighs against his head, urging him to give her more. Raymond was more than happy to oblige and increased the intensity of his kiss, lavishing her slick bud with his tongue. She felt her climax building again, but she needed Raymond inside her—now.

"I need. You. Inside," she cried as she came all over his face.

He drew her into his arms and they connected instantly. "Anything you want, baby," Raymond said.

Imani kissed her man slowly, sucking his bottom lip as he'd done to her the night before. Her kiss sent tingles from the top of his head to the tips of his toes. Raymond lifted Imani's leg and wrapped it around his waist, tempted to drive into her wetness without even protecting them. She was his woman, was going to be his wife, but they had to be protected. Imani slipped her hand inside his underwear, gripping his manhood with a tender touch. He moaned as her hand moved up and down, fast then slow. Slower, faster, slower, faster. She nearly brought him to climax as she stroked him and ran her tongue across his lips. He needed her right now. He reached down and peeled her panties off, inserting his finger inside her to torture her as she had been doing to him. Raymond wiggled out of his underwear when it became evident that Imani wasn't going to stop stroking him.

"I need to be inside you," he moaned as they broke off their kiss.

"Protection first," she said.

Easing away from her, he opened the nightstand drawer and retrieved a condom. In a quick motion, he opened the prophylactic and slipped it in place. Turning around, he saw Imani's eyes sparkling in the darkness. She wanted him just as much as he wanted her. She propped herself up on her knees and opened her arms to him as he made his way to her. "I want you so bad," he said before bringing his lips down on her neck. She parted her thighs and thrust into him. Raymond was enveloped by her warmness immediately. She was hot, wet, and fit him like a glove. As he ground slowly against her, he wondered how long would it be before this was their everyday routine? When would Imani become his wife and share this bed with him every night? Gripping her hips, Raymond slid back so that he was lying flat and Imani was on top of him, since they'd established that this was her favorite position. He could feel her juices spilling down on him as she gyrated against him. He was in total ecstasy as she tightened her walls around him, seemingly milking his essence out of him.

"Yes, yes," Imani moaned as Raymond pumped his hips into hers and palmed her breasts and fingered her hardened nipples.

"You feel so good, so good," he said as he lifted his head to take her nipple into his mouth. She arched her back as she felt her orgasm approaching. Raymond was near climax as well and he exploded when Imani clasped her legs around his waist and reached her own release. Imani rested her head on his chest and Raymond stroked her smooth back. Neither of them said a word as they held each other.

Chapter 21

Lying in bed with Raymond and being held in his strong arms made Imani think the world had just stopped spinning and they were in their own universe where time didn't matter. A cell phone, in her opinion at that moment, was nothing but a mood killer.

"You'd better get that," Raymond whispered. "It's been going off since you started snoring."

"Excuse you?" Imani laughed. "I don't snore."

"Yes, you do, but it's cute." The phone stopped ringing.

"I still say I don't snore," she said as she pinched his arm. The phone started ringing again and Imani reluctantly pulled herself out of Raymond's arms and got up out of bed.

"Imani, how do you know if you snore or not? You were asleep."

She shook her head and giggled as she grabbed her cell phone from the living room, thinking this had better be good.

"Yes, Edward?" she asked when she answered.

"Imani Gilliam, I hope you're sitting down," he said. "No, I hope you're next to your suitcase."

"Why?"

"Because you're going to LA tomorrow and forget about doing a screen test. You got the part, if you want it, and I know you do."

"What if I didn't like it?" Imani joked.

"Then I'd have to drop you like a rotten, hot potato. I don't know what you did or how you charmed Brock, but he went back to LA shortly after our meeting and has been raving about you to anyone who will listen. And get this, I may have found you steady work in New York."

"Doing what?" she asked.

"A new night time drama, called *Atlanta Confidential*," he said. "Baby, you are about to rocket right up into the heavens and be that shining star we always knew you were."

"Wow. So, when does filming start in LA?" she asked as she watched a shirtless Raymond walk into the living room.

"Next week," he said. "You're set up at the Regency and there will be a car waiting for you when you get to LAX."

"All right."

"And, don't miss your flight. First-class tickets don't come cheap."

"Bye, Edward," she said, then hung up the phone and rushed over to Raymond and leapt into his arms.

"Whoa. What's going on?" he asked as she squealed.

Sighing, she said, "I got the role in the Will

Smith movie. Of course, it doesn't have a title yet, but filming starts next week. I'm so excited."

"So," he said when he set her on the arm of the sofa, "when are you leaving?"

She fluffed her hair and looked into his eyes, and at that moment, her excitement began to wane. "In the morning."

"That soon?"

She nodded and Raymond cupped her chin. "Imani, I'm going to miss you, but you should still be excited about this. Your big return to the big screen. It's what you've wanted and now here it is." He kissed her gently. "I'm proud of you."

"Raymond . . ."

"Shh," he said, bringing his finger to her full lips. "How much time do we have left together? I don't want to waste a second." In a quick motion, Raymond scooped Imani up in his arms and took her back into the bedroom. He laid her on the bed, happy that she was still naked. He ran his tongue across her lips as he held her hands together above her head.

"Imani," he whispered before feasting on her breasts, licking her nipples as she moaned in delight. Slowly he inched down her body, exploring her smooth skin with his tongue until he reached her wet mound of femininity.

He looked up at her and asked, "What do you want me to do? This?" He pushed her legs apart and slowly kissed her tender folds of flesh until her desire stained his face. Imani screamed in pleasure as Raymond pulled back and slipped his finger inside her. "Or do you like this?"

"Oh," she panted breathlessly as he made circles on her sensitive bud, bringing her close to climax. Raymond reached for a condom as he continued his slow torture of Imani's sensitive body. When he was sheathed, he placed her hand on his hardness. "Or," he asked, "do you want this?"

"I—I want it all," she said as she stroked him, hoping to exact some sensual punishment of her own.

"You got it, all of it," he said, then gripped her wrist as he dove into her awaiting body. Imani screamed out his name and tightened her muscles around him as he moved in and out, in and out. Imani thrashed against him, matching him stroke for stroke. He loved the way she moved, the way she fed into his passion with raw desire of her own. He loved how quickly Imani learned about sex, but more than anything else, he loved her. Loved everything about her—her beauty, her heart, and her drive. Raymond didn't want to come, wanted to keep making love to her until the sun rose, but when she tightened her thighs together around his waist and licked her full lips as she reached her own climax, he was done.

Raymond collapsed on top of her, inhaling the cinnamon scent of her sweat mixed with his and the scented candles. She shifted underneath him before they both drifted off to sleep. Raymond didn't need to dream anymore; his number one fantasy was lying in his arms.

It was around three in the morning when Imani and Raymond realized two things—they were starved and she needed to pack and check on her flight arrangements. Still, as they lay across the bed facing the window, neither of them made a move as they watched the twinkling lights of the city.

"How do you sleep in here every night?" she asked. "I would just stare out of the window all night."

"I used to do that," Raymond replied, looking down at her. "But now, I have something better to look at."

Imani rolled over on her back and posed like Venus De Milo. "Just what would that be?"

"Oh, you know exactly what I'm talking about." Raymond drew Imani into his arms and brushed his lips across hers before devouring them in a hot kiss that made her shudder. Pulling back from her, he smiled. "I could look at you all night. But, you have a flight to catch in a few hours."

"I know," she said. "And I haven't packed a thing."

"Then it's time to go to Brooklyn."

"Yes," she replied. "But before we go, I need you to do me a favor." Imani stroked his hardness, working the length of his erection. Raymond inhaled sharply as her hand moved up and down.

"Ooh, anything baby," he moaned.

"Give me something to dream about on the plane." He spread her thighs apart, rubbing the tip of his hardness against her wetness. She wrapped her legs around his waist, drawing him into her wet valley. For a moment, neither of them thought about a condom as they melted—flesh to flesh—together. Imani had never felt such raw passion as every inch of Raymond filled her. She ground against him, rotating her hips and digging her nails into his shoulder as she exploded and her desire spilled down her thighs. Raymond quickly pulled out, though he wanted to remain buried in her hot body until he climaxed as she just had.

"Damn," he said. "I think I'm going to have those same dreams while you're on the plane."

The aftershocks of her intense orgasm left Imani speechless. He kissed her neck slowly and gently. "Mmm, ooh, stop," she exclaimed. "You're making it so hard for me to get out of this bed."

"I know, but we have to get up. You have a movie to make," he said supportively.

After a few more moments of just lying in bed, Imani and Raymond finally got up and dressed. Before heading to Imani's, they made a stop at Gray's Papaya for hot dogs.

"I'm going to make this a tradition," she said as she squeezed mustard on her frank.

"Packing late and rushing to the airport?" Raymond asked.

She smacked him on the shoulder playfully. "No, silly. Eating hot dogs before I go off to film a movie. Now, if it flops, then I'll have to come up with a new tradition."

"I think we have a great tradition," he said as he wrapped his arms around her waist. "Maybe when you get back from LA we should make it permanent," he said, then swiped a bite of Imani's hot dog.

"What do you mean?" she asked, nearly dropping her food.

Raymond grabbed her hand and saved her meal. "Just what I said. But right now, we need to get a cab and get you to Brooklyn before the sun comes up and you miss that flight."

"Wait, what do you mean by permanent? Moving in together? Marriage?"

"Yes," he said as he hailed a cab.

Imani tossed her half-eaten hot dog at the side of his head. "Yes to what?"

Raymond laughed as he wiped mustard from his ear with the edge of his shirt. "So violent," he joked. "Imani, we can talk about it when you wrap filming in Los Angeles and then we will see what our future holds. Brooklyn or Harlem. I'm really leaning toward Harlem."

Before Imani could reply, a cab pulled up to the curb and they were whisked off to Imani's home. All she could think about was returning to New York and becoming Mrs. Raymond Thomas and then winning her first Academy Award.

Three Months Later

Imani stared deep into Will Smith's eyes as he held her tightly against his chest. They floated upward on a hot air balloon and in a swift motion, he untied her skirt and it fell to the ground.

"You know I'm going to make you pay for that," she growled. "That was Prada."

"Baby," Will said, "you know I like to see you in nada!" Then he captured her lips and kissed her.

"And cut!" the director yelled. "That's a wrap, people!"

The cast and the crew of *Something Like the Wind* exploded in applause.

Imani and Will shook hands. "It was great working with you, Imani," he said before leaping off the platform and joining his wife and kids near the crafts table. Imani smiled as she slowly stepped off the platform herself.

Over the last three months, things couldn't have gone better professionally for her. She'd gained the respect of the cast and crew of *Something Like the Wind*, because she'd carried herself as a professional—showing up to the set early, going over her lines and treating everyone from the boom operator to Will Smith with the same respect. Damon Cartier, the film's director, had sung her praises in every interview he'd done about the movie, which was set to be released in the summer, as Will Smith didn't lose in summer blockbuster battles. Imani hoped that the movie would live up to the hype and the critics who'd called her "Flop Diva," would eat their words.

But at night when she returned to her hotel, she'd yearned for Raymond's touch and his kiss. Though they'd talk on the phone, with her waking him up in the middle of the night because of the time difference, she couldn't wait until she was back in his arms.

"Miss Imani," Damon said as she was leaving the set, "are you heading to the airport?"

"Unless you need me," she said, but silently prayed that he didn't. She'd been lucky enough to get an earlier flight.

He handed her a check and she furrowed her brow. "What's this?"

"It's for the clinic in Harlem you and Lloyd, the boom operator, were talking about. When you were on your break yesterday, I was going to ask you a question and I overheard you two talking. Marion G. Palmer, right?"

Imani nodded. "Thank you so much."

"My grandmother lived in the Bronx and hated going to the doctor, but if your boyfriend has a bunch of old women coming to his defense the way you described, then he is doing something right. It's not much, but I hope it helps."

Imani read the amount—$50,000—and nearly passed out, but she played it cool. "This will help Raymond and Keith a lot. Thank you, Damon."

"And I didn't make this donation so you will do the sequel, but please tell me you're thinking about it."

"Yes," she said. "I'd love to. She was a great character."

"The next movie is going to be filmed in New York, so . . ."

"Then I am definitely going to do it! I have to get out of here, but thank you for taking a chance on me."

Damon shrugged. "Thank you for being great."

When Imani finally arrived at her hotel, all she had to do was grab her bags. She could not wait to get back to New York.

* * *

Raymond read over Cortina Richardson's test results and smiled. Her cholesterol was down, her blood sugar seemed to be in control, and she'd dropped fifteen pounds. He loved it when his patients listened to him. As he closed the file, he looked at the calendar on the wall. Imani was returning today. The last three months had been hell on earth without her. Phone calls and Skype were not enough to quell his thirst for his woman. He needed her in his arms, in his bed, and more importantly, as his lawfully wedded wife.

"Raymond," Keith said when he popped his head into the office. "There's a woman out here to see you. What's up with that?"

"Just send her back," Raymond said.

"She's not Imani, and I know damned well—"

"Keith! Send her back. We have an appointment."

Scowling at his friend, Keith headed out front, then returned with the tall, buxom blond woman. She smiled at Keith and then turned to Raymond.

"It is good to finally meet you, Dr. Thomas," she purred. Raymond locked eyes with Keith, who was leaning against the wall in a stance that said he had no intention of leaving. Raymond laughed, figuring that his friend must have thought he'd lost his mind.

"Helen Jameson," Raymond said, "I'd like you to meet my business partner, Dr. Keith Jacobs. Keith, this is Helen, my jeweler.

"Oh," Keith said as he shook Helen's hand vigorously. "I'm sorry about the third degree I gave you out there."

She snatched her hand away from him and

offered him a plastic smile. "It's all right. Are you married?"

"Engaged. Why?"

She handed him her card. "I just get the feeling that at some point you're going to need to buy an apology piece for your future wife. My prices are pretty reasonable, but you might have to buy from the back row."

"That's funny," he said, but took the card anyway.

"Now," Raymond said, "can we get some privacy?"

"Sure," Keith said as he walked away.

Raymond laughed at his friend as he turned his full attention to Helen. She'd come highly recommended from Mrs. Wentworth, who'd told Raymond that Imani was not an off the rack kind of girl and he needed to show up at the airport with a special engagement ring for her.

"All right, Raymond," Helen said as she sat across from his desk and set her briefcase on top of it. "I have some custom pieces that I think you and your future bride will love." She opened the case and turned it toward Raymond, showing him a display of diamond engagement rings. "These rings are very rare and unique. This one," she said as she pointed to a three-carat princess cut platinum ring, "was made for one of J.Lo's engagements. She never got the ring because she and a certain mogul were involved in a shooting."

Raymond shook his head. "I don't want that one. I want something that . . ." He stopped talking when a sparkling gem caught his eye. It was a marquis cut diamond and emerald white-gold ring. It was odd, not your typical engagement ring. His eyes were riveted to it. It was perfect. It was Imani. Raymond reached for the ring. "This is what I want."

The woman smiled and took the ring out of the case. "Ahh, you have great taste. This ring was designed with Dorothy Dandridge in mind. You're fiancée is an actress, right?"

"She is, but more than anything else, she's just as unique as this ring," he said as he lifted it from the case. "What if I need to get it sized?"

"I can take care of that as well," she replied.

He held the ring up to the light; it sparkled like a thousand stars. Was he really ready to take this step? *Yes, I'm ready,* he told himself. He had never met anyone like Imani, a woman who supported him and the choices he made concerning his career. She supported him like no other woman ever had. She was the one. This was his destiny. He handed the ring back to the woman. "I want this one," he said decisively.

The woman pulled her card out of the side of the case and handed it to Raymond. "Just in case you have to call me again to have it sized," she said.

"All right," he said as he pulled out his wallet. "How much?"

"Twenty-five hundred," she said as she put the ring in a velvet box. "Cash or credit?"

Raymond pulled out his credit card and handed it to Helen. She produced a handheld credit card machine and ran the card through it. After receiving confirmation that the card was approved, Helen handed Raymond the box. "Good luck," she said as she turned to leave the break room. When she opened the door, Keith was standing there, holding a chart and trying to pretend he hadn't been eavesdropping on their conversation.

Helen shook her head. "Make sure you call me. Your fiancée is going to need a lot of jewelry," Helen said, then flounced down the hall and out the door.

Keith turned to Raymond, who was trying to hide the ring he had just purchased, but Keith grabbed the ring. "Now, you were in Hawaii when I went out to get Celeste's ring. I get to critique your taste," he said as he opened the box. "Damn!"

"Give me that," Raymond said as he took the ring back. "You're nosy as hell. What do you think, though?"

Keith rolled his eyes. "You know you just messed me up, right? When Celeste sees this, I'm going to be in a world of trouble. I guess it is a good thing that your jeweler did give me this card. When does your superstar fiancée get back into town?"

Raymond snapped the ring box shut and looked down at his watch. "I'd better get going. Her flight should be here in an hour."

"Raymond," Keith called after his friend as he dashed out the door. He'd forgotten to tell him that Elize from the network had called for him. Just as he was about to head out the door to grab Raymond before he got into a cab, Karen and Maria stopped him with two files he needed to look over.

Chapter 22

Imani had never been so happy to get off a plane. The trip from Los Angeles seemed to take thirty hours rather than five. She had been jolted awake when she heard the pilot announce that they were about to make their descent into New York's JFK Airport.

"The weather is clear in the Big Apple," he'd said over the public address system. "It's a brisk forty-five degrees and sunny."

Imani had sat upright in her seat and looked out the window. She couldn't help but smile happily as she saw the Statue of Liberty. "Home sweet home," Imani had whispered.

Her seatmate had cast an amused look at Imani. "You live in New York. Poor thing," the older lady said.

"I wouldn't want to live anyplace else," Imani replied.

"If I was young, I guess I'd feel the same way," she said. "But I'm just coming to visit my daughter. She goes to NYU and has some crazy idea about being an actress. I hope I can talk some sense into her," the woman said.

"Someone tried that with me once," Imani said.

"What happened?"

Smiling, she said, "I just finished filming with Will Smith."

"Whoa. I've been sitting beside a superstar and didn't even know it?" As the plane had bounced down on the landing strip, the woman had asked Imani for her autograph. Grabbing an in-flight magazine, Imani signed it for the lady: *Let your daughter make her own choices. She might surprise you and make a success of this acting thing. Imani Gilliam.*

Once Imani was off the plane, she rushed through the gate like O. J. Simpson in those old school Hertz commercials. When she saw Raymond standing near the baggage claim, she thought she was seeing a mirage. She hadn't told him that she was taking an earlier flight in.

"Are you just going to stand there, woman, or do I get some love?" he asked as he crossed over to her. Imani leapt into his arms and kissed him so slowly and deeply that his knees shook.

"Damn, I missed you," she said when they broke the kiss. "Three months was too long to be away from you."

"You're telling me."

"I'm glad you're here, but how did you know I was taking an earlier flight?" she asked.

"Call me Mr. Anxious," he quipped. "I left the clinic early and traffic was light on the way over here. I had no idea you'd be early, so it must be fate."

"Well," she said, "let's get these bags and get out of here, because I have a surprise for you."

"Really? I have one for you too."

Imani tilted her head to the side. "Can I have it now?" she asked.

"Absolutely not. Where do you want to go, Brooklyn, since I know you love that place, or uptown?"

"I want to be wherever you are," she said as her cell phone chimed. "Damn it," Imani muttered as she reached into her carry-on bag and fished out her phone. "Hello, Edward."

"I have some news that is going to knock your socks off," he said.

"Really?" she said, looking at Raymond and thinking of another way she wanted her socks knocked off.

"You've been cast for the show and after the glowing reviews Damon gave you, Gina can't wait to meet you. Kid, you're about to blow up."

"Wow," Imani said. "This is amazing."

"Are you ready for this?" Edward asked. "You've wanted to do a show on Broadway and now you have your chance. John Guare wants you in *A Free Man of Color.*"

"Are you serious?!" she shrieked. "Oh my God."

Raymond stopped in his tracks as he picked up Imani's bag. Turning to her, he mouthed, "What?"

"Why don't we get together tomorrow and talk about this?" Edward said. "I'm sure your man is at the airport waiting for you."

"He is and I can't wait to talk about this with you." Imani hung up the phone and jumped up and down as if she won the lottery.

"Okay, what's going on?" Raymond asked.

"Edward told me that I have a chance to finally star in a show on Broadway. Oh my God, that's one of my biggest dreams."

"One?"

"Yes. I have another one that I believe will come true as soon as we get out of here."

"That sounds good. Let's get out of here." Imani and Raymond rushed out to their awaiting cab and headed to Harlem.

"I was trying to wait for the perfect time to give you this," she said as she reached into her purse, "but I can't wait." Imani held out the check Damon had donated to the clinic.

"What's this?" He looked down at the amount of the check and let out a low whistle. "Oh my God."

"While I was in LA, when I wasn't running lines, I was talking about you and the clinic. Damon, the director, heard me and Lloyd, one of the crew members talking about you, New York, and the clinic. He was impressed and wanted to help—without getting his name in the papers."

"Well, you tell Damon thank you. This is going to help us get that MRI machine that we've needed for a long time," he said, then kissed Imani's cheek. "And that was amazing of you to go to Los Angeles and tell your colleagues about the clinic when you could've been gallivanting around Hollywood letting Paris Hilton write about you."

"You mean Perez Hilton," she said with a laugh. "You're going to have to get these gossip bloggers down. If this movie does as well as everyone expects, then—"

"I don't give a damn about a gossip blogger. I know what's real," he said as he cupped her face in his hands and kissed her—long and slow—until she moaned in pleasure. Imani had dreamed of this moment for three months. Kissing for real, tasting the sweetness of Raymond's mouth mixed in with the flavor of spearmint gum. His hands roamed her back, heating her up like a summer day. She wanted him, wanted to make love to her man as she slipped her arms around his waist and pulled him closer to her.

"Umm," he said as they broke their kiss. "I've been waiting for a kiss like that for the last ninety days."

"Me too," she said, then licked her lips. "When we get home, I'm going to show you what else I've been waiting for these past ninety days."

Raymond tapped the driver's seat. "Can you move this thing any faster?"

"Traffic," the man said, glancing back at Imani and Raymond. "Hey! You're the couple from TV. Why did you guys leave the show? That bitch who won, she was so annoying."

Imani and Raymond glanced at each other. "We didn't even watch the show after we left. Who won?" Imani asked.

"Some chick named Lucy and the fat dude who looked like the Penguin from those Batman shows. They won't be together long. I'm guessing they got married for the money. They were pretty funny on the reunion show pretending to be in love. That girl needs some acting lessons."

Raymond and Imani burst into laughter. "But," the taxi driver said as he turned down a side road, "I knew you two were real, even if she is an actress."

"Well, thank you," Imani said. When Raymond recognized the block where they were, he peeled off the cab fare and a hefty tip, then told the driver he and Imani could walk to his place.

"Are you sure? It looks like you have quite a few bags," he said.

"We're good, thanks, bud," Raymond said as they hopped out of the car and he hoisted her luggage out of the trunk when the driver popped it open.

Imani looked down at her feet, happy that she'd worn sensible shoes. Dana would be so proud, she thought as she reached for one of her bags. "So, are we walking so that we can get a wonderful hot dog from a street vendor?" Imani asked.

"Nope. We're walking because we're a half block from my place and I couldn't wait another second to get you in my arms." They half ran to Raymond's brownstone. Once they made it inside, they tossed Imani's luggage in the living room and wrapped up in each other's arms, clawing at each other's clothes. Imani ripped his Oxford shirt open, sending buttons flying across the room, as he reached underneath her skirt and tore her panties off, then turned her skirt upward. He lifted her into his arms and she wrapped her legs around his waist as he crossed into the bedroom. They tumbled onto the bed and Raymond kicked out of his pants as Imani kissed and sucked his bottom lip.

Damn, it felt good having her in his arms. Felt good to feel her heat against his cold sheets. He slipped his hand between her thighs, relishing in the sweetness flowing from her body. He stroked her until she screamed from the first sign of an orgasm, then he hungrily kissed her as his erection grew against her supple thighs. Darting his tongue in and out of her mouth, he savored her taste and teased her lips. Imani pressed her body against his, urging him to enter her awaiting valley.

"Love me," she begged. "Need you inside me."

"I need to be inside you. Need to feel you. I missed you." Raymond parted her wet folds of flesh with his finger and teased her clitoris until he felt her get wetter and wetter. Imani grabbed his penis, rubbing him fast as she felt an explosion building in the pit of her stomach.

Raymond tenderly pressed into her awaiting body. She moaned as Raymond buried himself in her G-spot. Raymond knew her body almost as well as he knew his. He knew when he pressed deep into her, she would dig her nails into his back. He knew when he slowly ground against her, Imani's legs would shake and she would quiver with delight.

Watching her reactions turned him on, made him do more to make her come, to leave her satisfied. He got his pleasure from pleasing her, from making her call his name and rain her love down on him.

When she rolled her hips, moving to position herself on top of him, Raymond let go to allow her to take control of his body, to give him what he wanted more than anything else—the chance to watch her explode. She placed her palms on his chest and bounced up and down in the throes of passion as she gyrated against him. He alternated kissing each of her breasts, licking and sucking on her nipples as she leaned forward. Raymond could feel an explosion growing in his shaft as Imani rolled her body across his. He grabbed her waist as he began to climax, slowing her down and relishing in the river flowing from her body. Raymond groaned like a wounded animal as Imani collapsed against his chest. He buried his face between her neck and shoulder as she wrapped her arms around his neck. "We should stay like this forever," he whispered in her ear. "But if we do, I can't give you your surprise."

"Umm, there's more?"

"Oh, yes," he said as they shifted positions so that they were lying face to face. Imani leaned in and kissed him softly.

"I love you so much," she whispered.

"Hold that thought," he said as he leapt from the bed.

Imani pouted like a child who had her toys taken away. "Where are you going?" she called out to his retreating figure. Raymond rushed into the living room and picked up his discarded jacket. He grabbed the ring box and then returned to the bedroom with his hands behind his back.

"I have a question for you. Well, two actually."

She tilted her head to the side, confused by his stance and the fact that he'd gotten out of bed when she fully expected that they'd fall asleep wrapped in each other's arms.

"Really?" she asked.

"Work with me, babe," he said as he crossed over to her side of the bed.

"All right, go ahead."

"What are the best-dressed actresses wearing in Hollywood on the red carpet these days?"

"That's an odd question," she said. "But I'm going to go with the guy who designed Michelle Obama's inauguration gown."

"Then, you're going to outshine them all if you wear this," he said as he pulled the box from behind his back and opened it. Imani's eyes stretched to the size of quarters. She brought her hands to her mouth as tears spilled from her eyes. "Is that . . . ?"

"Here's the second question," he said. "Imani, will you marry me?"

"Yes," she cried. "Yes, I will marry you."

Raymond took the ring from the box and slid it on Imani's finger. To his surprise, it was a perfect fit.

"Beautiful," he said, then kissed her hand. "I was told that this was designed for a famous actress and now one is wearing it."

Imani threw her arms around Raymond's neck and hugged him tightly. "You know what?" she said. "I never thought that I would ever meet a man like you and fall in love. You're the only leading man that I will ever need in my life and that's no act."

"I know, baby. Before I met you on that island, I really thought that I'd spend the rest of my life surrounded by little old ladies trying to set me up with their granddaughters, and then you burst into my life and turned everything upside down. I'm glad the clinic nearly went broke, because otherwise, I'd still be missing the best part of me."

As the tears poured down Imani's cheeks, she realized for the first time in her life that tears of joy were real.

Chapter 23

The next morning, Imani awoke before Raymond and stared at the ring on her left hand. It was beyond beautiful and she was over the moon with happiness. As she lay in the bed in the silence of the morning, she greeted that silence with a smile because all of the doubts that had been in her head before were gone. Raymond was the right man for her and if she was going to be the right woman for him, she could at least get up and fix that man some coffee. She attempted to slip out of bed, but Raymond tightened his grip around her waist.

"Woman, don't you get out of this bed," he growled.

"All I'm trying to do is practice being the good wife," she said. "I was going to make you coffee and get you a bagel."

"I know a better way you can practice being a good wife," he quipped.

"Didn't we get enough practice doing that last night?" she retorted.

Raymond nodded, then kissed her neck. "But

you know what they say—practice makes perfect. Although, we do have busy days today, don't we?"

Imani sighed. "Yes. I have to go meet with Edward and of course, if I don't tell Dana that I'm back in New York and about to marry the man of my dreams, I think she will write that tell-all book she's been threatening me with for years."

"Just what would she have to tell?" Raymond asked.

Imani yawned and smiled. "How I used to stalk Broadway directors, how I never leave the house without being camera-ready, and how I was a diva without a dime."

Raymond laughed. "I think I'd like to read that book. So, you and Dana came into this industry together?"

"Yes. She was smart, decided to do something that would give her a career right away. She has to take our wedding pictures."

"Of course."

"And I can actually pay her for her services for a change. She's going to be so happy."

Raymond laughed again and unwillingly got out of the bed. "I have a few midmorning patients and Keith still isn't one-hundred percent. But meet me for lunch if your schedule will allow it. I have to introduce my fiancée to the staff."

"I've met your staff."

"But you weren't my fiancée then," he said, winking at her as he headed for the bathroom.

While he showered, Imani headed for the kitchen and made a pot of coffee while she called Dana.

"Hello, superstar," Dana said happily. "I meant to go to your place and drop off all the press I've been collecting about you since you've been gone. Are you at home?"

"You could say that. I'm at Raymond's."

"I love you two as a couple," Dana said. "When will I be taking wedding pictures? It's obvious that he's going to pop the question soon."

Imani tried not to give anything away over the phone, but her silence told her oldest friend that the question had already been asked and answered. "My God, Imani. He proposed already, didn't he?"

"Yes!" Imani said, not hiding her excitement. "Last night, and I cried like a baby. I love him so much."

"I know you do and he's a great guy. Nothing like the asshole actors you used to date. Now I can ask you this; have you . . ."

"Many, many times."

"We must get together and dish. Because I have big news too."

"Tell me."

"When we see each other," she said.

Raymond walked into the kitchen, his blue button-down shirt open and his belt unbuckled. "That coffee smells good," he said.

"Are you pretending to be domesticated?" Dana asked. "Good thing you have the ring already. Call me when you get a chance."

"Just meet me at Edward's office. I have to meet with him this morning. Then you can share your news."

"See you there. Tell Raymond congratulations."

Imani hung up the phone and turned to her fiancé. "Dana says you're the luckiest man in the world," Imani quipped.

"Don't I know it," he said as he filled his travel mug with coffee. "I don't want to leave you this morning."

Imani crossed over to him and stroked his cheek. "I feel the same way. But we have the rest of our lives to spend as many mornings as we want together."

"That's why I'm marrying you, I love the way you think." Raymond gently kissed her and Imani buttoned his shirt.

"I think I could get used to this domestic thing," she said as she watched Raymond take a sip of his coffee.

"We're going to have to work on that," he said as he struggled to swallow his coffee. "If I finish that, I won't sleep for a month."

"Too strong?"

He held his thumb and forefinger inches from each other. "Just a little. I'll see you at lunch," he said, then swiped another kiss from her.

After Raymond left, Imani shut the coffee pot off, took a shower, dressed, and headed into Manhattan to meet with Edward and Dana. Once again, when she stepped out the front door, she was camera-ready in her black leather corset dress, cropped pink leather jacket, and black leather booties. And for a change, Imani didn't take the subway; she walked to the curb and hailed a cab. Three stopped for her at once and she couldn't help but smile as she climbed into the one she was closest to.

"Where are you going, beautiful?" the driver asked. "Come home with me and the trip is free."

"I don't think my fiancé would like that."

"He's no good," the driver said. "Dump him."

Imani laughed and gave him the address to Edward's office. For a change, her cab ride wasn't horrible. Traffic wasn't at a standstill and the driver seemed to know how to get around the city through back streets and side roads. When they arrived at Edward's office, Imani was happy to pay the fare and give the man a generous tip.

"If you want to leave that loser, remember old Rafe is waiting for you," he said, then blew her a kiss. Imani returned the gesture and headed inside.

In the middle of a phone call, Edward motioned for her to sit down as she walked in. "Great," he said. "I look forward to it. Thanks." He hung up the phone and looked at Imani with a huge smile on his face. "All it took was a little success to get you to start being on time, huh?" he quipped.

"That and I need my evening free," she said. Imani held up her left hand and wiggled it. "I have a wedding to plan."

"Wait a minute, when did this happen?" he asked. "You two have to go on the morning shows and tell the world about this engagement."

"Hold up," Imani said vehemently. "My private life is private and I'm not using my engagement as publicity."

Edward leaned back in his chair. "Unless Will

Smith gave you that ring and you broke up one of Hollywood's happiest couples, everyone wants to know about your marriage plans and your movie coming out as well as the upcoming Broadway show."

Imani shook her head furiously. "If Raymond was an actor, then maybe that would be all right, but I did the reality show to get a jump start in my career. My private life is officially private."

Edward threw his hands up. "All right, I can respect that and I won't call Elize back."

"Please tell me that's not who you were talking to," Imani groaned.

"Yes, I was talking to her because WAPC wants you to do a guest appearance on their top-rated soap opera, which will air before your movie premieres."

"Really?"

Edward nodded. "And if you show up on set sporting that rock, she's going to know you and the good doctor are getting married and she's going to try and get you two to talk about it. Your private life is over; you're a star now."

Imani was about to respond when Dana walked in. "What's going on, people?" she said as she crossed over to Imani and hugged her.

"Your friend is learning a quick lesson about fame," Edward said.

Imani frowned and shook her head. "Is it too much to ask to keep some aspects of my life private?"

Dana shrugged. "I've been getting calls about you this morning. The press thinks something is going on and I think it has something to do with your PDA at the airport yesterday." She handed Imani a copy of the *New York Post*. Right there on Page Six was a picture of Imani and Raymond kissing at the baggage terminal of JFK. The headline read, REALITY SHOW COUPLE GOING STRONG.

"Great," she said as she tossed the paper on Edward's desk. "I have to go talk to Raymond."

"I'm going with you," Dana said. "That way I can help you spot the paps. I knew this day was coming."

"What do you mean?" Imani asked as she rose to her feet.

"Welcome to stardom," Dana said. "Where there is a stalking photographer around every corner. At least your best friend isn't one of them." The three of them laughed as Imani and Dana headed out the door.

The clinic was once again abuzz with reporters and photographers. Keith shook his head as Maria and Karen booted another set of reporters out of the clinic, threatening to give them all flu shots with extremely sharp needles if they came back. Keith headed to the break room where Raymond had been hiding out and reading over patient charts.

"Coast is clear, buddy," he said. "Page Six. You're going about this the wrong way."

Raymond looked up at his friend and scowled. "As much as I want to be mad at you for getting the ball rolling on this, I can't be, since I would've never met Imani without that damned show. But this is too much. I can't kiss my fiancée in public without this media frenzy."

"And, the producer from the show called yesterday," Keith said.

Raymond groaned and dropped his head on the table, and then he sat up quickly. "There is good news today," he said as he reached into his pocket and handed Keith the check Imani had given him before he left the house. "We can buy the MRI machine that we need."

"Wow. How did she swing this?"

Raymond shrugged. "Her director thinks we're a worthy cause."

"Thank you, Imani," Keith said as he kissed the check. "So, when's the wedding?"

"A better question is how are we going to get married without the whole world and those damned blogs watching our every move? When are you and Celeste tying the knot? You can't keep milking the 'I'm in therapy angle'," he said.

"December thirty-first," Keith said with a slow smile. "What better way to put this year of ups and downs behind us than to step into the new year as husband and wife?"

Raymond nodded. "That is so sweet. Celeste told you to say that, didn't she?" Keith and Raymond laughed.

"But it's the truth. Look at this place. We thought we were going to have to close. Thought we were going to let Mrs. Palmer down, and now we're finally in the black," Keith said. "So what if we have to kick some photographers and reporters out because you can't keep your hands off your fiancée."

"You just gave me a great idea," Raymond said as he reached for his cell phone.

Keith shot him a confused look and shrugged his shoulders. "I'm a genius and didn't even know it."

"Edward Funderburke."

"Mr. Funderburke, this is Raymond Thomas."

"Hey, congratulations. Imani left here with a smile on her face and a sparkling rock on her finger. She's happy."

"And I want to keep her that way. I know her career is important to her and I fully support her on that," he said. "But I want our wedding to be about us."

"She said the same thing when she was here. I have an idea that may work."

"What's that?"

"Have you two set a date?"

"Not yet," Raymond replied.

"When you do, let me know and we will coordinate the plans."

"You mean plan my wedding around her film projects?" Raymond quipped.

"Well, yes. But I also know how you two want to keep your nuptials out of the media spotlight."

Raymond looked up and saw Imani standing in the doorway of the break room. She waved at him and smiled.

"I have to go, but we will talk about this later," he told Edward.

"I guess Imani is there? We'll get the details worked out."

"All right." Raymond hung up the phone and crossed over to Imani. Pulling her into his arms, he kissed her cheek. "Is it still crazy out there?"

"You mean all of the photographers and reporters asking if it's true that you proposed to me? Yes. Dana's out front telling them she has exclusive photo rights." Imani smiled and leaned her head against his chest. "This was never a part of my dreams of fame."

"So, what are we going to do?" he asked as he brushed her hair off her forehead.

"I know what we're not going to do. We're not turning our upcoming wedding into a feeding frenzy," she said angrily. "I think we should elope tomorrow."

"No," he said. "We're only doing this once and it's going to be special."

Later that evening, when Raymond walked into his house, greeted by the smell of jasmine and lavender. He dropped his bag in the foyer. The lights were low inside the living room and candles flickered in the distance. "Imani," he called out.

"In the kitchen. But I want you to have a seat in the living room," she commanded. Raymond took his jacket off and draped it on the arm of the sofa.

"Yes, ma'am," he said.

A few seconds later, Imani walked into the living room, dressed in an ivory lace and satin teddy with a matching garter belt and thigh-high stockings.

She carried a tray of raw oysters on the half shell, shrimp cocktail, chocolate-covered strawberries, and a chilled bottle of white wine.

Raymond couldn't take his eyes off Imani's body. The food didn't matter. His feast was setting the tray on his oak coffee table. "Wow," he said as she walked over to him with an oyster in her hand.

"Don't talk, I need you to eat. You're going to need your strength," she said as she placed the shell to his lips. Raymond took the succulent meat into his mouth, then pulled Imani against his chest.

He smacked his lips and looked into her eyes. "There's something I want a little more than an oyster," he said before covering her lips with his.

Imani pushed back from him. "Slow down," she said. "I have something I have to tell you." Imani sat down beside him and held his hand.

"I don't know if I'm going to be able to concentrate," he said as he lustfully eyed her.

"Focus," she said as she squeezed his hand. "Listen, I have the role of a lifetime. David Hershon's new film, *Watch Over Me*, is going to start filming in two weeks. Guess who has the lead?"

Raymond pulled Imani in his arms and kissed her face repeatedly. "I'm so proud of you. This is what you wanted."

She nodded, then bit her bottom lip. "The movie is going to be filmed in LA for the next six months," Imani said somberly.

Raymond loosened his embrace. "Six months? Whoa. I, um, that's a long time." He started thinking about the plans for the wedding. He couldn't tell her that he wanted to whisk her away to Jamaica and get married now.

"I know, but I have to do this," she said. "This will definitely make up for *Fearless Diva*."

Raymond looked at the excitement in her eyes. He was thrilled for her. Imani had told him how she'd struggled to make it as an actress, and when they first met how she was nearly kicked out of her apartment. Raymond wanted to take care of her and make sure that she never faced those kinds of situations again. But he also knew Imani had every right to bask in the glow of her success. While she gushed about the movie, Raymond swelled with pride. His fiancée was going to live her dream. "I'm talking too much, right?" she asked.

"No," he said as he stroked her cheek. "I'm going to miss you."

She leaned against his shoulder and wrapped her arms around his waist. "You can come visit me on the set. And just think, when we walk down the red carpet at the premiere, everyone is going to know what we have is real." Raymond kissed Imani's left hand and glanced at her engagement ring. "I don't think anyone will be looking at me," he said as he leaned over and picked up a piece of fruit. "I see you in some hot designer number with all the photographers snapping your picture."

"Please," she quipped, "you're going to be the hottest arm candy ever. They might forget about me." Raymond bit into the strawberry, then placed it to her lips. She bit into the berry. "Then," he said, "I guess we're going to be the heat of Hollywood."

"I love you so much," she said. "Thanks for supporting me."

"How could I not?" Raymond kissed her lips gently at first, but she turned up the intensity on the kiss, slinking her tongue in his mouth, pulling his tongue into her mouth. Imani climbed on top of him, wrapping her legs around him. Raymond felt heat radiating from Imani's center. He placed his hands between her legs and discovered that her outfit was crotchless. He slid his finger in the valley of her womanly mound, causing her to moan in delight. Raymond loved the feel of Imani. She was hot, soft, and moist. Her body seemed to be tailored to fit his. He knew where to touch to make her smile, make her scream, make her melt in his arms. He was going to that spot with his finger, wiggling it inside her. Imani clutched his shoulders as Raymond seemed to brand his initials inside her with his finger. With his other hand, Raymond fondled her breasts as they spilled out of her skimpy outfit.

Food was forgotten. The only thing that mattered was the aching in the pit of his stomach. Imani reached down and unbuttoned his pants, finding his manhood was poised and ready to burst out of his boxers. Raymond continued stroking her G-spot, making her shiver. He removed his finger as he felt her legs beginning to shake. He scooped her up in his arms and stood up. If he didn't feel her around him, he was going to explode. He needed her, longed for her, and ached for her. Imani rested her head against his shoulder and kissed his neck, setting him on fire.

Raymond couldn't make it to the bedroom fast enough with her tongue gliding up and down the side of his neck.

Once inside the darkened bedroom, Raymond laid Imani on the bed. He drank in her image. This was going to be what he woke up to every morning and what he fell asleep with in his arms every night. He licked his lips as he joined her on the bed. He spread her legs apart, kissing her inner thighs. Raymond headed for Imani's sweet nectar. He lapped up her delectable juices, sliding his tongue across her most sensitive spot. Imani moaned in delight as Raymond lashed her with his tongue and squeezed her breasts gently. Her nipples perked as his fingers grazed the tips of them. Raymond turned his kiss to her flat stomach. He couldn't wait until it was swollen with his child; their first son, maybe a daughter, but she would have to look like her mother. Imani wrapped her legs around Raymond as if she was urging and inviting him into her essence. Raymond kicked out of his boxers, pressing his hot, bulging manhood against Imani's thighs. He looked deep into her dark eyes. "I love you," he said. "More than I thought I could ever love anyone."

She gently stroked his cheek. "I love you too," she replied in a throaty whisper.

The phone rang before Raymond could say anything. He reached over to his nightstand and picked it up on the fourth ring.

"Hello?"

"Dr. Thomas?"

"Who is this?"

"This is Elize Harrington from APC Network. How are you?"

"I'm just fine," Raymond said as he wrinkled his nose. What did the network want? "What can I help you with?"

"I understand that congratulations are in order. You and Imani are getting married, right?"

I'm going to kill Keith, he thought before saying yes.

"Well, I would love to meet with you two and maybe discuss you getting married on our morning show."

"I don't know if that is such a great idea," he said. "Imani and I are happy in our private lives."

"We will pay for the entire wedding," Elize said. "And it is totally up to you how the wedding proceeds."

Imani was listening to the conversation now. "Just think about it before you say no," Elize continued.

Raymond looked at Imani and shrugged his shoulders. "I'll run it by Imani." Raymond hung up the phone and turned to his future bride.

"Who was that?" she asked.

"Elize Harrington. She found out about our engagement and she wants us to get married on *Wake Up, New York.*"

"How in the world did the network find out about us?" Imani asked as she swung her feet over the side of the bed.

Raymond raised his eyebrow. "Keith. He can't hold water. I should have known better than to let him see me with this ring."

"Well," Imani said as she fingered her hair, "it could be fun. The world saw us fall in love, why not let them watch us get married?" She walked over to him as he stood up and wrapped her arms around his waist. "And you can make the studio donate a big hunk of change to the clinic."

Raymond turned around and kissed Imani gently on the lips. "I like the way you think, lovely," he said.

"We should just run away to an island and get married without anyone watching," she said with a far-off look in her eyes.

"Mmm, what island would you choose," he asked, thinking of his plan to take her away for their wedding.

Imani shrugged. "Hawaii would be expected. But I love the sound of the ocean, almost as much as I love you."

"Do you want to sneak out of here and go eat some slices?" he asked.

"I'd love to," she said. "Let me call Dana. We were supposed to get together for a photo shoot, but I'm not really feeling it today." Imani reached for her cell phone and dialed Dana's number.

"Hello," Dana said when she answered.

"Hey, girl," Imani said as Raymond nuzzled her neck. "Would you hate me if I told you I wanted to reschedule the photo shoot?"

"Umm, diva behavior already," she quipped. "No, I'm cool with it. Guess what some tabloid offered me for pictures of you and Raymond?"

"A million dollars?"

"A measly ten-thousand. Like I would risk our

friendship for that? Ugh. And your movie hasn't even been released yet."

Imani shook her head. "You know I love you, right," she said. "And I hope this movie lives up to the hype and I don't get a new nickname."

"Please, the script was better and it wasn't shot with a HandyCam, you should be good."

Raymond whispered for the phone. "Dana," Imani said, "Raymond wants to talk to you." She handed the phone to him and he climbed out of the bed, speaking in hushed tones. As he headed out the room, Imani called out, "What are you two up to?"

"An exit strategy," he said over his shoulder. Returning to the call, he whispered, "Call Edward, tell him Imani and I want to get married in Jamaica next week and he needs to help me execute my plan."

"All right," she said. "But why are you whispering?"

"Imani doesn't know."

"I love it. She's not going to know what hit her," Dana exclaimed.

"I'd better get back to her before she gets suspicious," Raymond said as he headed back to the bedroom.

"Tell Imani I'll call her later," Dana said. Raymond clicked the phone off and handed it to Imani.

"So, what was that all about?" she asked.

"Dana said we're going to have to climb down the fire escape."

Imani looked down at her shoes and held her

left foot out to Raymond. "That's not going to happen."

He lifted her in his arms. "Baby, I got a strong back. I'll carry you."

She kissed him. "You know what to say to make a girl feel so good."

Chapter 24

When Raymond woke up with Imani in his arms, he couldn't help but smile, because tomorrow was their wedding day—only she didn't know it. He was amazed at how in less than a week, Edward Funderburke had pulled off the coup of the century.

Dana had been a godsend as well. She'd kept Imani busy with photo shoots and secret bridal gown shopping trips. While the plans for the wedding were being set into place, Raymond and Keith came up with a medical conference story so that they could take off for Jamaica before Imani and Dana arrived. He, Celeste, and Keith were scheduled to arrive in Negril this afternoon. He'd told Imani that he and Keith were going to a geriatric medical conference in New Orleans. It had taken everything in him to convince Imani not to join him in New Orleans.

"Come on," she'd said as they lay in bed. "I've never been to New Orleans and I would love to see the city. I hear it is magical."

"Baby, I'm going to be in meetings all day and

this trip would not allow us to spend any time together," he'd said. "I'm not going to be gone long, just two days."

"As much as I want to complain, I did leave you for three months."

He'd kissed her on the forehead. "Look at it this way. When I come back, we can put these wedding plans behind us and you'll probably have some new role that you will be excited about."

Imani had agreed with him. She had been scheduled to meet with Elize Harrington about her appearance on the network's soap opera. While she hadn't been excited about doing the show, Imani had agreed to make an appearance because Edward had told her that it would continue to help her career and would build an interest in her upcoming movie.

Raymond kissed Imani, waking her. "Good morning."

"What's good about it? You're leaving me," she pouted.

"Why are you acting like that?" he asked as he stroked her cheek. "I'm going to be bored and thinking about you every minute that I'm gone."

"You'd better," she said with a smile.

Raymond kissed her slowly and deeply, struggling to keep his excitement of their upcoming nuptials to himself. "I hate to do this," he said as he pulled back from her. "But I have to get to the airport."

"You're really going to leave me hanging like this?" she asked as she pulled him back in the bed by his shoulders.

"Baby, I'm going to miss my flight," he said, pulling away again.

Imani rolled her eyes and turned over on her side, watching Raymond grab his already packed bags from the closet. "Maybe I'll try that the next time I have to go out of town."

"What?" he asked as he pulled out his traveling outfit.

"Packing first, then going out for hot dogs," she said. Before Raymond could reply, Imani's cell phone went off with a call he'd been expecting.

"Hello," she sighed when she answered the phone.

"Imani, I need to see you in my office today," Edward said. "You will not believe this opportunity that just fell into my lap for you."

"What time should I be there?" she asked as Raymond padded into the bathroom.

"Noon works for me. I'm meeting with some potential clients this morning," he said.

"All right," she said. "I will see you then." After hanging up the phone, Imani decided that she would join Raymond in the shower. Walking into the steamy bathroom, she stripped out of her nightgown and stepped into the spray behind Raymond.

"I'll wash your back if you wash mine," she said as she took the soap from his hands.

"Talk about an offer I can't or won't refuse," he said as he turned around to face her. "But I'd rather wash your front." He pulled her underneath the spray and let the water rain down over her, then he took his soapy rag and rubbed her breasts until her nipples perked and called out for his lips.

Raymond licked and sucked her breasts until she moaned and her knees went weak.

"Yes," she moaned, "I like you washing my front." He lifted her leg and wrapped it around his waist and backed her against the wall of the shower.

"Then, you're going to love this," he said as he entered her awaiting valley and slowly ground against her. "Oh, you feel so good, baby."

"So do you," she groaned as he pumped in and out touching every sensitive spot inside her. Imani clamped her arms around his neck, bouncing up and down as she felt the waves of an orgasm coming down on her.

She licked the side of his neck and Raymond nearly exploded as she brushed her lips across his. She ground against him, gyrating faster and faster as she felt herself coming with a high intensity that she'd never felt before. Maybe it was because she knew that she was going to be without him for the next two days when she'd gotten so used to falling asleep in his arms, making love to him every night and sometimes in the mornings. And lunchtime, before she headed to Edward's office or rehearsal for her role on Broadway, to have a quickie in the break room while the rest of the staff was out of the office.

Sure, it was only two days, but still . . . Imani cried out in pleasure as he lifted her hands above her head and ground against her as he held her on the wall. The shower spray may have gone cold, but Imani and Raymond kept it hot in the shower as they reached an explosive climax. The couple slid down into the tub, holding each other tightly as they shivered.

"Baby," Raymond said. "I hate to let you go, but I have a plane to catch."

Imani sighed and nodded, though if she had her way, they wouldn't move from that spot ever. But she couldn't complain about her man being gone for two days when she'd be gone for months and months at a time because of a movie shoot. "All right," she said as he stood up and held his hand out to Imani. The melancholy look in her eyes killed him as he hugged her. "We'll be together sooner than you know," he said, then kissed her forehead.

"All right," she said. "I don't know why I'm tripping. You seemed to do fine for the three months I was in LA."

"No, I didn't. I was miserable. Just had a lot of work to keep me busy. As will you," he said. "I'm sure Edward will have scripts for you to read."

Imani nodded and stepped out of the tub and into the awaiting towel that Raymond held out for her. "Yes, he's been talking about something in Jamaica. But he's been sketchy on the details."

"Really?"

She nodded as he stroked her shoulders with the towel. "That sounds exciting," he said, then kissed her dry shoulder.

"Do you want me to make you some coffee? I've been practicing and Dana said my brew is much better," she said with a laugh.

"All right," he said. "But do me one favor."

"What's that?"

"Put some clothes on or I will never make my flight."

Imani smiled as she sauntered out of the bathroom not wearing a stitch of clothing.

"Whoa," he whispered. "Tomorrow, she's going to be my wife." Raymond rushed to get dressed and headed for the kitchen hoping Imani was telling the truth about her coffee-brewing skills.

Imani stood at the coffee maker, wrapped in her robe, sipping her coffee slowly.

"I will say it smells good," he said as he poured himself a cup. After he filled his cup with sugar and cream, he took a big sip and was pleasantly surprised that it had a decent taste to it. "That's it, I'm marrying you. This is pretty good."

"I told you I was getting better," she said, then kissed him on the cheek.

Raymond looked down at his watch, drained the majority of his coffee, and kissed Imani. "I've got to go," he said. "The car should be here shortly."

She walked him to the door as he rolled his luggage with him. "Have a safe trip," she said, and hugged him tightly.

When Imani closed the door behind her, she decided to get back in the bed, but her cell phone rang, interrupting the rest that she thought she was going to get.

"Yes," she said when she answered the phone.

"Imani, it's Edward," he said. "Remember that show in Negril I was telling you about?"

"Yes, the show that you won't give me the full details on? I don't think I want to do it."

"You have to do it," he said, his voice rising slightly. "Imani, I'm telling you that this is going to be the best thing that you've ever done. You have to do this."

"Why?" she asked. "You haven't given me one

good reason to take a break from rehearsals of *A Free Man of Color*, and let's not forget that I have an upcoming appearance on that soap opera. Going to Negril to talk about a role that I may or may not want seems ridiculous."

"You're going to want this role, it has Imani written all over it," Edward said. "And Dana's going to go with you."

"Why?"

"Ask her. I just know that I promised the producer you'd be down there today. Tickets are at the office."

"Edward."

"Have I ever steered you wrong?"

Sighing, Imani had to admit that Edward had her back and he'd been dead-on when it came to roles lately. "All right," she said. "I'll do it."

"Good. Then get your butt in gear and get over here so that you can get this ticket and get moving," he said.

"All right, I'm getting dressed," she said as she pulled herself off the bed.

"Make sure you pack a bag because you're leaving today. I'll have your travel details when you get here."

Imani hastily packed and headed to Edward's office. Whatever this role was, it had better be worth it. As she dashed outside and hailed a cab, she dialed Raymond's number, but hung up quickly. He was probably still in midair, so he wouldn't even get the call.

Her next call was to Dana. "Hello?"

"Dana, what do you know about Negril?" Imani asked. "And why are you going down there?"

"I have a fashion shoot."

"A what?" Imani laughed. "I thought you hated those fashion shoots."

"I do, but it's getting colder in New York and I want to go to Jamaica."

"All right," Imani said. "Well, at least we can laugh on the plane."

"Yeah," she said. "I'll see you at Edward's office."

A taxi stopped in front of Imani and she hopped in. Turning to the driver, she rattled off the address to Edward's office and leaned back in the seat, thinking about how weird this trip seemed. Dana never took trips with her, and Edward didn't book her for things with this limited information.

Just roll with it, she thought as the driver made his way through stop and go traffic. The only thing she knew for sure was that she would be back in New York by the time Raymond's conference was over. That would be nonnegotiable. Imani wanted a Valentine's Day wedding in Central Park. That was a lot to ask for in New York in the winter. She had to hope for no snow, an unseasonably warm day, and the right horse and carriage to whisk her and Raymond away after they said "I do."

"A girl can dream," she mumbled as visions of her perfect wedding flashed in her head. The last thing Imani wanted to be was one of those Bridezillas who freaked out when things didn't go her way. But she did want her day to be as perfect as possible.

"Lady," the surly driver said, "if you can stop talking to yourself, we're here."

She flashed him a sarcastic smile and handed him the cab fare and a tip. Imani hopped out of the cab, dragging her luggage behind her. When she walked into Edward's office, Dana and her agent quickly ended their conversation.

"What are you two up to?" she asked, looking from Edward to Dana.

"Nothing. Why are you so suspicious?" Dana asked.

"Because you all are acting funny."

"Well," Dana said, glancing at Edward, "I don't want to abuse our friendship and I was kind of scared to ask, but the reason we're going to Negril is because I'm shooting a spread for *Ebony Bride* and I didn't tell the editor that you were engaged, but they want you to be the model."

Imani smiled at Dana. "You know I wouldn't have turned you down. This is going to be fun." Imani clasped her hands together.

Edward nodded. "I love it when my clients work together. Here are the tickets and you two better get out of here. I'll call for a car."

Celeste walked through the grounds of the Negril Lighthouse. "This is beautiful. I can't believe you two pulled this off."

Raymond glanced at the grounds. The pathway leading up to the lighthouse where the minister would marry them was lined with pink, yellow, and purple roses. A red carpet was stretched out on the concrete walkway and an archway made of white roses and lilies covered where Imani and Raymond would exchange their vows.

"It's easy to do things when you love someone

enough. Imani and I wanted this wedding to be about us, close friends, and family."

Keith nodded. "And there was no way in hell that was going to happen in New York. The photographers and reporters staked out the clinic like we had the cure for cancer," he said.

Raymond laughed when he thought about how he fought not to do *Let's Get Married*. His life would be totally different had he not gone on that show. Turning to Celeste, he asked, "What's the word on the dress?"

"In her hotel waiting for her when she and Dana get here. I hope she likes it, because it is not your traditional wedding dress and she didn't pick it out herself."

"What does it look like?" Raymond asked.

"You'll see tomorrow. Can we keep some semblance of tradition going on here?" Celeste quipped. "And, Keith, this just raised the stakes on our New Year's Eve wedding."

Keith rolled his eyes and sighed. "Somehow, I knew that was going to happen."

Celeste sauntered away, smiling. "You shouldn't have showed me how capable you are, darling."

Once he was alone, Raymond stood in the middle of the walkway and smiled. This was the right thing, the wedding that Imani deserved. He didn't mind going all out for her because this would be their first and last wedding. At sunset tomorrow, they would take vows to spend the rest of their lives together.

Chapter 25

Imani and Dana landed in Negril at sunset after the most annoying flight in history. First, they were delayed for two hours because of a flock of geese on the runway. Once they were seated on the plane, one of the passengers, who'd spent at least two hours in the airport bar, was so unruly that they sat on the tarmac until security removed him from the plane.

Finally, once they were up in the air, the flight was hit by so much turbulence that Imani thought they were going to crash.

"This magazine shoot had better be worth it," Imani had said to Dana as she squeezed her hand.

"Ouch! It will be, but if you squeeze my hand again, then I'm not going to be able to shoot again."

Finally on the ground, they dashed through the airport and took the shuttle to the Xtabi Resort. Imani leaned back on the seat and closed her eyes.

"You're missing the sights," Dana said. "It is really beautiful out there."

"The only sight I want to see right now is the other side of my eyelids. I am drained and if you want me to look like something other than a beast for the shoot tomorrow, you're going to let me sleep," Imani said.

"I forgot how irritated you get when you're not properly rested," Dana said with an eye roll. "While you sleep, I have to go meet with the editorial director."

"Want me to go with you?"

"Absolutely not. I just want you to sleep and do something with your face," Dana said.

Imani squeezed her friend's arm. "My face is perfect," she said. "But I hope there is a nice hot tub in the room that I can soak in while you're working."

"Just rub it in," Dana said. "I think our room overlooks one of the cliffs. If you're up to it, we can jump later."

"Not on your life," she said. "Oh, I'd better call Raymond and let him know where I am. Shit, I don't even know if my cell phone will work over here. Can't you call internationally on your phone?"

Dana nodded but didn't immediately hand her phone over to her friend. "Let me call the editorial director first," she said. Imani shrugged and waited for Dana to finish her call.

"Here you go," Dana said as she handed her the phone.

Imani dialed Raymond's number and was excited to hear his voice even though he'd only been gone for half a day.

"Hello?"

"Baby, it's Imani," she said. "I was just calling to tell you that I'm in Jamaica."

"Really? What are you doing there?"

"A shoot with Dana. I should be back in New York around the same time you get back, but I wanted to let you know where I was just in case you called home and I wasn't there."

"Thanks for calling."

"How is New Orleans?"

Raymond sighed. "Without you here, very boring. I've been in meeting after meeting. Listening to doctors talk isn't that much fun when all I can think about is this hot fiancée that I can't wait to see."

Imani grinned from ear to ear. "And when you see said fiancée, just what are you going to do?"

"Mmm, hold that thought. My next session is about to start and I can't get into it. Love you."

"But—but." He'd hung up. She handed the phone back to Dana, saying, "He's busy."

"What did you expect that he would be doing?"

Imani tapped Dana on the knee. "Well, when we get back, I want to tell him about my plans for our Valentine's Day wedding."

"When? Four years from now? Not even with your newfound fame could you pull off a Valentine's Day wedding this late in the game," Dana said.

Imani sucked her teeth. "I can make it happen if I put my mind to it," she said. "But Raymond has a say in this as well. I don't want to be one of those brides who focuses more on the wedding and forgets about the marriage."

"That's what I'm talking about," Dana said.

After arriving at the resort, Dana rushed off to her meeting and Imani was so mesmerized by the view from the room that she forgot all about soaking in the hot tub.

Raymond rushed Dana into the room dubbed "wedding central." "Imani didn't follow you, did she?" he asked.

"Your fiancée is probably soaking her cares away in the tub. So, what time tomorrow do I need to have her walking down the aisle?" Dana asked.

"Sunset," Raymond said as Celeste walked into the room. She motioned for Dana to follow her.

"She gets to see the dress?" Raymond asked. "That isn't right."

"Hush up, Raymond," Celeste said as she and Dana headed into the adjoining room.

"She's going to love it," he heard Dana exclaim. Raymond couldn't help but smile. He only hoped that Imani would be as excited about the dress as her friend was.

Keith walked into the room with dinner. "Have Imani and Dana gotten here yet?"

"Yes. Imani called and I was almost busted when the steel drum band started playing. I damn near had to hang up on her in midconversation." Raymond and his partner laughed.

Dana and Celeste walked back into the room. "And our girl was not happy about that," Dana said. "I'm just glad I was able to call you and give you a heads-up that she was going to be calling on my phone."

"That was close because I would've ruined everything," he said with a laugh. "Now, how are you going to keep her busy all day tomorrow?"

"We're going to go to the lighthouse around four and take some shots. Celeste, I need the dress so that I can make sure it fits her and then we can get the accessories to go along with it."

"All right, but let me get the garment bag so that Raymond will be surprised by at least one thing on his wedding day," Celeste said as she headed back to get the dress.

"Dana, would you like to join us for dinner before you leave?" Keith asked.

"No, I'd better get back to Imani before she starts asking questions or comes looking for me. You know she's a very impatient woman when she wants to be." Dana laughed.

The warm air of Negril filled Imani's nostrils as she walked along the resort's grounds. She marveled at how close she was to the edge of a cliff, but at how safe she felt. One day she and Raymond would have to come here, maybe for their honeymoon. Looking down at her watch, she wondered what was taking Dana so long. She was starving and wanted to try some of the local cuisine. Of course they had Jamaican restaurants in New York, but the real thing here was going to be so much better, Imani imagined. She turned back toward the entrance of the building and headed inside. Dana, who was walking in from the other side, waved a garment bag at her.

"It's about time you made it back," Imani said. "What's in the bag?"

"The dress for the shoot. Let's order some curried jerk chicken and rum punch for dinner."

"Glad you know that I'm starving," Imani said. "That's a small bag for a wedding dress."

"It is, but you're going to love the dress."

"Not if I don't eat first," Imani said as they headed up to their room. Dana talked her friend into ordering room service and trying on the dress while they waited. Imani reluctantly agreed. She'd hoped to see more of Negril before she started working, but Dana made it seem as if trying on that dress was the most important thing in the world. But when Imani unzipped the white garment bag and saw the goldenrod halter dress with the fishtail and the matching lace wrap, she excitedly yelped. "This is beautiful. Who's the designer?"

Dana shrugged. "I have it in my notes. Try it on."

Imani carefully removed the dress from the bag and held it against her body. "It looks as if it was made for me."

"Can you try it on and make sure that it fits, please? I would like to eat sometime tonight," Dana said, smiling because she knew Imani would love the dress.

She watched as her friend dashed into the bathroom. Inside, Imani slowly slipped into the dress. The softness of the material against her skin felt like a lover's touch. And the fit was perfect. Rush-

ing back into the room, she twirled around so that
Dana could get a good look.

"As good as I look in this dress, I should be getting married tomorrow. It's chic, different, and
would make Raymond drool. Make sure you get the
designer's name for me," Imani said, then twirled
again. "I don't want to take it off."

"Well, you have to, because I've seen you eat.
This dress won't be sexy with jerk chicken stains
on it."

Imani smoothed her hands down her sides and
nodded. "You're right. Thanks for tricking me into
being your model. All you had to do was show me
this dress and I would've said yes."

After Imani had changed out of the dress and
into a simple tank top and a pair of denim cutoffs,
she and Dana decided to cancel room service and
head down to the resort's restaurant. Imani couldn't
wait to do the photo shoot tomorrow.

The next day, Raymond stood at the base of the
lighthouse nervously awaiting Imani's arrival. The
day had been a mix of bad weather, lost clothes,
and frayed nerves. But now, as the time drew near
for him to marry Imani, the weather was perfect.
The sky was putting on a show of colors—pink,
orange, deep blue—and the sun was leaving its
shiny footprints across the watery horizon.

"Are you ready?" Keith asked his friend.

Raymond looked down at his tan linen pants,
yellow shirt, and sighed. "I'm more than ready. I
hope she's ready."

Keith pointed at the walkway where Dana was walking backward snapping shots of Imani, who stopped Raymond's breathing when she came into view. "Wow," he intoned as he drank in her image. Hair pulled up in a loose bun with a white orchid behind her left ear. The goldenrod color highlighted her skin and made her look like a living doll, his doll.

Dana stopped taking pictures and stepped aside so she could see what was waiting for her at the end of the aisle. Imani focused on the scene before her, standing beneath the flowered archway. There was a man standing in the middle, looking like no pastor she'd ever seen in a pair of tan cargo shorts and a white tank top with a depiction of Jesus with dreadlocks in the center of his chest.

As she got closer, Imani realized that was no model standing in as her groom, that was Raymond. This wasn't a photo shoot, but her real wedding. A wedding that she knew nothing about.

Did she care? Nope. Before she knew it, Imani lifted the tail of her dress and took off running in Raymond's direction. When she made it down the aisle, she flung herself into his arms and kissed him, then, playfully punched him in the chest.

"I really want to be mad at you, but how can I when you've done all of this for me?"

"For us," he said.

The pastor laughed as he looked from Imani to Raymond. "I guess we are ready to get married," he said.

Raymond reached out and grabbed Imani's hand. "Oh, yes."

Imani nodded, her eyes sparkling with tears of joy.

"Then let's get you two married," the pastor replied.

Standing there, looking into Raymond's eyes, Imani knew she had found the love of a lifetime. She knew that this was the man she would grow old with and if fame eluded her, it wouldn't matter—because the most important thing was love. And as she pledged her heart, soul, and spirit to Raymond, she knew love was all she would ever need.

Don't miss

His Sexy Bad Habit

On sale now wherever books are sold.

Turn the page for an excerpt from
His Sexy Bad Habit . . .

Chapter 1

Serena Jacobs looked down at her pink brides-maid dress and shook her head in disgust. Sure she'd agreed to be in her best friend Kandace Davis's wedding, but she had no idea that she'd be stuck in pink lace looking like a bottle of Pepto Bismol.

She hated the color pink. In her mind it made people think women were weak. And the last thing Serena Jacobs was was a weak woman. She scowled as she fluffed her honey brown curls.

"Will you smile?" Jade Goings asked as she adjusted the bodice of her strapless dress in the mirror.

"Why would Kandace choose pink and gold for her wedding colors?" Serena asked as she smoothed her hands down the sides of her dress. "She could've gotten away with slinky black dresses."

Alicia Michaels ran her fingers though her wavy black hair and shook her head. "Only you would associate black with a wedding. At least we're part of this one," she said, then shot a glance at Jade.

"Am I ever going to live that down? It was a spur of the moment deal," Jade said of her Las Vegas wedding that her friends hadn't participated in. She and her husband, James, met and got married in Las Vegas nearly two years ago. Still, her friends weren't happy that they hadn't been part of the ceremony.

Serena went silent, thinking back to the wedding she'd almost had that would've left her friends out in the cold, too. Five years ago, she'd left Atlanta to chase her dream of screenwriting. But the first person Serena'd met in Los Angeles, renowned filmmaker Emerson Bradford, had told her that her future wasn't behind the scenes.

"What do you mean?" Serena had asked as she ripped her screenplay from his hands. "You haven't even read my script."

"I'm sure it's good," he'd replied with a 10,000-watt smile that made Serena's anger go from boil to simmer. "But you have the face and body of a star."

"What makes you an authority?" she'd asked, placing her hand on her hip. "I've never even heard of you. For all I know you could be some poseur hanging around UCLA hoping all the wannabe screenwriters are so desperate to get their foot in the door that we'll just fall for the first line you offer."

Emerson had stood there with a smile on his face. "I have the perfect role for you. Do you have your SAG card?"

"For the last time, I'm a writer. Why do I need a Screen Actors Guild card?"

"Because, you're going to star in my next movie. We can discuss it over dinner," he'd said. And despite her apprehension at who Emerson had said he was, Serena had agreed to dinner with him. But before they'd met for dinner, she'd headed to Starbucks and did a Google search of Emerson Bradford. She'd been surprised and satisfied to find out that he was who he'd said he was. According to *Variety,* Emerson had just signed a deal with Warner Brothers for a sexy thriller that could be a star vehicle for the right actress. The magazine had quoted Emerson saying he'd wanted a fresh face for the movie. *So, he's not full of crap after all,* she'd thought as she reread the article and studied the picture of Emerson Bradford.

She'd taken him as a handsome man with a caramel complexion and an air of sophistication. His hazel eyes had seemed to sparkle in the picture and she'd allowed her curiosity to take over. She figured even if Emerson had been trying to run that Hollywood game on her, she'd at least get a free dinner out of it.

Serena had blown off her shift at M Grill and called Emerson to get the details on his dinner offer. He'd informed her that he'd send a car to pick her up and he'd wanted her to wear the sexiest thing she had in her closet.

"Hello," Jade said, snapping Serena out of her reverie. "We have to go check on the bride."

"Yeah, yeah," Serena said as she retouched her lipstick, then followed her girlfriends out of the dressing room into the bridal suite.

As Serena trailed her friends, she tried to shake her mind clear of Emerson. For so many years, she'd buried those memories, not even sharing them with her close friends. The fact that they returned in full force today bothered her.

She'd never been the type of woman who envied friends who got married. *You're being a fool. Marriage is for women like Jade and Kandace, not you. Don't let the wedding bells play with your head,* Serena thought as Jade opened the door to the suite.

"Hello," Jade said to Kandace, who was sitting at the vanity toying with her veil. "Are you ready?"

Kandace turned around with a nervous look on her face. "Where the hell have you all been?" she asked. "I had to put my mother out. She was just too much to deal with."

Jade walked over to Kandace and fixed her crooked veil. "Why would you put your mother out?"

"Knowing Miss Davis, she was crying, wasn't she?" Alicia asked as she admired Kandace's ivory Vera Wang dress with intricate beading work across the bodice.

Kandace nodded her head. "I didn't think you guys were ever going to come in here and save me. Oh my God, I'm so nervous. There have to be twenty cameras out there and a bunch of people I don't even know."

"What did you expect when you said you would marry Solomon Crawford?" Serena asked as she handed Kandace a tube of MAC lip gloss. "I'm pretty sure half of New York is out there."

Kandace shook her head. "I knew we should've just kept it simple," she said as she slowly rose from her seat.

Alicia pinched Serena's arm. "You know how she is, especially after everything that happened in Charlotte. Don't make her nervous about those cameras," she whispered. Jade followed Kandace as she paced back and forth.

"Kandace," Jade said as she stopped her friend from pacing. "Today is your day. The only thing that matters is that you and Solomon love each other. This is your day."

Kandace smiled and nodded. "All right. You're right, my day."

"And all of those cameras are for you," Serena added. "So, don't worry about them."

The three women surrounded Kandace and hugged her, being careful not to wrinkle her dress or mess up her makeup. "Let's get you down the aisle so you can become Mrs. Crawford," Jade said.

"Serena, are you sure you're okay with taking over for me in Charlotte?" Kandace asked once the women stopped hugging.

She smiled at her friend. "I'm fine with it. I have some unfinished business in the Queen City."

"Antonio Billups?" Alicia questioned.

"Hello, let's focus on the bride," Jade said. "Then we'll talk about Serena and our contractor."

Despite the fact that Kandace had been nervous before walking down the aisle, she was the picture of grace and love when she and hotel mogul

Solomon Crawford exchanged their vows. Serena had to admit the ceremony was beautiful. She even felt a lone tear slide down her cheek as Kandace and Solomon kissed for the first time as husband and wife. As she linked arms with the groomsman she'd been paired with, all she could think about was the last conversation she'd had with Antonio Billups, the contractor who was going to revamp Hometown Delights after the horror that had occurred there last November.

Carmen De La Croix, or rather Chelsea Washington, had been obsessed with Solomon. When she'd seen that Solomon had fallen in love with Kandace, she'd stalked the couple and tried to kill Kandace in the restaurant. It was a messy scene and brought the wrong kind of attention from the media.

After Thanksgiving dinner, the women decided to redo the restaurant, which brought contractor Antonio Billups back into Serena's life since he'd been hired again, to oversee the renovations. Antonio intrigued her ever since they'd shared hot kisses in a room at the Westin hotel nearly two years ago. When he'd begun the initial work on the restaurant, Serena had thought she would've ended up in his bed by now, but Antonio pulled back. She felt as if he was hot and cold. Serena had done what she normally does when she doesn't get her way, tuned out emotionally—still, she wanted him and wondered what it would feel like to be wrapped up with Antonio.

Now that she would be in town she was going to get what she wanted from the sexy Mr. Billups. The thought of his naked body entwined with hers made her smile brightly as the photographer snapped a picture of the wedding party. She was definitely ready to head to Charlotte and oversee the renovation of the restaurant.

Antonio Billups yawned as he looked over the specs for Hometown Delights. He was set to start work on the restaurant when the owners returned from New York. Smiling, he thought about one of the owners in particular—Serena Jacobs. She had a killer body and lips that were soft like rose petals. But would she really fit into the life he had? He was a father first. Still, that didn't mean he wasn't a hot-blooded man who needed the comforts of a woman.

Could Serena offer him what he needed?

Looking out the window of his home office, Antonio thought back to the first moment he'd laid eyes on her.

She and Jade had met him at the property to talk about what renovations were needed before the restaurant could open. When Jade had gotten sick, Serena handled the meeting with him and Norman Engles, his business partner. Her deep brown eyes had struck him first. Then she'd smiled at him with a mix of seduction and desire dancing on her face as she'd extended her well-manicured hand and said, "I'm Serena Jacobs and I look forward to doing business with you gentlemen." Her voice had been melodic to his ears and his instant attraction to Serena had shocked him. It had been three years since he looked at a woman with lustful thoughts swirling in his head. Three years since his wife, Marian, had been killed in a collision with a drunk driver who was heading up the interstate going the wrong way.

But something in the way Serena Jacobs had looked at him awakened a dormant need. It had been a struggle for him to focus on business when he hadn't been able to tear his eyes away from her long shapely legs. It was as if something else had taken control of him when he'd said, "I can bring you the contracts for the project this evening and we can discuss them over a drink."

Norman had shot Antonio a stunned look. Asking a potential client out wasn't his partner's style, but he'd nodded approvingly at him when Serena had been talking to Jade on her cell phone.

"I was two seconds from doing that myself," Norman had whispered to Antonio. "She's a stone cold fox."

"And about twenty years younger than you," he'd replied to his partner as he patted the man's beer belly.

Norman sucked his teeth. "Just because it's snow on the roof don't mean the fireplace doesn't get hot. Just takes a little more time. I'm glad to see you coming out of the exile you put yourself in."

Antonio had shrugged his shoulders. "All I did was ask the woman out for a drink."

"I saw those looks you were giving her. This ain't about contracts or a drink," Norman had said.

Antonio had been about to deny what Norman

had observed when Serena sauntered over to them and said, "I'll be ready at eight to discuss the contracts and have that drink." Her smile had caused an ache in his pants and swelling in his boxers.

"I look forward to it, Mrs. Jacobs," he'd said.

"Please, call me Serena. Mrs. Jacobs was my grandmother," she'd replied in a flirty tone.

Smiling, Antonio had nodded in reply. "All right, Serena. Where are we meeting?"

"I'm staying at the Westin down—I mean—Uptown. I hear they have a nice bar there," Serena had said.

"Then I'll see you at eight." After they left, Antonio had headed home and called his sister-in-law, Casey, to watch A.J.

"What's going on?" she'd asked him after agreeing to watch her nephew.

"I'm meeting with a client," he'd replied, not wanting to tell his sister-in-law that he was meeting a woman. Though his wife had been dead for three years, he hadn't been sure Casey would agree with him returning to the dating world. Maybe she'd think he was betraying her sister and he hadn't wanted to have that conversation with her.

"I'd love to watch A.J. Should I come over there?" she'd inquired.

"Sure, he's getting ready to watch a movie on the Disney Channel. He's had his dinner and don't let him fool you into feeding him a bunch of ice cream before I get back."

"All right."

When Casey had arrived at his house, Antonio barely had said good-bye to her before he was out the door. His anticipation to see Serena had rendered him temporarily thoughtless. He'd sped from his northeast Charlotte home and arrived at the Westin in record time. The moment he'd stepped into the bar, Serena had met him, looking even more delicious in her black bandeau dress that skimmed her knees.

"It's pretty loud in here," she'd said. "Why don't we head up to my room and look over those contracts?"

"Are you sure?" he'd asked, not certain he'd be able to go into Serena's room and concentrate on business. Not the way she'd looked in that dress.

"Well, we can't talk over that music nor can we worry about spilling drinks on those important papers," she'd said, then ran her finger down his arm. Antonio had known Serena wanted to do more than talk business. Still, he'd followed her up to her room. Sure they'd gone over the contracts, but that took about twenty minutes, then she'd ordered drinks from room service and sat on the bed beside him. Their conversation had been light, talking about Charlotte's downtown area being called Uptown and how she got into the restaurant business.

She'd inched closer to him as he talked about how his company had worked on the Blake Hotel and helped turn the place into a boutique hotel that offered something different in the city. Serena had turned her head and their lips were inches from each other's. Antonio had expected her to turn her head away, but she'd pressed her lips against his and kissed him with a scorching passion that sent chills up and down his spine. He'd returned the kiss with fervor and zest that had allowed him to release years of pent up emotions, pent up desire and passion. She had melted against his chest and deepened the kiss. Their tongues danced against each other as Antonio had slipped his hand between her thighs.

Abruptly, he'd pulled back from her. "Whoa," he'd said, feeling like a teenager sneaking around with a girl. "This can't happen."

She'd raised her eyebrow and asked, "Why not? We're both adults."

"I can't do this. We're about to start working together."

Serena had risen to her feet and paced back and forth. "And? You're married, aren't you?"

Antonio held up his left hand. "I'm not married. But, like I said, we're about to start working together and I don't want to complicate matters with sex." He'd stood up and closed the space between them. He'd wanted to have sex with her, wanted to lift that little black dress above her head and see the splendor of her naked body.

Serena had seemed to notice his desire as she glanced down at the fly of his slacks. "I'm not a woman who plays games and I go after what I want," she'd said. "Since I know for sure this isn't one-sided, I'm telling you, again, we're adults."

"I know this," he'd replied. "But I have to try and be professional."

Serena had offered him a sly smile and pressed her body against his. "But I don't," she'd said and leaned in to kiss him again. Unable to resist, he'd cupped her bottom and started to inch up her dress. Before anything else could happen, the door had opened and Jade had walked in, causing them to break off the kiss.

That kiss still kept him up at night, even after all the time that had passed. It kept him yearning for more from Serena, but he couldn't get caught in her sexy web when he had A.J. and his business to run. Still, how much longer could he deny what he wanted?